Other Titles available; Diary of a Reluctant Psychic. Published by Flying Horse books 2014.

Amazon customer reviews

'Brilliant'
'Un-put down-able'
'Fantastic'
'Brilliant five stars'
'What a brilliant read honestly couldn't put this book down'
'A real page turner'
'Wow'
'Amazing'
'Thought provoking'

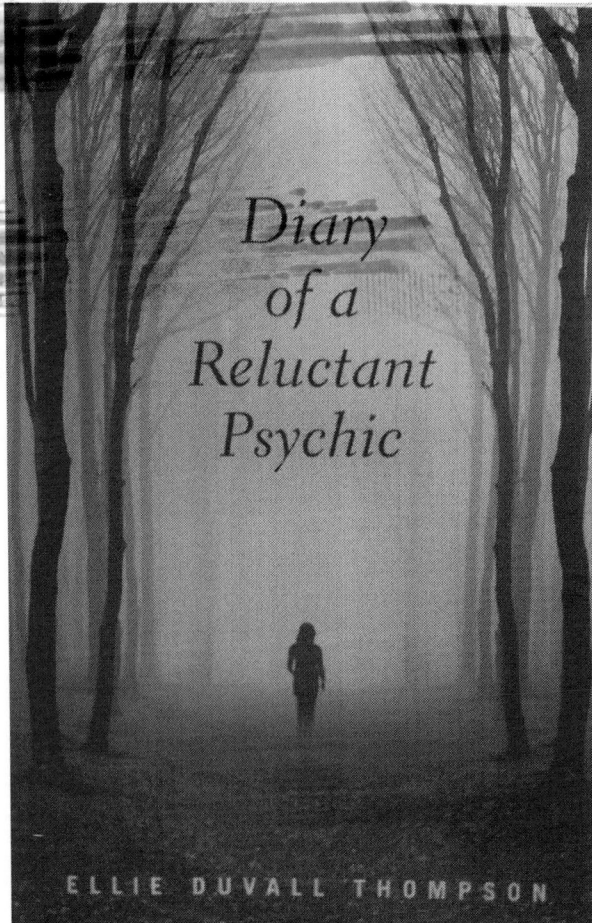

Children's Books also available from this author.
The little girl in the Woods
My little alphabet book of animals
Cecil le plop
Fairies in the night

Amazon reviews

'The poetry is captivating, and the illustrations are eye-catchingly wonderful. A great read for children'

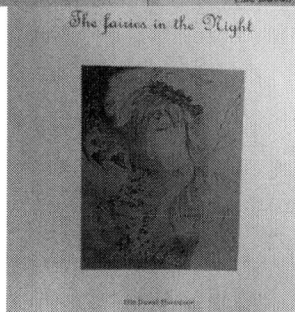

The Little Girl in the Woods

Ellie Duvall Thompson

My Little Alphabet Book
Of
Animals

Ellie Duvall Thompson

Cecil Le Plop

Ellie Duvall Thompson

The fairies in the Night

NANCY

ELLIE DUVALL THOMPSON

Twisty Whistle Books

Published in 2016

By

Twisty Whistle Books

ISBN-13: 978-1523472819
ISBN-10:1523472812

This book is dedicated to all the hormonal, post pubescent & menopausal women of this world.
You are beautiful, strong, amazing, remarkable creations of society.

****

Special thanks have to go to, my family for not institutionalizing me, whilst in the full throws of a hot flush or a total menopausal breakdown moment.
I also have to give special thanks to Michaela & Amy, for being amazing friends. To Margaret for trying to teach my dyslexic brain to function properly and to Sara for being a wonderful person.

Prologue

I realize most books start with an introduction to the story and a brief outline of what is to come. But I thought to myself I shall be a little bit different and use these first few pages to give some practical advice. To which you, the reader, I'm sure could add too. Then pass on to any daughter, granddaughter, niece or any other post puberty young female who is about to make her mark on the world.

We are going to begin our journey and talk about the species of human, known as MAN. There are many types of MAN in this world. Some of which will, no matter how hard you work those hormones, ever change!

All women can be prepared for child birth, hard work, stomach cramps, hot flushes, but the most difficult deed we will ever embark on is to be able to understand the 'penis people' we choose to share our lives and this planet with.

They say women and their hormones are hard to understand and deal with. Tell that to a female who has been married for twenty six years and she will give you another side to the story.

We shall call the introduction to this book 'The True Definition of'. Then we will begin the tale of Nancy. A woman of a certain age who is proof that all woman have, as much fight, strength, determination and stamina as any man.

The world will realize one day that a pinch of hormones is stronger than any chemical weapon, nuclear device or even a room full of testosterone driven 'penis people'. I do not mean that in a burn my bra feminist sort of way. More in a manner of 'don't mess with me, my family or my life'. Because in the end somehow, someway we women will always show you we are by far, the stronger sex.

The True Definition of;

<u>Penis person</u>; the male of the species. A human being with the ability to not only use his genitalia for reproduction but also act like a gigantic cock most of the time! There are many different types of penis people, each have their own unique style and each are in a league of their own!

<u>Neanderthal 'P P'</u>; His appearance often resembles being un-shaven. Nine times out of ten he will have a muffin top hanging over his jeans he will argue with you till you are blue in the face, that the overhang is just relaxed muscle. Women are not stupid and know it's actually caused by too much beer, burgers, pork pies and sitting in front of the television watching some other types of 'P P run around a pitch, field or court. They seem to have a great fear of water and soap and will only scrub their bodies when they are out on the town to share a night in some back street boozer with other like-minded P P's. The top button of their trousers is normally undone

(due to the size of their gut). They will once again argue with you telling you the makers of said item must have changed its sizing guide or you have quite simply, shrunk them in the wash. Their role in society is simple they are here to annoy the fuck out of you. They have not evolved as quick as some of the other 'P P's and their views on the role of a woman have not changed since they first grabbed you by the hair and dragged you around on course rough ground. They think your job in their life's are to wait on them hand and foot, cook the hunt of the day (which by the way you would have bought from some local supermarket). They will also expect you to be a vixen in the bedroom and pamper to their every wish. Sex with them is a mission. There will be no foreplay whatsoever. The chances are they will just launch themselves on top of you, pound away at you in no real rhythmic fashion. Crush and pulverise you and pummel your lady parts until they have finished (normally this will take approximately 3 minutes but that's only if you are lucky!) He will then lay there saying

"God I'm good, bet ya enjoyed that didn't you?"

Because you are a well-mannered partner/wife you will off course reply with some positive comment. Then you will turn over, close your eyes and dream and fantasise about one of the other types of 'P P's. The Neanderthal P P's are hard work, one can only hope that evolution catches up with them and they realise women are not just here for their pleasure or to bow down to their every whim.

'Poseur PP': These types often pretend to be something or someone else. They will always leave you with a puzzled expression on your face as you can never quite work out who or what they are trying to be. Unlike some of the other types our 'poseur' grows and develops into this form of 'PP'. As appearance goes they often look smart to the onlooker, but as they get older they will have a tendency to dress like some fourteen year old teenager. They hate growing up as turning into an adult scares the fuck out of them. They will use every toner, moisturiser and cleanser you own. Grecian 2000 was invented for them. The mirror is their best friend and normally their only friend, as no one can ever try and compete with their feminine need to pamper themselves. In-between the sheets they are no different. Whilst engaging in some form of sexual pleasure they will continue to admire their bodily movements in the mirror and can often be seen to stroke their own arse or slick back their hair in the middle of gyration. As foreplay goes they will engage but not at the risk of messing up their hair or chipping a nail. If you are dating a 'Poseur' then make sure you have had a full Brazilian wax as one of their greatest fears is getting something stuck between their teeth. They have spent possibly over four thousand pounds getting them whitened or veneered and the very last thing they want is a stray pubic hair getting caught in them! If you like 'pretty' boys then this type of 'PP' are for you, but you will have to prepare yourselves for the competition you face throughout the whole of your life. Every shop window you pass they will be staring in looking at their own reflection, every new beauty product that goes on sale they will buy, every t-shirt or shirt they own will have to be crease free, ironed and folded in the correct manner . They are arrogant and pride is their biggest issue, they are in love with themselves and no one else will ever do!

Foetus PP: These types are the babies of the bunch. They refuse to cut the ties of their mother's apron strings and she is you're biggest threat. They will phone their mother or even drop everything to go round to see her after you have had a blazing row. You can forget about colour scheming your own home as this 'foetus's PP's' mother will have complete control. She will also have control and power over when her son is allowed to see you. BUT if she does not like you after the first meeting forget totally about forming a relationship with him. The chances are you will on occasions have disturbing images of her still nursing him. The facade they go for is normally one that is clean and tidy (but this is only because their mothers have bathed, shaved and chosen what clothes they should put on) He will always have an emotional attachment to his mother and you will never win! In the bedroom department expect him to pick up the phone half way through and check that he is doing it right. He will become obsessed with your breasts but be extra careful here as too much mouth action will probably mean he will be asleep in a matter of minutes. He will expect you to run his bath after a hard day at the office, he will also expect you to chop up his dinner in small bite size mouthfuls and feed him from a spoon. He will not have a clue whilst out shopping as to what socks, boxers or shirts to buy and if you ever send him out to buy bra's or knickers he will return with something that his mother wears which will be in her size too. The reason for this is because he didn't actually buy them but he phoned his mother who went shopping on his behalf. If your ideal partner is one that you want to care for and nurture then a 'foetus PP' is your perfect partner. Just as long as you can accept the fact that you will have three people in your relationship. Good luck!

Jerk face PP; This PP has many names, douchebag, wanker, arsehole, twat, jackass, dipshit, nimrod, chode, prat and the most commonly used one c**t! He is the one guy you never really want in your life but you will feel drawn to him the moment you lay eyes on him. He is the one who will shag anything that moves irrelevant of what they look like. His main aim is to bed as many women as possible. His belt buckle and bed post will probably be scratched to ribbons as he has run out of where to place the conquests he has bedded over the years. He probably started his sexual exploitation when he was about 13, or as soon as he realised just what his penis was actually for. Sex with him will be amazing. He will know just what to do and how to do it. If you have never experienced an orgasm or would like to know just what a multiple one feels like, take a chance and go with him. Plus an added bonus is your mother will love him because of his way with words and pleasing appearance. But here comes the BUT you will never be able to tie him down. His life is about sex, and he has the aptitude, qualifications and capacity to carry on screwing anything with a vagina or a hole come to that! He is a man whore and will leave you crying into your cornflakes on more than one occasion. Treat him as he treats you, like a friend with benefits and nothing more.

<u>Ring bearer PP</u>: Not much can be said about him except don't go there! He is married! He will do one of two things, remove his ring, but you can catch him out as the visible marks of his wedding band will still be on his finger. If you notice this ask him about why you can still see said marks. If his reply is "we have just separated" laugh in his face and walk away. His other game plan will be to start a conversation saying how bad his life is and how his wife does not understand him again do not fall for this old chestnut. He is married. He will not leave his wife for you and will keep you hanging on to boost his self-esteem and use you till he has found another gullible woman to take your place. In the bedroom he will be tender at first then do as he pleases but expect him to shag you exactly the same as he does his wife. If you can imagine his wife to be a ploughed field, you are his nicely mowed lawn. You really have to remember all nicely mowed lawns get churned up, walked over and sooner or later have the same appearance

as that ploughed field. If your happy being 'his bit on the side' that will never quite get to owning all of him and are good at sharing, then you two are made for each other.

BOF PP: He is the 'boring old fart'. He is Mr 'I'm always right'! Which means no matter what you say, however much you argue your case there is not a hope in hell of you ever being right or winning an argument. This type should not be confused with a geek. A geek is a young person male or female who has a reason to be clever. A BOF on the other hand has the mental capacity of an earthworm; actually an earthworm probably has more data and facts' running through their bodies than the BOF has in his little finger. (My apology to earth worms). Everything you say he will auto correct you, and will go out of his way to make you look like an absolute div. His overall and far reaching views on everything to the meaning of life or how to bake the best Victoria sandwich will over rule anything you have to say, even if you are an expert. In the middle of a sexual encounter he will in all probability and without a shadow of a doubt explain to you why his penis has become erect. Why he has ejaculated, and the total scientific evaluation as to why you haven't managed climax. This PP should only really have sex with himself and his right hand because he will bore you and any normal hot bloodied female. If you would rather sit and talk about sex than do it he is your man, the only issue you will have is the constant bickering about which one of you is right. May the force be with you!

Beefcake PP: Everywoman likes a bit of beef every now and then! The trouble is the beefcake PP's are normally only seen on programmes like Spartacus or True Blood. These men really know how to make an entrance, and if there are any women in the room when they enter do expect a few jaw dropping open mouth gasps, sighs or groans.

Your biggest challenge with a beefcake is not, I repeat NOT, other women oh no your biggest rival is a pec deck, hack squat and an Exigo Strength Adjustable Dual Pulley Compact! You will have to get used to spending many an evening alone with a duvet, a glass of wine and Spartacus on repeat. You will also have to get used to them standing in front of the mirror kissing those huge pumped up guns. A tape measure is a must for these types as they will need to measure their growing muscles every minute of every day, but they will also use it to measure the size and girth of their man hood. Just to make sure the old myth about penis shrinkage does not take place after pumping all that iron. They are the sportsman of our bunch. They will be spectators when they cannot take part in their chosen sport any longer and once they get to their mature years they sadly do have the traits of our good old Neanderthal man. Enjoy them while they are in their prime because once the ability to exercise has gone you have to get used to that muffin top hanging over their jeans! In the bedroom they have the energy of a wild dog and will keep going for as long as it takes. Stamina is not an issue for them. Make sure you have a good supply of bed linen though as those oil stains are a bugger to remove! There is nothing wrong whatsoever with a 'Beefcake PP' unless you are a vegetarian off course.

Jealous PP: If you can handle being told what to do and have the desire to be owned like Anastasia Steele then a jealous type may be your perfect partner. Most women though would end up getting so bored and frustrated with a 'jealous PP' that they would either dump them at the first opportunity or just come out and blatantly lie and say they have turned into a nymphomaniac lesbian overnight just to escape their clutches. This type will follow you round like a lap dog; check your phone, your bank statements and could actually sniff your knickers just after removal to verify that you have not been unfaithful. At the beginning of the relationship you may feel like they are head over heels in love with you. By about six months in they will suffocate you with demands. These demands will normally be, 'don't do that, don't wear that, why are you going out? Who are you going with? You will either have to be one strong woman to cope with their dictatorship personality. Or a woman that likes to be controlled. Sex will be about a 7/10 as they will want to please you in order that you stay with them. Your relationship will be a volatile one and he will not be interested in your side of the story. His face will go a sickly shade of green when you are talking to another man. He will be envious of you spending time with your own family or close friends. By the time you have worked out what an absolute wanker he is, the lust you once had for him will have mutated you into a woman that turns his Thom Browne fine wool and silk suit into some ripped torn Halloween costume from jokers masquerade. Nice to be desired but don't get confused between desire and possession. Just watch The Exorcist to see what happened to her!

The True Definition of the Female

The Bath: The one pleasure no woman should ever have interrupted. You will find the average time spent in the bath for a penis person is anything from fifteen to thirty minutes. A female on the other hand takes a lot longer. Here's why; a woman has to ensure that there are just the right amount of bubbles in her bath. Not for cleansing purposes, but to cover all her floating parts. Too few and her frustration levels will build, to many and she will feel like she has been attacked with some cyber goo from the planet Zirgon! And the same goes for the temperature of the water. In the words of Goldilocks "It has to be just right". Once a female has stepped into the bath you will hear the hot tap being turned on again. Every woman has the ability to use her toes for this procedure. We learn it from a very young age. It is a gift we never forget and one that stops us from having to heave our naked bodies to an upright position. Once comfy she will then proceed to shave. Her legs, her arm pits and her nether regions. Be warned if yours is the only razor about, it will quite probably end up shaving the hairs around her bum! Once shaving has taken place it will be time to wash. The hair first. To which the conditioner will be left on till the very last minute and only rinsed before the climbing out of the bath procedure begins. The body will be lathered and by this point the occasional straggly pubic hair will be stuck to the soap. Now comes the relaxation point. A woman will lay there (topping up the hot water with her toes obviously!) for another twenty or thirty minutes. You will know when she is ready to leave her now bubble-less bath as she will scream as the hot water has run out. The departure of the bath is another well taught trick. She will grab her towel but not depart the vessel of cleaning immediately. You see she has to let gravity take hold and she has to let her vagina release the water it has managed to suck up in the hour or so she has spent in the bath. Depending on how good her 'sucking' system is, will depend on how long she stays in a vertical position over the bath. The bath, not to be confused with 'I'm pretending to be on the loo, to have a break from the kids' moment.

The big O or ovulation: Every woman will at some time in their life's experience the big O. This should not be confused with the other big O that many are lucky enough to have experienced once in a while. This O is also known as the big ouch. It is that one time in a woman's cycle when the ripest egg in ones ovaries gets released into ones fallopian tubes. Many perceive that PMT (Pre-menstrual tantrums) actually start about a week before ones period. This is sadly not true. PMT often begins at the centre point of a woman's cycle.

And the cries of "I NEED CHOCOLATE" can be heard in every household around the country. This is when every penis person should really tread carefully. If he doesn't want his partner to chop of his genitalia with a blunt object then he really needs to learn the rules of ovulation or the big O.

1) Under no circumstances patronise your partner your life will be at risk if you do.
2) If your partner wants chocolate do the decent thing and go to the nearest shop and purchase some. Word of warning buy every bar you can possibly afford because if you come home with just a Twix in your hands she will undoubtedly want a mint Aero. Do as Bear Grylls does and always be prepared for every eventuality.
3) There is a high chance that your partner will suffer one of the following.
    i)   Extreme pain whereby she will need to sit on the toilet seat and bear down due to a heavy feeling in her

pelvic regions. This could go on for a couple of minutes or in some cases over an hour. The chances are her bowels will open at this bearing down point which actually brings a moment of relief for her. Be sympathetic!

ii) She will want to rip your clothes of and have passionate sex with you. Under no circumstances go to the pub, watch football, or fall asleep. It will probably be another month before these unbridled extensive feelings of lust and hunger for sex strikes again. If you choose to go to the pub instead be aware you may be replaced with a vibrating object!

4) Above anything else stay calm the big OUCH only lasts a day or two and then all you have to prepare yourself for is menstruation itself ☺

<u>Menstruation:</u> The day has finally arrived. The build-up and tension of the last few days has led to this day. It will normally begin with a tight sensation in the groin area. Followed by a rather disgusting coloured spotting of 'stuff' in her pants. After an hour or two the flow of blood decides to descend and with it comes extreme stomach cramps, the monthly period headache and the over bearing desire to have her 'period poo'. Sorry to talk about poo, but us women have to deal with this every month. It does not matter what the hell we eat at this time in our cycle our bowels seem to have a mind of their own. So a word of warning if your partner is about to have her period poo, vacate the house, buy extra air fresheners, burn incense or essential oils. A penis person's hang over poo has nothing on the female's period poo! Once this constitution has taken place slight relief can be felt for the female. But the next few days really do have to prove the point that we females really are the stronger sex. As we can bleed, do mundane chores,

work, look after children and still not die from losing what feels like a gallon of blood. All at the same time as our stomachs feel like they have been kicked by a dinosaur and are heads are about to explode not only with pain but the, shall I punch someone or cry buckets emotions. The period, a time in a woman's life when, she really hates being a woman!

The other BIG O or Orgasm: Every penis person would like to assume that every time they ride their partner like a rodeo king, the inevitable will happen. Sorry to burst your bubbles boys. The female has many gifts and one of them is 'pretence'. Let's give you some tips to help you realise all what you do is really not necessary.

1) Foreplay is a must! That does not mean a text from you saying your chosen football or rugby team has just scored. If you want to score with your partner. Try

snogging her, tickling her feet, back or stomach. Very softly and tenderly.

2) Once your partner is aroused, DO NOT assume this is the moment you insert your man parts into her. Keep her panting for a while. Anticipation is the best aphrodisiac out there.

3) You will learn in time when your partner needs a good old fashioned pounding or a soft delicate approach in love making. Let her guide you, choosing the wrong option will leave her reaching for the latest model of a battery operated device!

4) So you want a bit of anal do you or you are transfixed with the female's star fish. Tread carefully if she is un-prepared you will castrated quicker than a room full of men waiting a vasectomy.

5) Stop watching porn and expecting your partner to behave in this manner. Not all woman have a cervix the size of mount doom, and most DO NOT scream the

OOOOOOO's and RRRRRRR's in the same way as a porn princess.

6) At some stage in every man's life they will be out on the town with a belly full of beer. On their return home they will get a little fruity and want more than a Horlicks and digestive biscuit before bedtime. PLEASE brush your god damn teeth and wipe the burger and chips with extra sauce from your faces, before embarking on any form of passion. Beer breath and burger sauce IS NOT A TURN ON.

7) Dildos and vibrators. All I can say there is LOL. If you purchase one of these to add lust to your sex life. You really have to be prepared for your partner to choose these over your penis. They go where they are supposed to, they have just the right amount of power, an on off switch and they do not ejaculate over parts of your body you do not wish to get ejaculated on.

8) Hand cuffs, whips, cable ties, gags, bondage wear, nipple clamps and any other piece of equipment should only be used with consent of both parties. But remember what's good for the goose is also good for the gander. It works both ways! Unless you are Mr Grey off course (selfish man!)

9) A woman will become highly conspicuous about parts of her body. It happens to us all at some stage. Do all us women a favour and don't prod the bits we are not happy with. You will not do yourself any favours! And remember as our female form grows older so does yours. Shrinkage really does happen. Sorry.

10) Nobody wants to sleep on the wet patch. Do the gentlemanly thing and make sure all activities are on your side of the bed. Trust me she will remember ☺

<u>Giving birth:</u> If you are a first time father the words of Captain James T Kirk are all you have to remember, "You are about to go where no man has gone before". You will see things that make Alien vs Predator look like an episode of Pepper Pig. In time, you will be able to view your partner's lady parts as a sexual object again. But for a while the stretching and expulsion of a baby will change your views! Please don't be like most men or partners who moan on and on about being exhausted as you have not been to bed for seventy two hours. Oooo my heart bleeds! Remember your partner. Yep, she is the one that has had her vagina stretched beyond measure. Who has probably suffered the embarrassment of her bowels opening as the contractions became stronger. She is the one who has probably vomited in a little paper bowl due to the pain killing drugs she has succumbed to taking. She is the one who has got into a highly undignified position with one Doctor

or Midwife poking her bits continuously She is the one who will squeeze your hand, dig her fingers nails into your skin, call you every obscenity under the planet and turn into Linda Blair from the Exorcist. She is the one who will now spend the next year of her life, scrubbing baby sick from her clothes, from the floor and from the wall. She is the one that will deal with the night time feeds, have her boobs looking like she has had a treble H breast enlargement. She will be walking around like a zombie, going shopping in her pyjamas, forgetting who the hell she is any more. Dealing with 'new mum syndrome' and their constant stares, jibes and comments about her new baby (this gets worse as the child grows). She will be having to deal with the terrible twos, threes, fours, fifteens, twenty ones and thirties (yep it goes on forever) and your complaining about being a bit tired! Welcome to mother hood.

'M' word (The Menopause): Meaning when is my life gona return to fucking normal! And also the period of time a middle aged women will self-combust from the inside out & feel hypothermic in a spate of five minutes. She will feel sick, dizzy, sneeze and piss herself (even after religiously doing her pelvic floor). She will forget who her children are, including their names and dates of births. Cry when peeling a potato and say sorry to it for boiling it alive. Have uncontrollable urges of I really need to be taken from behind and shagged senseless or the total opposite and begin to feel like a nun. She will have an irrepressible and unmanageable urge to punch a stranger in the face because she just doesn't like the look of them, or hug random people and become a throw back, from the sixties spreading free love all around her. She will forget what she is supposed to be doing and leave taps running whilst filling up the sink only to return a few moments later to find the kitchen floor flooded. She will place raw food in the oven on a low heat to cook slowly sending the chunks of meat in the dish into a mouth-gasm but realising just as she is about to dish up the oven hasn't actually been turned on. She will not have a period for months then when it finally happens her guts feel like they are being shredded by a blunt pair of scissors. Her groin will ache like a complete and utter bitch where some deformed creature is playing ping pong with her ovaries and her knickers will look like road kill on the M25! 'M' word a confused state of mind that affects 1 in every 3 women. And those who do not get affected by it FUCK YOU!

Which leads us nicely onto Nancy, a hormonal woman who finds herself and her world turned upside down. It's the little things that change us women. But for Nancy it was the little changes that turned her back into a woman of fortitude and strength.

Chapter 1

The night was damp, cold and uninviting, the rain poured down, the wind howled and there was an icy chill in the air. Oh who am I kidding! In Nancy's bedroom it was like an oven. An oven that someone had just thrown her into slammed the door and turned the controls onto 250 degrees!

Nancy laid there on top of the covers, in nothing but a pair of pants. It has to be said these pants had seen better days. Which on occasions these thread bare accessories would see a bit of sexual activity by being ripped off by her husband's teeth. Just not for a very long time!

Her legs were spread eagled searching for a cool patch on the bed. She was mimicking a snow angel on her sheets. Feeling her way for that one spot that hadn't yet been warmed by either herself, her husband or one of her rather large German Sheppard's that they shared their bed with. Sweat poured out of every orifice. For the gazillionth time that night she was in the middle of yet another hot flush! Oh how she loved being middle aged. And thought what stupid twat came up with the saying 'life begins at forty'.

"Maybe for a penis person it might"

There was no cool spot to be found and all that strenuous leg searching made Nancy's body heat up quicker than a marshmallow that had just been thrown onto an open fire.

In all Nancy's frustration she spoke loudly not caring if she woke her husband, the dogs or even the dead.

"Oh for fucks sake"

 Not only was she in the full throws of a physical internal combustion moment but her bladder decided it would burst at any given time. And as everyone knows a menopausal woman's bladder is a force of its own. No woman can dither about when the pangs of 'I need to piss' make an appearance! If they do then the consequences are fatal! Tena lady was invented for a reason you know! All hail the penis person who invented them at least one of the 'P' tribe managed to do something right.

Nancy sat perched on the toilet staring down at her feet. A nippy fresh breeze of the outdoors was gently blowing onto her neck through the small bathroom window.

Nancy sighed

"Bliss"

After thirteen years of being perimenopausal Nancy knew that she had approximately 36 seconds , to wipe, flush, wash her hands and snuggle up to either her husband's warm body or the dogs. Either or, she just knew she was going to need one of them before the aftermath of a hot flush hit her. And what prey tell is the aftermath? The cold flush of course. Actually it's the 'oh my bejesus, Mary and Joseph I'm dying of hypothermia flush.' Which sends your body into convulsive shivers, where goosebumps upon goosebumps appear on your skin and the undesirable need to piss like a race horse once again takes over your every movement.

The night to say the least was a long one.

"Mum, Mumm Mumma, mom, ma, are you awake" Daisy poked Nancy in her closed eye sockets "Are you dead?"

Nancy's reply was short and sweet

"Yes GO AWAY!"

Daisy was Nancy's third born daughter that she made with her husband Ralph, on one sultry night in June. Passion and lust took hold and Daisy was conceived on the kitchen floor of their rented accommodation. But if anyone ever asks her she always told them she was an immaculate conception. That some alien being from a faraway distant planet placed in her womb, after doing some weird and wonderful experiments on her one humid summer evening. Actually she always announced quite loudly that all of her three daughters were not made from a night of passion and lust but were the after effects of being violated by some extra-terrestrial being from outer space. It soon shut people up. Nancy could never understand why people continuously asked, how, why and where after someone announced they had become pregnant. Surely to god after centuries of women growing babies in their uterus folk would have worked all this shit out by now!

"Mum, it's nearly 10 o'clock, and I can't believe your still lying in bed, you lazy old trout! Daisy carried on poking her mother's closed eye sockets with her finger.

Nancy opened her blood shot eyes and lifted her head from her pillow. Her short blonde highlighted hair stuck to her forehead, her mascara she had applied the day before was smudged around and down her face. Her eyelashes looked like some deformed spiders legs sticking out of her eye lids and the ominous dried dribble stains were stuck to the corners of each side of her mouth and down her chin. She looked like a mixture between Sloth from the Goonies and the Alien in the film with the same name.

"Rough night, mother dearest? Anyway I really, really, really need to tell you something it's really, really, really important" the urgency in Daisy's voice sounded well........ urgent.

Nancy stared at her daughter, and tried her hardest to show the interested mother face. You know the one; eyes slightly pursed together, lips at a semi pout, head tilted. Before Nancy could say anything, Daisy's gob opened quicker than she could pee, wipe, wash and be snuggled back in her bed before the 'cold flush' occurred.

"Well" Daisy announced "You know the twat of an ex-boyfriend, he has only just gone and knocked up Felicity, but that's not all, before he donated his sperm to her she found out she had Percy's!" Daisy fell about laughing like she had just been to the dentist and inhaled too much nitrous oxide.

Should really explain who these two people are and the story behind why Daisy feels a bout of genital warts is so hilarious. Felicity was Daisy's old house share buddy. Daisy moved in with her over a year ago. Things were going quite well really apart from the fact that after a very late night in the tattoo shop where Daisy worked inking stranger's skin every day, she arrived home only to find Felicity and her now ex- boyfriend Phil, top and tailing each other on the living room floor. After an awful lot of 'effing an geffing, the occasional plate, cushion, and Felicity's laptop being thrown, Daisy was back home in her old bed within an hour of the horrendous totally unpleasant and appalling sluttish behaviour of her house mate and the man whore. Who Daisy described more often than not as having a penis smaller than a fish finger and ejaculated quicker than she could blow out the candles on her birthday cake!

Daisy still laughing to the point where your stomach muscles go into total spasm finished off her morning gossip with

"Karma's a bitch in it, but fucking worth waiting for!"

With that Daisy planted massive kisses on her mother's morning breathe lips and left.

"Well at least someone's happy this morning" Nancy said to herself as she heaved her rather middle aged shattered body from her bed.

Her shower that morning was set to 'cold' in a bid to 1) wake her up a bit and 2) to hope that cooling her body down to a point of my fingers and toes have gone blue would stop her body from heating up again. She knew it wouldn't work but she had tried every herbal remedy that she had seen via adverts on the internet claiming they could 'cure your menopause in an instant'. Needless to say they didn't do nothing but make her a few pounds poorer. It was that bloody magnet she bought that was the biggest waste of money and personal embarrassment. She done what it said on the leaflet, she positioned it at the top of her pelvic bone, in the place her uterus was. One side touching her skin the other on the outside of her knickers. The instructions tell you to wear it day and night for a couple of weeks to feel the benefits of this rather heavy, cold bit of metal. Well after an hour or two Nancy lost it. No really, I mean she lost it. The outer part was stuck in her jeans trouser leg but she couldn't find the other bit. She had removed her trousers, her knickers but the offending object was nowhere to be seen.

"I wonder" Nancy thought

As she inserted her finger into her own vagina, she felt around for a bit and kerboom there it was! Nestled in the cushiony part of her cervix was the other half of that blasted magnet. It was an unwanted and an unnecessary wasted hour of her life and not to mention the money she spent on this miraculous cure. She wasn't against any form of manual gratification but the sheer panic she felt thinking she would end up in accident and emergency with some random Doctor poking around in her privates sent her heart rate into super speed mode, her stomach fill with fear and her legs go all sort of quivery. The same leg shake women always get when they are lying on the Doctors couch waiting for them to perform the every six month smear. So the jubilation she had when she found it was to say the least a very happy moment.

Nancy took her time getting ready after all it's not like she had a job to go to. Just the normal hum drum routine of feeding the families three dogs, hamster and a hundred tropical fish. Then the daily dog pooh clearing up, the house work, washing, preparing the evening meal, decorating, shopping, paying the bills, cutting the grass, tidying the garden, sucking up the hundreds of wet leaves that had fallen the night before, brushing the dogs, then hovering again after the dog hair encouraged itself to haphazardly puff around the room. Helped with each dog leaving a flurry of fur as they escaped her clutches and the dog grooming brush, and of course trying to run away from the day time hot flushes too.

Her housework used to be done in record time and so did all the other chores. She liked nothing more than to be up at the crack of dawn, whilst everybody else still lay in their beds, and she always had the majority of her daily housekeeping jobs done before 10am. As the years have moved forward so has her natural alarm clock that used to get her up when the birds just started their dawn chorus. But since the good old 'M' she is lucky if sleep has happened before 6am, and lucky if her body came out of her semi-comatose state before 10am.

All of the housewifey stuff had to be done slower as the slightest form of physical assertion would bring about the sickly rising sensation in the pit of her stomach before it spread upwards and turned her face bright pink, made her neck tingle and her head spinning like a child's after they have gone round and round in circles for too long. And last but not least the need to evacuate her bladder.

A wife and mother was all Nancy knew, it was all she had done since falling pregnant in her late teens. And now twenty seven, nearly twenty eight, years later and with two of her three daughters now living in their own home she was at a bit of a loss with what the hell to do with the rest of her life. Apart from wasting the hours of a day manually extracting magnets from her bearded clam, and forgetting what the hell it was she went into a room for.

For a brief second her motherly instincts seemed to return, as she picked up her mobile phone and text her youngest daughter.

"Daisy its mum, just had a thought about what you said this morning and Phil having warts, don't you think you should get checked out just to be on the safe side, love you" xxx

****

"Mum you don't have to tell me it's you when you text, I have you plumbed into my phone lol, I already have, I may be twenty two, like thrash metal, and seem a bit of a doughnut but I go to the gum clinic at least once a month or after any relationship breaks up just to make sure my snatch hasn't caught some disease. Love you morererer......p.s can I have fish fingers for dinner so I can pretend I'm biting really hard on

Phil's todger (in an evil, spiteful and malicious sort of way) (x)

****

"Fish fingers for dinner it is then" Nancy smirked as she headed to the freezer not to stick her head into it to cool down, but to make sure she had some unreal frozen penis's to cook.

As a mother, and not in a pervy sort of way Nancy was going to enjoy pretending she was afflicting imaginary physical pain on the young skanky douchebag that broke her daughters heart, whilst eating a plate of fish fingers, chips and peas! But if the enlightening bite down on a fish finger was going to give her that much pleasure she could only imagine how much satisfaction Daisy was going to get.

"Best cook all 20, just to make sure Daisy's contentment and pleasure has a long lasting effect, no man or beast should stand in the way of a heart broken, angry, incensed female" She told her reflection that was visible in the oven door. The oven door didn't answer, but at least her reflection made it appear she was talking to another human being and not just an inanimate object.

Chapter 2

Nancy dipped her paint brush into the newly opened pot of paint and began splashing it onto the wall. Splashing being the very lose way she painted. Any qualified painter and decorator would have possibly had heart failure at her distinct painting methods, but Nancy didn't care as long as the job got done. The only thing she had to ensure was that there was enough dust sheets covering every inch of the floor as she really didn't want to spend hours scraping off those little specks of dye that decided they would look better on the floor than the wall. 'Overtly Olive' was the colour she had chosen and in typical Nancy fashion she went into 'think mode'. Something every woman does, but a menopausal women's brain is hard wired to 'over think' things and the 'think mode' becomes second nature.

"I wonder who actually comes up with the spelling of words. Cos surely 'overtly' should be spelt 'oh-vurt-lee'." She pondered for a moment

" I wonder if there is a locked darkened room somewhere that hides away a little man who has to come up with the one and only way to spell a word? And that is all they do day in day out, until the day comes when they are all worded out and have no more use, I wonder what they do then?........ They become politicians" Nancy laughed out loud

Politicians were the people in life she had no time for. She never voted and when election time came and they banged hard on her door begging for her vote she would in no uncertain terms tell them to basically "fuck off" or do the total opposite (depending what sort of mood she was in) and stand there arguing with them until they couldn't answer her questions. They would give up sooner than she would but she loved nothing more than to antagonize, alienate and oppose these hounding power hungry individuals that in her words "didn't give a shit about anyone and all talked bollocks anyway". Politicians were not deemed rational people in her eyes and she considered all of them to be corrupt wankers, male or female!

BC (before children) Nancy was a total activist and would fight for anyone or anything that she thought needed protecting or changing. She would fight for the weak, animals or the disabled and Nancy would stand against any political structure that she could. Motherhood soon changed her wild woman of the woods approach to life but buried deep inside was that woman who would go out on a limb to stop the hunt and stand at the front line with placards. She would scream until her voice left its box and retreated further back down her throat. How Nancy missed those days where she used her untamed, primitive and feral instincts. She was an indigenous woman, a woman so free that she ran naked in the woods, washed in a freezing cold stream and sat every night by a bonfire discussing what cause her and her innate freedom fighters were going to battle against next.

She met Ralph at a 'stop the hunt' march. He was employed by the organizers to erect fences at the point of start, as rumours were spreading that Nancy's group of libertarians were going to cause some trouble. Trouble never! Nancy and her friends never caused trouble but they did make their voices heard and their points made. They would never hold violent protests, naked sometimes but never violent!

Nancy could not take her eyes of Ralph as he hammered hard down on a wooden fence post. He was young, tanned, muscular, and wearing a cut off pair of denim shorts and no shirt. His shoulders were rounded, his stomach ridged, his legs were well toned. She watched as beads of sweat trickled down his neck onto his smooth chest.

"Views good isn't it" Joe said, giving a little wink

Joe was her very camp, very gay best friend that she shared her sleeping bag with on many nights. He had perfect hair, perfect nails, perfect teeth and would have been her perfect partner if it wasn't for the fact he preferred men.

"It's a very, very good view Joe" Nancy sighed deeply

Joe shouted in Ralph's direction

 "Excuse me"

Nancy stared at Joe questioning him with her eyes. She wondered what the hell he was going to do or say next.

Ralph looked up.

"That's an impressive tool you have there?" Joe smiled

Nancy squirmed. Whilst Ralph just replied with a confused tone.

"Errmmmmmm thanks...I think"

Joe raised his eyebrows at Nancy and gave a cheeky grin

"Do you want a cock I mean a coke, coke I said coke"

Ralph walked towards the duo as Joe reached into his ruck sack and pulled out a warm can of coke and handed it to the half-naked, tanned succulent male.

"Thanks, it's much appreciated"

Joe had the unique ability to gather as much information about people in record time, which was probably down to the fact he came right out and asked just what it was he wanted to know.

"So, do you live around here? Do you have a girlfriend or even a boyfriend maybe?"

"Well" said Ralph "you don't beat around the bush when trying to find out a person's life history do you?"

Joe smiled before concluding the conversation

"No my dear friend I can honestly say I've never been one for a bush, trimmed or otherwise! I prefer a more solid hard forceful approach" Joe sighed winked and left Nancy and Ralph to get better acquainted.

Ralph gulped down another mouthful of the dark sweet liquid.

"He's a bit of a character isn't he? So do you do this sort of thing often?"

"Actually all the time"

"Why" Ralph enquired

"Because I enjoy it, I feel like I'm making a difference no matter how small it is. It makes me feel good, plus I love being outdoors."

"Same as, the being outdoors bit anyway" Ralph looked at his watch and picked up his rather impressive tool once more

"I, I better get back to it, before you lot start stampeding all over this posh blokes land"

Nancy nodded and began walking back to Joe. Her mind was all hazy and all Nancy could think of was the three second rule. If he turns back in three seconds he was interested. She counted slowly holding her breath far too long between each number, one, two .....

Ralph turned and looked back in Nancy's direction.

"I was just wondering" Ralph shouted "If you would you like to go for a drink sometime...obviously after the hunt has finished and you chased a few coppers away?"

Nancy's alter ego punched the air, and then she felt the heat rise in her cheeks and the butterflies in her stomach had turned into dinosaurs playing a game of football with her appendix!

Nancy took a deep breath in a bid to try and slow her heart rate as it was getting to the point of beating out of control. She was sure he would be able to see it pounding away under her thin cotton vest. If she didn't calm herself soon she would end up fainting and that would probably mean he would change his mind and she really didn't want that to happen

"I'd love to, I'll meet you here at shall we say around seven"

"Seven it is then" Ralph smiled before once again resuming banging in the fence posts.

Nancy felt like she was flying high. As if Tinkerbell had just sprinkled magic fairy dust all over her. But then reality struck. She hadn't washed in over a week, her hair was a tangled mess and her legs were hairier than a grizzly bears arse!

 Nancy screamed so loud that if there were any foxes in the vicinity they would have been more frightened of her banshee roars than any horn ordering the chase.

 "JOEEEEEEEEEE"

Joe's little ruck sack had everything needed to make an impression. Shampoo, conditioner, razors, deodorant, needle and thread, buttons, condoms, K Y jelly. The only thing he didn't have was the kitchen sink and an excuse for having K Y Jelly in his bag.

After the hunt was finished Joe and his ruck sack of goodies went to work on Nancy. He combed out Nancy's mousey hair, she was shaved and plucked within an inch of her life and some random scent was sprayed all over her body. Joe placed a kiss on her forehead and a condom in the back pocket of her jeans.

"There you go my little lady of the woods, you are shaved, pruned, washed and good enough to eat, and if I wasn't a huge bit gay I would eat you myself, nom, nom, nom. Now go and have fun lots and lots of fun. Oh and Nance, there is a little something I slipped into your back pocket"

Nancy frowned as she pulled it out.

"Don't frown at me young lady, you know what Uncle Joe always says. If you're going to be a lover, wear a cover. Now go, go, go, go. And don't do anything I wouldn't do"

Which Nancy knew wasn't a lot!

As Nancy got close to the clearing Ralph was already standing there leaning on one of the fences he erected that day. He had a tight black t-shirt on and a pair of stone washed Levi jeans. Nancy couldn't help but breathe a sigh of relief that at least he hadn't chosen the typical 80's very loud Hawaiian shirts, and chino trousers! Even at eighteen she knew what she liked in a man and what she liked was a man who looked rough and ready for anything and everything.

After a very shy hello and a timid smile they went to one of the local pubs that was just a short walk from where Nancy and her friends had set up camp. It was the typical old fashioned quaint little country establishment. There specialty was chicken in a basket and a pint of beer. Not one for beer Nancy opted for a glass of coke. The typical flat coke that pubs of this sort always served. But the meal made a nice change from the burnt sausages cooked over an open fire and shoved between two pieces of rather dry stale bread. The conversation went well too. She found out that Ralph was the younger of two brothers, left school at the age of fifteen due to the fact he didn't quite get on with the whole education thing and started work immediately as a builder's apprentice. He came from a working class background lived in a tiny two up two down in the town close to the camp and had just broke up from the girl next door. Both his parents and the girl's family thought that Ralph and Theresa would stay together forever. They went to primary school and secondary school together and were inseparable. Till Ralph caught her with her knickers down doing some doggy type breeding with his own brother Mark.

Nancy had told him her parents split up after her father beat her mother up, after being an alcoholic for many years. Then they got back together again after he promised to stop the demon drink. That lasted precisely four months before he started hiding bottles of scotch under the sink or wrapped up in towels in the bathroom cupboard. So she gave her mother the ultimatum that if she stays with him she would move out. Needless to say Nancy's mother chose the fists of her husband rather than the love of her daughter. So Nancy went on the road, until she found the group of people she now calls her family. For now he did not need to know any more about her, her family or her past.

"Don't you miss your mum and creature comforts?" Ralph asked

"Erm yes of course but I couldn't watch Mum being controlled by him any longer and to be honest it got to a point where I think she actually enjoyed it. I know that sounds wrong but she liked the attention, she liked people being concerned about her. It's as if it became her drug her fix of some sort. But as for creature comforts shit yeah! I miss a warm bath, a flushing toilet, decent food and a soft bed with a snugly duvet, but these people give me freedom to be who and what I want to be. Living in this manner is in my blood and you know what they say, blood is thicker than water. And anyway there is more to life than a mortgage, a nine to five job and all the stress that goes with it. Joe's crew are my irrational, dysfunctional, creatures of society but I so love them!" Nancy sipped her coke "You should so try it some time, you should take all your clothes off and just run as far as you can with nothing but the wind in your hair and the sun beating down on your skin.....Just a word of advice though don't do it when Joe's around cos you will probably get more than you bargained for and it won't just be the thorns that give you a bit of a prick!"

The conversation continued without any uncomfortable pauses and before both of them knew it last orders had been called.

"I'll walk you back to your camp" Ralph said as he downed the last mouthful of his beer "Can I possibly see you again sometime?"

"We are only due to stay for another two days then we are off up North somewhere" Nancy said "But there is always tonight, life's about making memories isn't it?"

Nancy leaned over the table and kissed Ralph on the lips. Her heart was beating so fast she thought she was going to die at any time. Never had she ever been so brazen before. Well except once at a school disco when she saw Sarah Chivers swooning all over Christopher Adams. Nancy had fancied him for ages and had decided in her History lesson that tonight she was going to make him know just how much. Nancy and her best friend Charlotte (Char for short) had come up with a plan that at the beginning of the evening Nancy was to start dancing right in front of him. Which for Nancy was a task in itself as she had two left feet and was going to wear a pair of neck breaking stilettos that Char had pinched from her sister for her. Between the two of them they had chosen a skirt so short that her knickers could be seen from any angle and a low cut chemise style top which to the trained eye would have probably been better being worn to bed rather than an end of term disco. The evening arrived soon enough and Nancy's face was made up like a china dolls, rouge that hadn't been blended, multi coloured eye-shadow and strongly outlined lips. Obviously if Char had been a true friend she wouldn't have let her best mate even leave the house as Nancy sort of resembled a clown from a circus and some rain forest tribe member that was preparing for 'the hunt'. Charlotte had told her she looked gorgeous and if he wasn't interested in her he 'must be blind or gay!'

Nancy was unsure, but her best friend wouldn't lie would she?

Nancy put those disgusting yellow neck breaking shoes onto her dainty feet, pushed around her heavily back combed hair and re-arranged her boobs so that at least it would appear she had a cleavage of sorts. At fifteen Mother Nature was being a bit slow on the breast development and Nancy had wondered if her boobs would ever grow instead of looking like two fried eggs all alone on a dinner plate. Unlike the well-formed bust of Sarah poxy look at my big tits and my perfect figure Chivers!

In typical Nancy style she fell over her own feet landed face down on the hard wooden school hall floor and blood began seeping from her nose. Not the best way to try and make someone fancy you, but Nancy didn't give up oh no she cleaned up her face, re-arranged her attire and headed back to where the gorgeous Christopher was standing. Only to find that Sarah bloody Chviers had stepped into her place, gyrating her backside right in front of him to Relax by Frankie goes to

Hollywood. Everyone fancied Sarah, everyone loved her abnormal sized breasts, perfect skin and designer clothes!

Bitch!

Nancy bent down took off those man made distasteful yellow scaffolds and marched right up to Christopher making sure she pushed the villainous Sarah out of the way she grabbed hold of his cheeks and shoved her tongue right down his throat. Nancy had assumed that kissing him was going to make her fall more in love with him than she was already but his breath tasted of cheese and onion crisps and he didn't even use his tongue! So that was the end of that love affair and the end of her friendship with Charlotte. As the following day at school she caught her laughing about how stupid Nancy looked the night before in the science blocks toilets with none other than SARAH PERFECT PANTS CHIVERS!

But Nancy felt she had the last laugh as the day she walked out of her mums at the tender age of seventeen she spotted Sarah Chivers standing at the bus stop soaking wet, twenty stone heavier, a face full of acne and pushing a pram, Whereby Nancy on the other hand was a sumptuous size ten with a 34DD breast long flowing blonde hair and a spot free face.

Karma strikes again!

****

It only took minutes for the two young people to reach the clearing. The warm summer air hung to their bodies as the nightingales sung their favourite tunes with the odd owl and grasshopper joining in every now and then. It was so quiet and peaceful unlike hours before when the hippy reprobates where running and jumping across fields and brooks shaking old plastic bottles filled with stones. The metal tins used to cook and serve dinners were being banged hard to scare any foxes away from the stampeding horses. The pack of hungry dogs and all those jumped up toffs in their red coats with shiny buttons. Nancy and her posse of dirty proletariat commoners felt extremely happy that no fox got caught today and no novice hunter got blooded. The fact that no one got arrested and thrown into a cell for the night was also seen as a good result. The hunt may have been fueled with slightly drunk flask drinking redcoats and the bohemian non conformists but at least a life was saved that day, which put everyone in an exceptionally favourable mood. Except the redcoats of course!

Ralph stood by one of the fence posts and started picking at the pale wood. Nancy was standing a few feet away staring longingly into his eyes. May be it was down to the warm summer evening, the fumes from that rancid beer or just the way he made her feel so comfortable but the image of Ralph covered in sweat hammering the fence post earlier was transfixed into Nancy's mind. She wanted him, she needed him and so did the fire that was building inside her.

"So" said Ralph as he kicked a lump of dried churned up mud "What did you mean by 'life is about making memories'?"

Nancy moved a little closer to him and brushed off a bit of fluff that was on his shoulder

"Well none of us know if we are going to be here tomorrow, and we as people waste so much time on worrying about all the unimportant things in life we tend to miss out on all the good things. You know happy moments that really can make a difference to our lives and how we feel" Nancy paused and stared up into the night sky "Tomorrow never knows" she said in a whisper

Ralph stretched out his arm and pulled Nancy towards him. Nancy did not retreat and positioned her arms around his neck. Their eyes were riveted on each other as their lips touched. Their tongues moved and swayed in each other's mouths like cobra's moving to a dancing flute. In a silent swift motion Ralph's hands transcended down onto Nancy's buttocks and he pulled her close into him their groins now touching. Nancy could feel him pulsating, her greed and rapaciousness as the hunter was growing, he was her prey and she wanted to devour him in any way she could. Nancy felt for the top button of his Levi's and she undone each button in turn, the heat from his crotch sent shivers down her back. Ralph lifted up her arms and pulled off her top to reveal Nancy's firm breasts his fingers began caressing her ever growing nipples and his tongue licked the bare flesh of her skin. Nancy gasped. Ralph moved his hands slowly down her spine making her back arch and her head fall backwards. Ralph stopped and gazed into her big brown eyes

"You are so beautiful"

Nancy did not reply but she smiled and removed her jeans. She was now totally naked and vulnerable. Her body was intoxicated with his scent her groin yearning for pleasure.

Never had she hungered for anyone like she did him, for tonight anyway he was hers.

was stunning. Her long auburn naturally wavy hair hung around her shoulders like a lions mane, her eyes were as green as emeralds and her figure was one any other middle aged woman would have died for. She was crazy yes but she was the one person that Nancy could be herself with and when they both got together the exaggerated comments seem to grow to that gargantuan proportion.

They often put the world to rights and no one could get a word in edgeways once these two women got going. Michele's taste in men was more burger king than a Michelin star restaurant. She liked her men like she liked her food quick, easy on the eye and even easier to digest. Michele attracted the bad boys. She never planned on this, it just seemed to happen. She had nearly all the types of penis people that were out there so now at forty five she decided that she was going to become a female that would use men for their genitals and nothing more.

She reached this conclusion after being told by her last boyfriend that he had arranged for some wild night of fun for the pair of them. Michele like most women thought of a nice restaurant a hotel room and some very rough and passionate rumpy pumpy. The shock on her face said it all when he took her to a semi-detached house with a nicely mowed lawn and trailing petunias regimentally planted in some hanging baskets. She entered the house to find a thick brown shag pile carpet and pictures of Her Majesty hung above an old electric fire. Flying ducks were on one of the other walls and the place stunk of 'shake n vac' and cheesy feet.

"Shag pile carpet who the fuck has shag pile carpets in 2009!" Michele thought.

Ten other couples where there in the distastefully decorated abode, all laughing and holding their 1970's style glass and nibbles holder delicately in their hands. This house was a time warp and so were its occupants!

A large middle aged man with a huge beer belly dressed in a rather loud Hawaiian shirt and white chinos held out his hand to Michele. Not knowing if she should shake it or tell him to wash it, get a manicure or put on a pair of marigolds she begrudgingly held the tips of his fingers and said

'Hello, pleased to meet you'

Michele wasn't one to make a scene....not then anyway...and smiled sweetly as he reached in for the ultimate HUG. His wine breath was blowing down the side of her face and he placed his left hand on to her hip

"Ewwwwwww" Michele thought and wanted to gag …..lots…!

"So pleased you could join us, my name's Graham, would you like a drink" he asked, his huge arms still draped around her neck like some scarf in a snow storm.

"Erm yes a glass of red if you have it" Michele answered still totally unsure of the fact if she had just walked through a time loop or if her date had forgot to tell her tonight was a themed party.

Graham walked towards the old 1970's mahogany effect drinks cabinet, its doors wide open revealing a selection of cheap red and white plonk and a lonely bottle of brandy. In the door its self were ledges that held numerous size glasses. No cut crystal but Asda specials that cost £2.99 for six. The sort of glass that was as thin as paper that would break the instant you put it into hot water. Which you then cut your finger on as it somehow almost always got stuck around the plug hole.

Graham unscrewed a bottle of red wine but even though Michele didn't have her glasses on even she could see in big bold letters on the label GOURMET CLASSIC DRY RED WINE and proceeded to pour the cooking additive into the sub-standard, poor quality drinking utensil. He walked back over to Michele who by this point was standing all alone as her date had minced away to chat to some of the other guests. Graham handed her the tawdry crude drink.

"Ere you go love, lovely glass of red that, it'll make your toes curls too or maybe I could do that later" he winked and swaggered off to the center of the living room and spoke aloud to all the guests in his home

"Ladies and gentleman, thank you for coming to our humble abode. I must say it's nice to see a few new faces here tonight "Graham looked in Michele's direction, dried spit was resting in each corner of his leering mouth. Michele began to feel immensely uncomfortable. Graham continued

"I hope you all enjoy tonight's activities and each other's company, so without further ado let's get on with it." He guffawed loudly.

Out of nowhere and in 'Ta Dah' Paul Daniels sort of way a short dumpy lady appeared wearing an orange jump suit with a yellow sash tied tightly around her waist, her hair was the colour of Birdseye custard powder that flicked out at the ends and on her feet were a pair of fluffy pink kitten heel slippers. She was certainly no Debbie Magee! The rather bizarre looking female tottered into the center of the living room carrying a large round Pyrex bowl and in seconds each guest in turn put their car keys into it.

The penny dropped.

"Oh my God" Michele screamed "Your all fucking swingers!"

Every face turned to look at Michele. The dumpy woman who looked like she had just walked out of a re-run from the 1970's show Butterflies addressed Michele's outburst.

"Oh deary! Do not call us swingers" Her tone held an element of sarcasm "We are F.L.I's, Free Loving Individuals, and we give each other love and affection once a fortnight!"

Michele stood still her eyebrows raised and biting the sides of her cheeks glanced once more around the room.

"Call yourselves what the hell you like love but none of you aren't getting anywhere near my lady garden!"

Michele left at a fast pace. She didn't see her date again after that night and that's when she denounced to the world that all men are condescending pricks and she would only touch a male of the species again when her vagina yearned for fulfilment. Or at that time of the month when the rampant pangs of ovulation struck.

Chapter 4

Nancy was not one for dressing up, and being in a room of gaggling horny women was not really her ideal way to spend an evening. All she really wanted on this chilly February night was to try out a new home made face pack made from one hundred grams of porridge oats, a tea spoon of honey, a squeeze of lemon juice and soya milk. But Michele was going to pick her up in under an hour so they could both spend the night at the local rugby club, gawping at a bunch of spray tanned American males dancing with their willies hanging out. Before pushing the offending objects into the faces of the audience. Note to self-Nancy thought "sit at the back of the club"

Nancy really didn't want to go but hurriedly bathed, shaved and plucked her body, applied her make-up and dressed casually in a pair of Levi's and a long sleeve slubby t-shirt. She had been to one of these nights before but last time she dressed to kill in her one and only posh

frock and a pair of five inch heels. Minutes
into the evening some concupiscent female
had spilt a glass of rum and coke down her
dress whilst another puked on her smart
suede shoes. Tonight she was going prepared,
jeans, t-shirt and a leather pair of boots. Her
short blonde hair was styled within an inch of
its life instead of just being held back with a
bandana. Her dark brown eyes were given the
smoky effect and her lips just a neutral shade
of gloss. She reached for her handbag and
made sure she had everything required, door
keys; check, phone; check, lip gloss; check,
money; check, baby wipes; for clearing off any
drunk woman's vomit; check, needle and
thread; for emergencies; check, ear plugs; in
case music is too loud; check, tickets; Michele
has them, condoms for Michele; check (she
always forgets them!) A get out of jail free card
and a monopoly boot which had been in her
handbag since last summer. She had no idea
why and just threw the card and boot back in
her handbag with her evening essentials and

went down stairs. Ralph was sitting on the sofa with a can of cider, his hand down the front of his tracksuit scratching his man parts and watching Police, Camera, Action on the tele.

"How do I look" she asked

No answer, Nancy repeated but a little louder,

"How do I look?"

No Answer

Nancy walked in front of the television but shouted her question. "HOW DO I LOOK?"

Ralph pulled his hand out of his tracksuit, she finally had his attention

Ralph's voice was raised in an agitated manner "Get out of the light woman!"

Nancy didn't even bother asking again and walked into the kitchen shaking her head. Just as she felt the pangs of rejection and the tears building in her eyes she heard a BEEP BEEP from outside.

"I'm going now" she said

NO ANSWER. Nancy picked up her hand bag, swallowed back her tears and left without even a "you look lovely, have a nice time" or even a kiss goodbye. Nancy felt rejected.

A long queue greeted them as they parked the car in the heaving car park. Hordes of already slightly tipsy women were all standing in a very haphazard line waiting for the doors to open. Most were dressed in attire that would have been better for the summer months. Miniskirts that didn't leave much to the imagination, neck breaking heals and camisole tops that were low enough to show off bulging breasts. Breasts that had been pushed together by an Ann Summers instant boob job bra. The first thing Nancy heard when she stepped out of the car was the tune of clattering teeth. Michele looked at Nancy, Nancy looked at Michele. Both just couldn't help themselves and broke into fits of hysterical giggles!

The doors opened and as the tickets were not numbered it became a race to get to the front of the seating arrangements. Nancy and Michele instantly sat at the back of the club and were very soon joined by a small group of women. All of which must have been a good twenty years older than themselves. Michelle leaned over and whispered in Nancy's ear.

"I'm sure that the women next to me is a friend of my Mum's and the one on the end is married to the vicar of St Margaret's."

"No way" Replied Nancy "Are you sure? So they know what tonight is all about don't they?"

Michele shrugged her shoulders and smiled.

"It's going to be interesting finding out" she laughed "What ya' want to drink, stupid question, mineral water ice and a slice maybe?"

Nancy smiled and nodded.

Everyone was settled in their seats when the lights went out the place was in total darkness.

Michele's Mum's friend poked her in her ribs and leaned over in her direction

"Hope they hurry up and turn the lights back on I can't see my knitting or my sherry!, I do hope they do a bit of Tom Jones tonight, oooo I do love a bit of Tom you know especially Green, Green, Grass of Home having that old tune played at me funeral you know "

Nancy and Michele both inhaled deeply between pursed lips. If nothing else tonight was going to be an attention grabbing experience especially for these old dears.

The lights were now back on and the compare took his place on the stage. He was dressed in a black tuxedo, and couldn't have been more than five foot tall. He shuffled from one side of the stage to the other and resembled penguin from the old Batman TV programs. In a Dick van Dyke accent and a constant repetition of "hello guv'nor" he started the show. A few slightly inebriated females thought he was highly amusing and giggled in a childish teenage way especially after he jumped off the stage and put one of their hands down his trousers!

"ladies I will not keep you in suspense any longer, please give a good old English welcome to Shawn and his sensual salamander and after tonight ladies y'all know why"

The stage went dark again and Dizzee Rascal's 'I don't need a reason' began vibrating out of the speakers that were placed in every corner of the club. The lights came back on and in the middle of the stage stood a man of six foot six, with a body to die for. A body that had muscles where Nancy had never seen muscles before, bulging and oiled up to make them more prominent. He was dressed in a tight black pair of leather trousers and a crisp white shirt that was opened to his navel. He had his back to the audience and began gyrating his hips to the beat of the music. Nancy looked at Michele, Michele looked at Nancy both looked at the old ladies sitting with their knitting next to them. But these old ladies eyes were transfixed to the stage and the pulsating thrusting groin of this gorgeous god like creation. With one hand he gradually undone each one of the buttons on his shirt and with the greatest of ease removed it throwing it to the side of the stage. Shawn the salamander flexed his biceps and stroked his smooth skin. He contracted his shoulder muscles and then moved both of his hands down to his tight buttocks. With slow movements he stroked them gently. Shawn turned and faced this highly excited crowd and jumped of the stage into the audience below and began grinding his crotch in the face of a willing female. He unbuttoned his trousers and began sliding them down his toned legs. He sat on the edge of the stage and beckoned another willing female to pull them from his feet. The randy libidinous crowd cheered and whistled as he leaped back up onto the make shift platform wearing nothing more than a skimpy black thong. Constantly propelling his hips that pivoted forward and backwards he placed his fingertips around the edge of his tight black thong. He teased the gawking crowd, pushing it down and then stopping until with the last line of the song he yanked them off. Everyone could see now why they called him Shawn the Salamander! The sex starved randy women cheered, whooped, whistled and clapped as he bent down to take his bow.

Michele open mouthed looked at Nancy, Nancy open mouthed looked at Michele, once again they both looked at the sixty pluses with their knitting. Michele's Mum's friend looked at them, swallowed hard and said

"Think I need another sherry"

Three strippers in, it was interval time and everyone jumped out of their seats and made a mad dash for the toilets or to go outside for a cigarette to cool their lustful ardour down.

Nancy squinted her eyes as the main lights were all turned back on she began jiggling about in her seat "God I so need to pee!, But I will wait till the second half as the queue will be so long, really don't know if my forty seven year old bladder is going to hold out though Chele I may have to borrow your glass......Chele, Chele?" Nancy turned to look at Michele but she wasn't there "Where the bloody hell has she gone?" She spoke curiously to an empty chair.

After ten minutes the lights dimmed again. There was a mad rush as women of all shapes and sizes hurried to find their seats. Most of them by now were filled with unbridled lust, a stomach full of cheap wine, vodka and Bacardi breezer's. Their faces flushed and glowing and with the help of the alcohol each one had taken on a demonic need to see yet more dis-robed men. The vicar's wife from St Margaret's, Michele's Mum's friend and the rest of the antediluvian women promptly took their seats, all smiling with eagerness and zeal.

They must have got through at least three bottles of sherry between them and their knitting was now in a tangled mess on the floor beneath their feet.

Nancy was still sitting with a ready to explode bladder wondering where Michele had disappeared too. She didn't want to just get up and leave the coats and bags unattended but was getting just a bit worried about her BFF. The Danny DeVito compare with his penguin suit, pointed nose and pathetic Dick Van Dyke impression once again took the stage. He was really beginning to grate on Nancy's nerves but her soon to be exploding bladder was annoying her more. Nancy was just about to get up and head to the ladies as her bladder began threatening to empty its contents down her leg when an out of breathe Michele quickly took her place by her side. As Michele sat down Nancy turned to her and with an earnest tone to her voice asked.

"Where the fuck have you been? Actually don't tell me I so need to wee right now and if I don't go I'm really going to piss myself!"

She gave Michele one of them motherly disapproving stares before exiting her seat and rushing to the loo. She was so very relieved that there was no queue and she had the choice of any cubicle she desired. The first one was blocked, the second one had vomit all over the floor but just like Goldilocks the third one was just right. Sort of clean, but with no puke, and a working flush. Heaven!

As Nancy sat on the toilet breathing a sigh of relief at her emptying bladder she heard the door open and a man singing Journey's 'Don't stop believing'. He had a really good voice but what the hell was he doing in the ladies Nancy thought. She sat there a few moments longer before wiping and flushing. She opened the cubicle door and saw one of the erotic dancers grooming himself in the mirror. He smiled at her. Nancy blushed and smiled back.

"Are you enjoying the show" He asked in a BRITISH ACCENT

"Oooo erm you're not American" she answered as she squirted soap onto her hands

"No love, I'm from Uckfield, between you and me the only one that's from the big old USA is Kevin"

"Kevin?" Nancy inquired

He lent against the sink, the eye candy was now dressed in a tight white t-shirt and a pair of Hollister straight legged jeans that fit snugly around his buttocks. Nancy couldn't help but stare at the size of those biceps and the contours of his beautiful face and square chin. The Adonis started to run his fingers through his dark brown shoulder length hair. Nancy sighed, as she looked into those crystal blue eyes, she was feeling a hot flush coming on and not of the menopause variety either!

"Kevin's the compare and to be honest a complete prat too when he is on stage!" he announced "Anyway you haven't answered my question, are you enjoying the show?"

Blushing again and feeling the heat rise ......in-between her legs..... Nancy answered stuttering like a stupid teenage!

"ermmm yyyyyes it's, it's a very good show and I'm having a lovely time, ermmmm ttthank you"

Oh for god sake Nancy's alter ego said, "Pull yourself to bloody-gether, he is young enough to be your son and wouldn't even think twice about looking at some middle aged women that stutters!"

Mr. Biceps, leaned over towards her placed his hand on her bum and kissed her gently on the cheek.

"Good I hope you enjoy the rest of the evening just as much and maybe we can meet after in the bar for a drink? " He blew Nancy a kiss as he walked out of the door. Nancy's heart was palpitating faster than he could move those hips. She splashed cold water on her face, took a huge deep breath and tried to recompose herself, before venturing back to her seat.

Pete the python was sitting legs straddled on some women who he had pulled out of the audience, his manhood being covered by another of those tight fitting black thongs. As he rubbed his concealed penis in the woman's face Nancy sat back down in her seat.

"So where the hell did you get too? "She asked Michele

"Well you know the third act we saw tonight, I know him, I know him very well in fact."

"Eh what how?"

"Well do you remember that bloke I met a few times the one that I sort of had sex with over the bonnet of his Mini Cooper"

"You mean the one you did have sex with not sort of had sex with, the one who you put handcuffs on and lost the key?"

"Well" Michele said her eyebrows raised "Ed the eel is actually Simon from Sussex,"

"No way?"

"Yes way, I thought I recognized that tattoo on his arse, so I needed to go and check, and well we sort of well……. we actually got a bit re-acquainted in the interval"

"Please don't tell me you had sex with him"

"Erm well maybe just a tinsy winsy bit"

"What do you mean just a tinsy winsy bit!" Nancy was just about to go head long into a lecture about safe sex and condoms when a sweaty arse was pushed right into her face. Nancy leaned right back on her chair, her eyes flicking from side to side as Pete the python pushed his groin closer into her face. Nancy was blushing beyond compare as Pete placed her hand on his thong and whispered in her ear

"Pull it off"

Nancy had nowhere to run so with one eye open and the other closed she yanked off the thong, but couldn't help but laugh.

"Why you laughing" he asked as the crowd began whooping

"Well" said Nancy quite flippantly "Pete the python you most certainly are not I've seen more meat on a butchers table!"

Pete grabbed back his thong, bowed to the rest of the audience and scowled at Nancy.

Chapter 5

At 1.30am Nancy pulled up onto her drive. She sat staring at the front door of her home but couldn't seem to muster enough energy or enthusiasm to get out of the car. Michele had drunk far too much and Nancy took Michele's keys away from her a couple of hours prior to leaving the club. After all the performers had finished the male strippers re-grouped in the clubs bar for photographs. IPhone's were clicking away everywhere you looked which was preceded with the said photos being uploaded to Instagram, twitter or Facebook. The vicar's wife from St Margaret's who was by now as drunk as a skunk must have had a picture done with every one of the men that entertained the sex starved females. She also squeezed each and every buttock and kissed every pair of lips. She even tried giving her number to Kevin the twat compare, which to give him credit he didn't throw back in her face but said thank you and put it in his pocket. What was her Vicar of a husband going to say when he found out? Her outlandish antics would have made a good Sunday sermon.

Nancy sat sipping her mineral water and did what she liked to do best, people watch. It's at times like this she is so glad she doesn't drink. In the corner of the room one women was throwing up in a bin, another who had just left the toilets was walking round with her skirt tucked into her knickers and half a toilet roll was being dragged behind her. Then there was the ones that threw themselves and their breasts at the Adonis men, grabbing their crotches and trying their hardest to be as sensual and as sexy as possible. But most of them had by now smudged make-up around their eyes, lipstick anywhere but on their lips and they could barely stand. They looked like their movements where being controlled by some puppeteer with an evil sense of humour. Nancy was actually enjoying this after show more than the real performance, and made a mental note never to start drinking!

Michele was busy getting better acquainted once again with Ed the Eel or Simon from Sussex. It had been a little over a year since she saw him last. He used to work for the same company as she did but he was based in their London office. It was a brief but erotic fling whereby they had slightly illegal sex at every opportunity they could. Emotions did not play a part in it either it was sex, sex and more sex. Just the way Michele liked it. No attachments, and commitments, just pure unadulterated passion. Simon was seated on a bar stool and Michele was standing in-between those firm thighs. They were giggling and whispering in each other's ears as Simon pulled her closer into him. Nancy couldn't help but feel pangs of jealousy. Michele was free to do just exactly as she chose. She had a good job was totally independent, owned her own flat and car and shagged whomever she wanted when she wanted. Unlike Nancy whose house and car was in her husband's name only, no job and a sex life that died about eight months ago. She wasn't even needed by her children any more except when things in their own lives went wrong. Nancy felt unimportant, unattractive, unloved, old, past it, menopausal and bored! How she hated her life right now and seeing just how free Michele was made her feel even worse than ever. Nancy let out a huge yawn.

"Are we keeping you up?"

Mr. Adonis from the toilets, stood right in front of her, with that rather large package in her direct eye line. Stuttering Nancy was back.

"Ermmmm yyyyyes, nnnno ssssorry I mean no, oh bloody hell I don't know what I mean!"

Nancy looked up from that rather well-endowed crotch into the deep penetrating eyes of this stunningly beautiful creation. God he was gorgeous!

"Can I get you that drink now" He asked as his eyes leisurely gazed down at her breasts.

Mother Nature had been very kind to her so far in her middle age. Yes her breasts where ok a little less firm than BC (before children) but they still had there voluptuous appearance and even though she had gone up in size around her mid-rift she still managed to squeeze into a size 10 pair of jeans when needed. Her tummy didn't have any stretch marks (well maybe one or two) and admittedly her toned strong stomach muscles were a lot less taut nowadays but her figure was holding its own.....just....

"No I'm fine thanks I was just about to leave anyway" a blushing Nancy answered

Dream boat bent down and kissed Nancy on one check then the other and then moved his mouth to her lips and kissed her again.

"Is there anything I can do to make you stay" His voice was....... god his voice was so sexy!

"Erm well.....erm you do realise I'm old enough to be your mother don't you?"

He smirked

"Old enough, sober enough and so pleasing on the eye" he kissed her cheek again "Plus older women are so much more attractive and have so much more to give than younger women, they know how to please. …If you know what I mean?"

For the first time in months Nancy's blocked vaginal chimney that was covered in cobwebs finally began to heat up! She tried her hardest to compose herself

"I'm so sorry my darling I'm married"

"Well I won't tell the husband if you don't" he placed another of those soft sweet kisses on her lips

Nancy jumped to her feet grabbed her bag, her jacket and looked at this beast of a man. A man who she would have eaten for breakfast, lunch and supper and may be a mid-morning and midnight snack too.

"I'm sorry I just can't"

She hurriedly walked to Michelle who by now was playing tonsil tennis with her fuck buddy.

"Chele I'm off are you going to be ok?"

A rather hot faced dry lipped Michele answered in a croaky sort of way

"Yep, just fine and dandy, dandy and fine, I will ring you tomorrow, and come pick my car up just don't know what time as I may be rather busy for the next twenty four hours or so" she gave a tantalizing provocative smile.

As Nancy reached the exit she glanced once more at the Mr. perfect, who by now was being pulled, groped, and stroked by a gaggle of six women. Their IPhone's were clicking wildly as they begin pulling him in every direction. He stared right at her, Nancy smiled back and mouthed 'bye' as she pushed open the door and made her retreat.

The drive home cooled her ardour down and now she was sitting watching the darkness of her house. Normally the porch light was left on when any member of the family were out for the evening but tonight the house was a blackout zone. Nancy got out of the car and fumbled to find the lock. She knew Daisy wasn't going to be in as she was staying over at a friend's house after going to a Defeater concert. Ralph was supposed to be in tonight to look after the dogs. Nancy fumbled in the darkness for the light switch and entered the kitchen. Each one of her four legged companions greeted her.

"Why are you all shut in here? "She asked them as their tails wagged with excitement.

Nancy flipped the button of the kettle, got a cup out of the cupboard and started making herself a cup of tea, but the cold chill in the air and the fact that Michele's heater on her car didn't work meant her bladder demanded her complete attention...... again!

After peeing like a race horse she walked into her bedroom only to find her bed was empty, she looked in the other two bedrooms, Ralph wasn't there either, actually he wasn't anywhere in the house.

In typical menopause fashion with a hundred and one paranoid thoughts racing through her brain she checked her phone for messages. No messages. She clicked play on the answer phone. There was only one message, from some sales company in a random part of India, telling her that her computer does not work properly and to call this number for some instant help. Nancy dialed Ralph's number, it rung and rung until going to his answer phone. With one failed attempt after another to contact her husband she left a message.

"Where the fuck are you?"

That night's sleep was even more unsettled than normal her anger and frustration at not knowing where Ralph was made the night time flushes seem even more potent than ever. The duvet was on then kicked off by her irritated legs. She pounded the bed with her fists which didn't actually make the situation any better it just made her dogs jump from the bed and hide in another room, just far enough away from this crabby irked female.

Somewhere between four and five o'clock she dozed into a resentful sleep. The thing about being a mother is a deep sleep, you know the ones where nothing not even an atomic bomb could wake you hadn't happened for many years so as soon as she heard a key turn in the lock down stairs her eyes were wide awake and her heart began palpitating. The clock on her phone read 5.36am.

A drunk Ralph entered the bedroom, stinking of alcohol and tripping up over his own feet. Nancy pretended she was still asleep. He crawled into the bed beside her and instead of putting his arms around her he instantly turned the other way, farted, and snored his way into oblivion.

The following morning Nancy was sitting at the dining room table trying to read her new Natural Remedy, cure for everything book, when Ralph got up. She started chewing on the inside of her cheek unsure of how to begin a conversation between them. Over the last couple of months they only spoke to discuss the kids the dogs or the colour of paint. Monday nights he was at the driving range hitting stupid little balls with a stick, Tuesday was his curry night with mates, Wednesday was gym night (his relaxed muscle didn't seem to be getting tighter though just a little more beer gut like) Thursday was spent at home (Hooray!) but he would always be in front of the tele, with Magners cider in hand, watching some totally crap program about some stupid bloke getting arrested under SECTION 5. Fridays was pub night. Saturdays was rugby and Sundays was the day all the family got together, had their typical roast dinner (unless it was summer then the rusty BBQ got used). Where Ralph would at 2.30pm on the dot fall asleep with a belly full of food and acid farts due to the Paxo stuffing and three types of veg. The joys of married life!

Nancy was looking at the pages of her book, her curiosity built to a level of exceeding the boundaries of its limitations.

"So where were you last night then, I thought you were going to stay home to look after the dogs for once?"

Ralph reached in the cupboard for some Anadin extra and poured himself a glass of water "They are dogs for Christ sake they can be left once in a while you know, and please don't speak so loud I've got the worst hang over ever!"

Nancy closed her book and walked into the kitchen.

"I wasn't actually shouting, I just thought you were staying in that's all" she paused "So where did you go till gone five thirty in the morning anyway?"

"Nowhere special"

"Well you must have gone somewhere? Or did you just sit on piss head Phil's bench up the town drinking the night away?"

Piss head Phil was the towns local alcoholic. Who spent each and every day sitting on the same old broken rickety bench in the high street by the war memorial. Only moving for the Armistice Day service every November. This was also the only time he looked clean shaven, washed and wore a smart suit. The rest of the time he had a can of Tennents extra in his hand, filthy smelly clothes, urine stains down his trousers and breath that could knock out Mike Tyson.

"So where the hell were you" she asked again impatiently

"I went to The Frog & Bucket met up with some mates and then went back too…" he stopped dead in his tracks

Nancy was getting very tetchy at Ralphs inability to answer

"Then went back to where?" she asked again her voice sounding peeved

"Oh my god, I went back to Lucy's ok! Now please can we talk about this later my head is banging like a bitch!"

Nancy flared her nostrils like a charging bull.

"You went back to lurid Lucy's and her loose labia" Nancy snorted "Oh so what was it this time, did the poor little cow break a nail or did she stub her toe and needed you to carry her home cos the pain was unbearable!"

Ralph tried to throw his glass in the sink but it missed and broke into a thousand pieces over the floor. (Yes it was a Asda special £2.99 for six)

"Now look at what you made me do for fuck sake woman!" he bent down to pick up the large shards of glass "If you really want to know she is having a bad time with her husband....."

Nancy interrupted

"Oh don't tell me, her husband is away a lot on business and he doesn't understand her and they haven't had sex for ages and she is lonely and has to look after the house all day in her Armani frock, Jimmy Choo mirror leather sandals with her fat arse bleached blonde hair, false nails, push up bra and spoilt brats for kids. Am I right or am I right!" she screamed with rage, resentfulness and a full blown hatred of that bloody lurid Lucy whose labia was as loose as a un-buckled belt

"I don't need this shit!" Ralph yelled as he threw the broken glass back onto the tiled kitchen floor. He picked up his van keys and stormed out of the house.

The tears began falling from Nancy's tired eyes as she bent down to clear up the broken glass. One tiny shard pierced her finger and blood poured from the open wound. Nancy sat on the cold hard floor, unable to stop the tears and the blood. It wasn't just that god forsaken cheap glass that was broken and shattered Nancy's heart was too.

Chapter 6

The end of February and the start of the new month had been a roller coaster of emotions. Ralph and Nancy hadn't spoken to each other since their argument. Each time Nancy would try and have a rational conversation with Ralph he just gave her a shake of the head and walked away. She didn't try any more after the last dismal attempt of reconciliation.

She had begun sleeping in the tiny box room that was full from floor to ceiling with years and years of clutter, old books, her daughter's school reports, photographs and boxes of memories. Memories that showed her a time when things were good, and a few that were not so good. But most were of happy times and times when the only things that were important was her, Ralph and their children.

Nancy was fed up with moving each box every night before she could squeeze into bed and decided to have a sort out and try and make her nightly visit to sleep on the ten year old mattress a little more bearable. She began sifting through each box. But like it does with most people when she got to the box that held years of photographs she sat down on the floor her back leaning up against the wall and picked every picture up in turn. Most of them were pictures of her daughter's, days at the beach or park, old family pets but then she found one of her mother and her drunk heavy handed father. Her mother was sitting on an old swing in the garden of her Auntie's house. Sharon wasn't her real Auntie but was one of the only people Nancy kept in touch with when she walked out of home. She was a good friend to her and always tried to take care of her mother after her Dad went on a week-long drinking binge. Nancy's dad had his arm draped over her mother's shoulder a can of Stella in his hand. Nancy remembered that day well. They had gone to her Aunt Sharon's for her birthday. The day was going really well until Nancy's dad decided to down a large tumbler full of Scotch. He then preceded to have a go at any one including Sharon's husband who was a lot bigger, stronger and sober. The day ended in tempers being lost, fists being clenched and blood being spat out of Sharon Husband's mouth as her own father had lamped him in the gob with one of the kids tennis rackets. Oh and her dad being arrested. Typical day in her household when she was young. Nancy run her finger tips over her mother's smiling face and a sense of guilt transcended down her body. Two years after Nancy left home her Mum died. She suffered a severe bleed on the brain and never regained consciousness. There was a lot of speculation about why, but Nancy's dad told the police and everyone else that she fell out of the loft hatch. Nancy and her Aunty Sharon just knew this wasn't the real truth but they had no proof so the police dropped the case. They stood together at her mother's funeral, both refused to speak to Peregrin, Nancy's dad. Who stood at the graveside with his two brothers, Percival and Pethius. Nancy gave her two uncles a nod of the head. There was only one person she really wanted to see that day and that was her Grammie, her dad's mother, and the woman she was named after. But she was nowhere to be seen. For all Nancy knew her father was still standing there today or dead in a ditch a bottle of scotch in one hand and a clenched fist in the other.

Nancy ripped of the side of the photo where her father was standing and tore it into a thousand pieces. She kissed her mother's face and put the torn picture into her pocket.

Time got away with Nancy and before she knew it, it was 6.45pm and Ralph's van pulled up on the drive. Normally she would have felt guilty at the fact that a hot meal was not cooked ready and waiting for him by the time he arrived home. But since there lack of contact she had downed tools, she hadn't cooked for him, done his washing, ironing or cleaned the house in the anal way she used too. She heard him enter the kitchen pull open the fridge and pull out a cold cider.

"Someone's gotta swallow their pride and give in, it might as well be me" she said to her reflection in the dressing table mirror.

Nancy removed her oversized baggy jumper that had man made holes in the cuff. Holes that were just the right size for her thumbs to lodge themselves into whilst the rest of the threadbare woolen stocking stitched cuff nestled itself comfortably over her knuckles and hands. Her blue scope neck loose fit swing vest was covered in the typical bleach stains. The scruffy old cleaning top may not have done much for her appearance but her ample breasts made this unsexy garment look rather fetching on her. She rearranged her breasts to form a welcoming cleavage, touched up her lips with a pot of Vaseline rose and almond lip therapy balm and checked her hair was ok before going downstairs.

"Ralph can we please stop all this crap now" she begged standing in a more upright position so her breasts stood out that little bit more." I really can't be bothered to argue anymore and hate it that we are not speaking"

"Well you've got to stop being so jealous then" he answered in a sardonic tone

"Sorry....I'm not being jealous I just don't understand why you feel the need to go round other women's houses to sort out their problems that's nothing to do with you, that's between her and her husband not you!"

"Fucking hell Nancy! I was helping out a friend!"

"A friend" she screamed "She's a slut everyone knows it, she's always having an affair a few months back she was screwing an eighteen year old boy! But no good old Ralph to the rescue he sees a damsel in distress and whoosh like a flash of lightening he's on his sturdy old steed sword in hand! Really Ralph when are you going to wake up? She wanted to get into your pants, you were her target, her shag. You were a way to get back at her husband that's all!"

"I wasn't just her shag" he stopped taking very abruptly

Nancy's cheeks were glowing red, a sick feeling was beginning to rise in her stomach, and her heart was beginning to beat fast inside the cavity of her chest.

"What did you say? You wasn't just her shag? What the hell does that mean? You slept with her didn't you?"

Ralph turned his back on his wife, his hands were resting in front of him on the kitchen worktop. With a hesitated response he said

"Yes, I mean not really, I mean we touched that's all"

"You touched!.....you touched her what intimately?"

Ralph slowly turned round to find Nancy only inches away from him. Tears were streaming down her cheeks. Her hands were clenched into two tight balls by her side and her eyes were wide open awaiting the anticipated prognosis of Ralph's betrayal.

Ralph looked at the cold tiled floor and swallowed hard.

"Yes" he said

Nancy froze, the anger that was holding her together like super glue vanished and her free flowing tears stopped cascading down her soft flushed cheeks in a precipitously manner. She lifted up Ralph's face so he was staring into her eyes.

Nancy's voice began to shake as she spoke "So you kissed her, you, you groped her. For Gods sake Ralph tell me what did you do! "

Ralph edged himself away from the mother of his children.

"Well......yes ok yes we kissed, we groped"
Ralph rubbed his forehead with his hands
"She sort of gave me a blow job and yes I sort
of returned the favour, I'm so sorry Nancy, it
was an accident it just seemed to happen"

Shivers travelled down Nancy's spine and her
stomach cramped into a tight spasm. Nancy's
heart began to fracture and splinter beneath
her rib cage and her eyes burned as she
suppressed the cloudburst of water wanting to
escape them.

"YOU BASTARD" She screamed

Chapter 7

Nancy could not muster another word to say to her lying cheating husband and headed for the door. Not even bothering to put her seat belt on, Nancy put her foot down hard on the gas and accelerated of the drive. She drove for miles with her vision constantly being impaired by the deluge of tears. Her mobile phone vibrated repeatedly in her back pocket, she ignored it. Nancy's head throbbed and her brain pulsated inside her skull. Memory after memory flashed before her eyes until she was blinded by pain and by the image of lurid Lucy with her loose labia going down on her husband!

She pulled the car into a lay by and wept violently continuously hitting the steering wheel with her hands over and over again. A heavy nauseous feeling was rising in her stomach, she opened the car door and vomited a sour tasting bile. Nancy sat there for a few moments longer gasping in deep breaths and forcibly stopping herself from retching again. It could have been the chill of the March night the shock over Ralph's betrayal or the fact that in her haste to leave the family home Nancy was only wearing her old cotton vest covered in bleach stains. But Nancy's body temperature was dropping quicker than Lucy's knickers. She turned on the ignition of her car and put the heater on high, a prickly sensation crept its way through every artery and vein in her body as her body established a near normal thermal reading.

Nancy took her mobile phone out of her back pocket and stared at the screen. Twenty two missed calls and ten voice mail messages. Five where from Willow, two from Daisy, four from Poppy and the rest from her dishonest two timing husband! Who thought helping a friend out meant bringing her to climax with his tongue!

Nancy sucked in a huge amount of the warm air through her nose that was circulating the car in a bid to stop her gag reflex taking hold again. As she typed a group text message to her daughters telling them not to worry, she will be ok and that she loves them more than a dung beetle loves poop. She toyed with her phone for a few minutes longer before pressing play on the voice mail messages from Ralph.

"Nancy please I'm sorry, just come home so we can talk about it. It shouldn't have happened I know that, but you've got to admit things between us have been shit these last few months, I was drunk and she needed a friend. I'm sorry please call me back I love you"

But Nancy didn't call him back and searched her phone book for the one person she knew she could trust and loved more than she loved her own mother. Joe.

"Hey beautiful" Joe's soft voice said "Long time no speak"

Nancy automatically relaxed but the misery inside her built again and the warm translucent water fell from her bulging eyes.

"Oh Joe" she sobbed "Everything has gone so terribly wrong"

Joe's impassive serene voice answered

"Hey, there's never a problem that can't be sorted-where are you?"

"Erm I'm not sure, I think I'm near Heathfield"

"Brilliant" he responded "That means you are not actually far from me. Have you got the maps app on your phone?"

"Yes" Nancy replied

"Jolly good, right if you put me on loud speaker and go to your maps app and your 3G is working ok you will get a definite position of where you are....got that"

"Yes ok, you will have to wait a bit cos I still don't understand these blasted contraptions!"

There was a long pause until Nancy finally worked out where she was.

"Ok Joe I'm on the A265"

"Awesome, ok, well I want you to keep going in a straight line then turn right onto the A267, you will get to a T junction when you do turn left onto the B2203. Go down this road for about five minutes and you will see a wooden post banged into the ground. The top of the post is painted in bright yellow fluorescent paint so you can't miss it. Turn down this road. It's a bit dodgy down here as there are no street lights and there are big dips in the road so take it slow. I'll be waiting at the end…..and Nancy "

"Yes"

"Welcome home"

Chapter 8

Ralph was sitting on the edge of his bed his eyes felt heavy and there was an empty dragging pain in the middle of his gut. He bent down and stroked Jovi one of their dogs who was laying by the side of the bed at his feet. Nelson was where Nelson always is, stretched out on top of their bed and Elsa their beautiful pure white German Shepherd bitch hadn't moved from her place by the front door. She had laid there when Nancy stormed out and was still in the exact same position with her head laying across her front paws. Ralph had tried to get her to eat her dinner after Nancy left but Elsa refused. Even Ralph could not face any solid food and just consumed one can of cider after another. The energy in the house was low, the dogs felt it and so did Ralph.

Ralph recollected the evening's events in his mind and the look on Daisy's face when he told her what had happened.

Daisy came home from work at around seven thirty. She was in one her typical 'I love life moods'. She walked into the living room the French doors where wide open and Ralph was sitting on the step looking straight down the garden.

"Jeeezzzzzzzzzzzzzz Dad its bloody freezing in here" Daisy said pulling her jacket tight across her chest.

"Daisy" Ralph turned to face his youngest daughter "I think I've done something terrible, actually I don't think I know"

Daisy walked over to her Dad and rubbed his shoulder

"Well you know what Joe always says, and that's there's never a problem that can't be fixed"

"Oh for fuck sake Daisy shut up about bloody Joe, that's all I hear from your mum, Joe this and Joe that, good 'ole fucking gay take it up the arse Joe"

"Alright dad calm it down! What the hell's got into you and what have you done so terribly wrong anyway?"

Ralph forged ahead telling Daisy every sordid detail. The one thing both Nancy and Ralph always agreed on was under no circumstances will they ever lie to their children (which isn't quite strictly true, but you will soon find out why) If they are old enough to ask then they are old enough to know the truth was Nancy's moto. Well some truths anyway, some things should always remain a secret. But the thing about lying is one day the truth will always out itself.

Daisy stood quiet and still as she listened to her father's unfaithfulness and treacherous deception. She shook her head and bit her bottom lip.

"You total bastard Dad! How could you do that to Mum? And with that old troll Lucy to! She glared at him with hatred in her eyes. "So tell me I have to know, how many times have you been with her?"

"This was the first time I promise," Ralph claimed as beads of sweat dripped from his forehead.

"Mum really hates that woman Dad, from the first time you became friends with her over fucking Facebook. She told you she was after you, but you wouldn't have it would you?"

"Oh god Daisy what have I done?"

"You've cheated on the one woman who loved you more than anything that's what you've done Dad"

A dispirited Daisy turned and walked out of the house in the same disbelieving manner Nancy had. With trembling hands she telephoned both her sisters and told them what their father had done. Poppy picked up the phone straight after and screamed like a woman possessed down the phone at her father. Willow on the other hand went straight round to the family home. She didn't exchange any words with him but slapped him hard across the face and left.

Ralph shuddered and let the flashbacks of the last few hours leave his conscious mind. He sat still on the edge of the bed in a pair of tatty old tracksuit bottoms and a threadbare sweatshirt. His melancholy train of thought was disturbed by his phone acknowledging he had received a message. He patted Jovi and reached over to the newly painted shabby chic dressing table that Nancy had just spent the last few weeks doing up and picked up his phone. It was from Lucy.

"Hi stud, husbands gone away again! Mums got the kids and I'm all lonely"
;-) x

Ralph's gaze looked fixedly at her message, and before he knew what he was doing he text back.

"So am I, why don't you come over I could really do with a friend"

Lucy pulled up on his drive in her latest 'if you don't buy me this car, I'm not having sex with you bribe to her husband, as predicted he bought it for her. A brand spanking new black 3 litre Range Rover Sport with its contemporary design features and five digital camera technology.

She rat-a-tat-tatted on the door with her keys. Ralph hadn't been able to shift Elsa so had to step over her to open the door.

"Dah'ling" said Lucy leaning forward and kissing him on both cheeks

Elsa began to growl and for the first time that evening stood up, her ears pointing high and her hackles on her back standing to attention.

"Elsa enough! Down girl!" Ralph ordered

Elsa promptly obeyed her master's commands and laid back down on the floor her head once again positioned across her paws.

"Hi Luce, please come in" Ralph said his voice a low murmur

Lucy hesitantly stepped away from Elsa giving her an incriminating look and followed Ralph into the kitchen.

"So where is the frigid one tonight then?" Lucy asked as she began stroking her poker straight hair.

With a downbeat expression on his face Ralph took out a bottle of wine from the fridge.

"I told her about us and I think she may have left me Luce"

Lucy removed the wine form his clutches and placed it onto the kitchen worktop. She moved closer to him, her finger tips lightly brushing the side of his face.

"What a witch! Just because you took solace in another woman, she left you? Well Ralph that just proves how little she does actually care for you in my book"

She edged closer to Ralph her breast's touching his chest. Lucy kissed him and with no hesitation Ralph kissed her back. She pulled away with a sultry look in her eyes and dropped to her knees. With both hands she gently dragged down his tracksuit bottoms. His semi erection was growing with every stroke of her tongue, she looked up at him as she took him fully in her mouth. Ralph gasped. He closed his eyes. The image of Nancy filled his mind. Regret was building in his chest as his eyes began filling with tears. Ralph grabbed hold of Lucy's hair and lifted her head. As he stared down at her, he thought for one split second it was Nancy's dark brown eyes he was gazing into. But it wasn't, it was Lucy, with her poker straight blonde hair, blue eyes and pouting lips looking back up at him. Ralphs fingers let go of her hair as an undaunted Lucy continued to caress him. He was lost in the moment. With one final surge of guilt touching every nerve ending in his body he climaxed.

Chapter 9

Joe was waiting for Nancy as she finally reached the end of the long potholed road. An old tartan blanket was swathed over his shoulders. Even in the dimly lit area Nancy could see just how dashing and well-groomed he still looked even though he was now in his late fifties. Nancy climbed out of the car and collapsed into his waiting arms. Joe held her tight and wrapped the blanket over her bare shoulders. Neither one speaking they embraced each other in total silence. Joe tenderly placed a kiss on her head and he held her close as they walked into the house.

Once inside Joe held Nancy at arm's length and scrutinized this disheveled looking creature.

"Oh my Nancy would you just look at those bags under your eyes but don't worry my little lady of the woods a bit of Preparation H will soon sort them out!"

Nancy couldn't help but smile, trust Joe to think of her inflamed puffy eye bags and hemorrhoid cream.

"But first things first" he said pulling the blanket snugly around her " A nice cup of cranberry and chamomile tea and you can tell your uncle Joe all about what the hell's been going on"

Nancy held on to the edge of the fraying woolen sheath and for the first time that night she began to relax

"Joe"

"Yes" he replied as he filled the old fashioned looking kettle and placed it on top of an ancient Aga

"Have you got any P G tips? Cos I really hate all those fruit teas you forced down my throat all them years ago.

Joe laughed

"For you my little princess anything" he blew her a kiss.

Joe held her hand tightly as she told him of Ralph's infidelity. She only paused to wipe the tears from her weeping eyes. Her body felt drained of any energy and her head was throbbing with sadness. Joe squeezed her hands in his before letting go and pulling out a small brown bottle from his trouser pocket.

"Right young lady, you've got it all off your chest and now you are going to bed!" Joe opened the bottle and shook two tablets into the palm of his hand "Take these don't worry they will just relax you enough to drop off to sleep"

Nancy placed the tiny white tablets onto her tongue and swallowed hard.

Joe helped Nancy to stand and led her down a small corridor. He stopped by a door which had a hand painted door plaque hanging on it. 'JOE'S ROOM ENTER BY INVITATION ONLY'.

The wooden door creaked as he pushed it open.

"We can sort something else out tomorrow" he said "But for tonight you can sleep with me, but I warn you any snoring or farting and you will be in the decrepit garden shed with the woodworm and spiders"

Nancy smiled as her eyes scanned the room. In the corner of the room an old log burner was lit. It filled the room with a sweet smell of cedar. The duvet was already pulled back on the small double bed and two half-filled glasses of wine were positioned on the dark oak bedside table. It became obvious to Nancy that her erratic telephone call had interrupted his evening. She felt instantly guilty.

"Oh Joe I'm sorry was you with someone tonight?"

"Shh child, it was nothing that can't wait, anticipation can sometimes be the best aphrodisiac drug in the world" Joe winked as he undressed this shambolic female "Come on into bed"

Nancy lay eyes closed with his strong arms holding her tight, he held her like a father would his daughter. Nancy felt safe, she felt secure, she felt loved and within minutes she was asleep.

Chapter 10

The sound of laughing chattering voices and footsteps walking up and down in the corridor outside her room woke Nancy from her slumber. Her body ached as she stretched out her legs. She arched her back her spine graciously said thank you as it clicked in response. As she peered over the top of her covers she could see the fire had since died down and was nothing more than a pile of ash and dust behind the glass door of the burner. The strong cedar smell still hung in the air and made the room instantly feel warm and cosy. At the windows was a dark blue heavy lined pair of velvet curtains that was blocking any natural sunlight from entering the room. In the left hand corner by the fireplace stood an old desk stained in the same dark oak as the bedside table. On it were piles of books, an assortment of papers and a painted tin can filled with an array of pens and pencils. Nancy grinned. Remembering how Joe re-cycled everything he could including old baked bean cans. The dark wooden floorboards were bought to life by a handmade braided rug. The room was quaint and nostalgically attractive.

Nancy looked at the alarm clock by the bed it read 10.30am and scanned the room for her clothes but they were nowhere in sight. Instead in a neat pile at the foot of the bed was a white bath towel, a pair of grey marl Nike tracksuit bottoms, a tight fitting white V-neck T-shirt, a pure lace molded baby pink bra and briefs set and a tube of preparation H.

Nancy covered her naked body with the towel, picked up the assortment of clothes (and of course the tube of hemorrhoid cream) and opened the bedroom door. The passage way had now fallen silent as she began searching for the bathroom. There was another three doors on this level and Nancy peered into each room. The first room she tried was smaller than Joe's and had two single beds pushed together, folded sheets and blankets lay on top of the bare mattress. It had a single wardrobe with doors opened standing in the alcove by the window. The next room she went in had two sets of bunk beds, all the beds were unmade dirty garments were thrown on the floor, hiking boots and steel toe-capped Dr Martens that looked like they had been removed at some pace were left in an untidy pile. Sods law dictated that it would be the last door she opened that would be the bathroom. In the middle of this room stood an old cast iron roll top bath. The panels on the wall had been painted white. In fact the whole bathroom was white apart from a small grey jug on the window sill that was filled with a herb bouquet which let a sweet smelling aroma fill the room. She filled the bath with a rich liquid that she poured from an ornate glass bottle decorated in black onyx jewels and silver twists. Nancy let her towel fall from her body and stepped into the frothing water and sublime suds. The water cascaded over her and for one brief moment she felt her body unwind and she dismissed from her mind everything that had happened in the last twenty four hours.

Chapter 11

Ralph got awoken by a rather hairy black German Shepard. Whose tongue was washing his face as if it was a prime piece of rump steak. He pushed him away and was just about to turn over and cradle his wife in his arms when he saw a comatose Lucy laying in the place Nancy should have been. Her long blonde hair was fanning out over the pillow case and a wheezy snort was escaping her opened mouth. Guilt and regret once again dragged its way through every molecule of his middle aged body.

The black fluff ball jumped up onto the bed. He stood towering above Lucy, his tongue hanging out of the side of his mouth as he breathed dog breath over this strange woman's face. He lowered his head and sniffed the top of hers.

Lucy woke with a startled expression on her face and stared into those deep orange eyes "Get that disgusting creature away from me!"

she bellowed as she pulled the floral Laura Ashley duvet cover up over her nose, which made her look like she was wearing some form of flowery burka.

Ralph realised at that point Lucy was no dog lover, he clicked his fingers and gave Nelson an authoritative instruction to get down off the bed. Nelson's head tilted to the side but the furry four legged beast obliged with a disapproving look in his eyes.

Ralph grabbed a pair of boxers of the floor and made a hasty retreat out of his bedroom. He didn't have a clue how to behave or even what to say to the sexually frustrated married nymphomaniac that he shared his marital bed with. His mind was all over the place and was a complete mess but it wasn't just his jumbled thoughts that was in a disordered condition so was his once spotlessly clean house.

Empty cider cans, three empty bottles of wine and a takeaway pizza box were disseminated around the living room. In a heaped pile on the dining room table were enough tissue's to make a whole nine pack of Andrex loo rolls. Which were used to mop up the bodily excretions after Ralph and Lucy had full penetrative sex on the living room floor and over Nancy's highly polished antiqued dining table with turned and faceted legs. The clues were obvious as to what had happened the night before but Ralph was suffering a bad dose of alcohol induced amnesia. All he remembered was Lucy removing all her clothing and masturbating in front of him till he succumbed and became a husband having an illicit affair rather than just a spouse who had a brief one night stand.

He felt like his stomach was churning as he began self-condemning his behavior last night. His misconduct and failing's as a husband made him remember the unfavourable memories he had of finding the love of his life shagging his own brother. And now after many passing moons he had made another human being, his wife and the mother of his children endure the same malady and torture that once ripped out his heart and left him with an inability to trust another human being......except Nancy.

Ralph sat down on the large brown leather arm chair as the full effects of too much cider, cheap red wine and dehydration took hold. He dozed off into a trance like state as his imagination became a force of nature. His mind conjured up a scenario of a court room. He was the one standing in the dock, the jury were his children, his close friends and members of his family. The judge his tormented wife.

The court usher handed a folded piece of paper to Nancy the high court judge.

Nancy began unfolding it as she sat behind a raised bench her body being camouflaged with a scarlet robe with fur facings and a winged collar. Her hair was covered by a long wig. She spoke to the seated jury members.

"Is this the verdict of you all?"

"Yes" they all said in synchronicity.

Nancy turned her head, her stern expression gazed directly at Ralph. In a bull-headed obstinate way she addressed the accused.

"You have been charged with sleeping with Lucy. A complete slag of the first degree. Who is known as a manipulative serial adulteress and whose legs seem to have an inability to stay closed! You have also been accused of lying to the one woman who loved you more than life itself and thinking more of Lucy's vaginal needs before your wife's emotional one. I would like to make you aware that God has given you ten free minutes of Babestation a box of tissues and your right hand if you felt the wanton lustful urges to expel the contents of your testicles. But you took it on yourself to destroy your marriage and sleep with a woman that exhibits behavioral problems because of her over indulgent spoilt brat attitude. The verdict of this jury is…

Nancy lifted up her hand and smashed the hard wood gravel down on the sounding block.

"GUILTY!"

A stunned and stupefied Ralph sat bolt upright and awake in his chair. He was guilty and damned.

Chapter 12

The solid oak door to the kitchen was ajar and Nancy could hear many voices in a rather heated debate. She stood still for a moment unsure of whether she should enter or walk back to her room until the faceless ensemble had calmed down. But it was too late the floor boards she was standing on creaked loudly and the raised voices ceased all communication with each other. Nancy took a deep breath in and pushed open the wooden barrier.

Joe was seated at the top of the table, three other men and one woman sat emphatically on the other chairs. Strewn across the article of furniture was an assortment of papers and maps, coffee cups and a white porcelain serving plate half full with croissants stuffed with soft cheese, bacon, roma tomatoes and red onion which took centre stage on the assiduous overloaded table.

"Oh awake are we" Joe said

Nancy blushed as she made her way to the one spare chair, smiling at the new faces in turn as she sat down.

Joe began to gather up all the papers and maps into a neat pile.

"Everybody this is Nancy, Nancy this is everybody"

Nancy's shyness took hold and she coughed a quiet response

"Hello, everybody"

"There's no point telling her your name cos our Nancy is totally menopausal and will forget it anyway" Joe brusquely replied

Nancy knitted her brows and gave Joe the evil eye.

"Oh thanks for that Joe!"

"Only being truthful Nance" Joe shrugged his shoulders "Right my fellow comrades I think we are done for today. It's a lovely crisp morning out there so why don't we all take the day off and resume our discussions tomorrow"

All the other heads nodded in agreement and took their leave, apart from the female of the group. She couldn't have been taller than 5ft, and she was certainly no more than a size 8. She was dressed immaculately in a pair of black suspender tights with a decorative bow, a meshed ruffle mini skirt and a boyfriend shirt tied in a knot at her waist. Her nails were painted in a vibrant magenta and her long auburn hair was pulled back in a high pony tail. It was obvious to Nancy that Joe had influenced this beautiful young woman. She stood up and took hold of Nancy's hand

"At last" she said "Another female! I'm Sasha but everyone round ere calls me walnut not because I like them but because I'm allergic to the little buggers! Make me swell they do and go all sort of blotchy, horrible, horrible little things they are!" She didn't even take an intake of breathe as she continued to say "It's lovely to meet you, cant bloomin' wait to get to know you better, Joe has told me so much bout you"

Nancy turned to look at Joe her eyes brows raised high on her forehead

"You have?" questioned Nancy

Joe lifted up the plate of croissant's and shoved them under Nancy's nose

"Only the good stuff Nance, promise, croissant?"

Nancy removed her grip from Walnuts hand and took one of the tasty filled pastries.

"You seem very young Sasha I mean Walnut to be part of Joe's gaggle, if you don't mind me saying"

"She's two years older than you were Nancy my dear when you joined us. Another injured seagull trying to fly free of life's troubles and woes eh Sasha?"

Sasha placed her arms tightly around Joe's neck, stood on her tip toes and kissed his cheek.

"But I'm rescued now aren't I Joseph" she let go of her saviour's neck as one of the men called her name "May be we can have a girly chat sometime Nancy, Joseph is good but it would be lush to talk to another female for once?"

Nancy nodded

"I'd like that" she said. Her maternal instincts were telling her that it wasn't a female she needed but a motherly aspect and outlook on all things feminine, but was Nancy really the right woman to take on this role?

As Sasha run out of the door Nancy got up from the table and glanced outside the kitchen window. In the darkness and her disordered and grieved state the night before she didn't see just how beautiful this place actually was.

A post and rail fence bordered both sides of a gravel drive. With two universal five bar gates securing the property from the rest of the world. To Nancy's right was a small pond with geese, mallards and drakes swimming gracefully on the quiescent water. A few large stone pots were dotted around, each one holding beautiful evergreen shrubs. The ground was covered with random spouting daffodils and blue bells and deep in the distant Nancy could see the welcoming site of a bewitching and mystical forest.

"Beautiful isn't it?" Joe asked as he gripped her around her waist

"I'm truly lost for words Joe"

"It's taken me a good three years getting it to look like this. Remind me to show you the before pictures"

Nancy turned round to face Joe. She stared up into his piercing grey eyes.

"Has it really been three years since I saw you last Joe?"

Joe removed his arms from her waist and looked at his watch

"Actually my darling it's been three years, eight months, four days and thirty eight minutes. Not that I'm counting. …..The last time we actually saw each other was at Taylor's funeral?"

"Now I feel bad. We have only lived forty five minutes from each other for three years and yet I've been so wrapped up in my own life that I I I…" Nancy sighed "Do you still miss him Joe" her voice sympathetic and full of remorse.

"He was the love of my life, no one will ever replace him Nance……but he's still around me I can feel him and every now and then he visits me in my dreams, he's gone yes, but he will never be taken totally from me" Joe kissed her forehead as both of them gazed at the splendour and tranquility of the view from the window and an old dirty khaki green land rover pulling up at the other side of the gates.

Nancy's jaw dropped open as she saw a dark haired figure jump out of the driver's side of the land rover and push open the gates.

"It can't be" She said out loud "Oh my GOD it is" Nancy's eyes were wide open and her mouth even wider "Tttthats Shawn the salamander!"

Joe let out a rowdy laugh.

"You've met our Malachi then have you?"

"Met him!" Nancy screeched "I've seen every orifice and dangly bodily equipment he has!"

Joe shuffled away from the window still laughing and began gathering the plates and empty cups from the table. Nancy still stood admiring the view.

"He's just one of my boys, the three men you saw earlier are also my boys"

"I'm confused one of your boys?" a bewildered Nancy asked

"Taylor left me a bit of insurance when he died that paid for the mortgage and renovations on this place and I invested some of it, but I still needed something to live on, so I came up with 'Let Them Rip"

A shocked Nancy gaped at Joe

"What? You mean you own Let Them Rip?"

"Yep, built it up and own it all and don't be so shocked Nance sex sells it always has and it always will. Plus it enables me to do all the other stuff I need or want to do in life and its totally fabulous having such dishy youthful men around the place" Joe winked, Nancy just drooled.

Nancy turned on the taps and filled the butlers sink with water. She allowed the warm liquid to run through her fingers like melting ice cubes in the hot summer sun. Her stomach felt nervous and she imagined ten thousand ants with steel toe capped boots playing football inside her gut. She hadn't felt this way for over twenty years. The last time was when she met Ralph.

"Ralph" she thought

Her hands began shaking and the ants inside her turned into monsters in her belly fighting their way through her stomach lining. Confusion and panic started to build. Nancy inhaled deeply

"Are you ok Nance" a concerned Joe asked

"I just got a case of the collywobbles Joe….oh my god I haven't even text the kids today to let them know I'm ok..shit!"

"Relax princess I've done it. I spoke to Willow first thing this morning. I told her you would ring them in a couple of days"

"What would I do without you Joe…..I love you so much"

"Ditto"

Chapter 13

Nancy felt her face turn a deep shade of pink as Malachi entered the kitchen. She was so glad the ants were back crawling and tickling around inside her. But she did feel somewhat pathetic. A women of her age getting excited about meeting a tall, dark, sensual, tanned, gorgeous, enchanting, beautiful, dreamboat of a man. No of a God!

Malachi threw his back pack on the cold black slate floor tiles and walked straight over to Joe and gave him a man hug. He didn't pay one bit of attention to Nancy as she stood leaning against the sink with a cup of tea in her hand.

The chatterbox in her head was telling her to "stop being such a fool, he probably thinks you are the cleaner, or basically just some old hag that's popped in for tea. Pull yourself together for Christ's sake Nancy"

But try as hard as she could her eyes would not leave the tightness of his backside in those jeans. She scrutinised every inch of his body, and as she looked up into those intense eyes. He met her gaze. She swallowed hard as the fever in-between her legs was growing.

"I know you don't I?" Malachi inquired his eyes still fixed on hers

Oh here comes stuttering Nancy.

"errmmmmmmmm yyess we, we sort of met at the show you done at the rugby club in the ladies loo" her face was redder than a bowl of beetroot soup

"Yep I remember now, you were the middle aged married one that revoked my advances"

Nancy's chatterbox returned. "See! He thinks your old married and a frigid fossil. Bloody hell women grow the fuck up! And whatever you do don't sneeze or you will probably piss yourself! And then he will think you have just been let out for the day from some special hospital that treats horny menopausal incontinent females! "

Nancy thought it safer not to answer and just gave a one sided smile and turned back around. Once again she was looking out onto the gravel drive. She inhaled deeply, very deeply.

It was now Malachi's eyes that were paralysed on the back view of Nancy. The tracksuit pants hugged her bottom, the indentations of her waist and her elegant neck made his knees tremble and his heart quiver with excitement.

Joe just stood and watched but the awkward silence was killing him.

"So tell me Mal how long have we got you here for?"

Malachi shook his head to break the hypnotic sensations

"At least a month, or maybe two" Malachi looked at Nancy. "I'm going back on the road after the demonstration, summer's our busiest time, but your bank balance already knows that mate" he laughed "Am I in the same room as always?"

"You are indeed my friend"

Malachi fidgeted on his heels and mouthed to Joe

"Is she staying here to?"

"Oh what am I like" Joe exclaimed "You two need a proper introduction, Malachi this is Nancy, Nancy this is Malachi. Nancy is my dearest friend and will be with us for as long as she needs. She will be staying in the boudoir."

"Eh what?" Nancy turned to face the two men "The boudoir what the bloody hell is that when it's at home"

"Come this way Nancy dearest and I will show you"

Nancy stepped past the gorgeously tanned Malachi. Trying her hardest not to look back in his direction. But she did. Malachi smiled at her, with his perfectly white teeth that were whiter than a virgin's tunic! Her heart missed as many beats as the England football team missed goals in the World Cup. Nancy turned her head back abruptly before it stopped beating altogether and saw an impatient Joe waiting for her at the foot of the staircase. Ornate pictures in a mixture of dark oak and gilded gold frames hung in a systematic fashion on the white painted walls. At the top of the stairs Nancy could see four other oak doors.

"Shut your eyes Nance"

Nancy closed her eyes tight as Joe took hold of her hand. She heard him turn the original hard wood door handle with brass fittings. A breeze brushed past her face as the door opened.

"Now open them Nancy"

Nancy gasped as she gazed around the room. A cream wall to wall carpet made of the softest fibres was beneath her feet. The panelled walls had all been painted in a smooth cream. Each panel was edged in gold. By the foot of an antique four poster bed that was draped in white linen and stuffed full of faux fur cushions, stood a small two seated high backed chaise longue with crystal buttons. At the other end of this ostentatious room was yet another restored roll top bath with gold painted feet.

Nancy walked over to the bath and rubbed the shiny glossy enamel with her hand.

"Joe this is just ……..oh my I'm lost for words, it's just beautiful"

"Isn't it just…..It was going to be mine and Taylor's room but I've never had the heart to use it since he died. Climb into the bath I want to show you the view"

Nancy climbed into the bath as Joe opened up two French doors which led onto a Juliette balcony with black painted railings. Nancy lay in the empty bath and stared at the Orphic forest in the distance.

She had no words that could express her amazement at what she was seeing. It was charming, it was alluring, it was pretentious but it was a haven of calmness and solitude. It was a utopia in the heart of Sussex.

"Look up Nance, nobody ever really looks at the sky. They shout at it often, but never really see its full beauty."

Nancy tilted her head upwards and watched the gossamer clouds float aimlessly through the alluring sky

"Joe this is just mesmerizing but I can't sleep here. This is your room. Yours and Taylors. It wouldn't feel right. I will sleep in one of the other rooms next door"

"Well if you want to sleep in one of the other rooms you will be sleeping with a pasting table rolls of wall paper a jig saw and some nails. Please Nancy you deserve a break, you deserve a small slice of comfort with no rushing around worrying about what to do for supper, if the kids are okay or if the dogs have been fed. You are my guest and will be treated like one all the time you are staying here..........oh and by the way behind those doors over there" Joe pointed at two large heavy doors painted in the same cream colour as the walls and edged in the same gold leaf.

 "I went and done a bit of shopping this morning. There's enough clothes in there to keep you going for a while, and if I may say so some rather sexy underwear too." Joe made a purring sound with his tongue.

Tears formed in Nancy's eyes as an amiable smile spread across her face

"Joe I wish you hadn't, you shouldn't spend your money on me. For one, I have clothes at home and for two, I actually can't think of a two right now but I will. Nancy climbed out of the bath and hugged Joe so tightly "Joe I love you so much, thank you"

"The pleasures all mine Nancy the pleasure is all mine"

Chapter 14

Nancy had been with Joe and his freedom fighters for a little over a week.

In the whole time she only saw Malachi once. No conversation was shared just a few rather long stares and the occasional smile. She still hadn't spoken to Ralph either and the constant bombardment of text messages and voice mails had ceased about three days ago. She rung her daughters daily just to check they were eating properly, and made sure they kept a close eye on Poppy and her frequent morning sickness and also Elsa who was still in a state of grieve over where her two legged mother was. She wanted to ask about their father and Lucy but couldn't bring herself to mention it. She knew deep in her heart the girls were holding something back from her, but she really didn't want to be told anything more right now. The bars that imprisoned her for over twenty years had finally stated to corrode and warp and Nancy was able to walk through them, holding her head high (except when she had a hot flush then her head was more often than not placed between her legs to stop her passing out, throwing up or both!)

The antiquated house was empty of all its occupants. It had been since 7.30am that morning when all the other house mates jumped into Joe's off road Subaru for a day trip to London. Joe had meetings with the powers that be regarding the demonstration that was planned for June, and typically Joe wanted to walk the complete course as his OCD would have gone crazy if he wasn't a 150% prepared for every circumstance.

Nancy was still tucked up in bed with the fluffy cushions and crisp cotton sheets. She wrongly assumed she was going to be spending the day alone, relaxing, chilling and sorting out her jumbled brain, but may be its not her brain that needed sorting, it was her chimney with those darn cobwebs that resembled a scene from Indiana Jones and the Temple of Doom.

The typical April weather threw out some shockingly heavy showers. But as the rain was Nancy's most favourable weather condition nothing or no one could keep her inside when the skies turned into a grey sheet and the liquid sunshine fell from the heavens. She launched herself out of bed, threw on an old sweatshirt and jeans and headed out into the dampness of the world outside.

Nancy was standing on a rickety old bridge watching the rain drops fall into the stream below when she felt a hand tap her on the shoulder. Nancy lost in her own thoughts jumped out of her skin.

"What the fu….." she said as she did an about turn

Malachi was standing behind her

"Oh I'm really sorry I didn't mean to startle you" he said his hair dripping with rain

Nancy's steely expression said it all

"You shouldn't creep up on people like that especially woman"

"I know I'm truly sorry"

Nancy took the authoritarian role in this conversation as she wiped the rain drops from her cheeks

 "Well you still shouldn't have done it! How long have you been standing there staring at me!"

"About ten minutes......you look so,so....."

Chatterbox brain interrupted his sentence "You look so old and fat and ugly and wet through and old and even older than old and......"

"Beautiful"

A nervous laughter escaped her throat

"Are you laughing at me" he asked

"Am I laughing at him or am I laughing at me" Nancy thought

She pushed back her short blonde hair and lifted her gaze to his

"I'm not sure?" Just say thank you chatterbox told her "I appreciate your compliment but it still doesn't change the fact I'm old enough to be your mother. Would you tell her she was beautiful?"

"If she was alive I expect I would. If she was as beautiful as you anyway"

Chatterbox head to the rescue "Oh Nancy you are such a pleb! He is telling you, you are beautiful in a motherly sort of way not a drop dead gorgeous I want to shag your brains out manner!...Just say thank you for Christ sake and he will go!"

"Thank you Mal"

Nancy felt her heart pound deep inside her chest and waves of nauseous nervous tension and excitement shot electric currents through her body as she stood waiting for his response.

"May I stand with you for a while?"

"Erm if you really want to but I'm getting a little cold now so will probably be leaving very soon"

Malachi removed his Ralph Lauren embroidered combat jacket and cloaked her soaking wet shoulders. He held on to the edges of the jacket as Nancy's eyes fixated themselves on his oversized biceps and the rain that dripped methodically down his bronzed arms. Lustful urges oscillated through her veins. She tried hard to think of dirty socks and overflowing bin liners, but nothing was distracting her shameless thoughts.

Malachi still held tight to his jacket as he bent his head forward and kissed her gingerly on the lips. Nancy retreated.

"I I I'm sorry" he said "I thought"

"You thought what Malachi?"

"I thought you wanted me too?"

Nancy halted her reply but inwardly breathed a massive sigh of relief as she sarcastically answered her 'chatterbox' "you were wrong!"

She lifted up her arm and smoothed away a single rain drop from the side of his face. The scent on his skin was driving her insane.

Malachi once again pressed his lips to hers. Nancy pulled away again.

Malachi stood perplexed by her withdrawal

"What's wrong?"

Nancy soaked by the driving rain, as apprehension flowed through her veins, she looked up into his beautiful eyes.

"Tell me how many women have you been with Mal"

He took a step back and seemed somewhat agitated with her question

"I don't understand what has that got to do with me trying to kiss you? "

"Please just answer the question"

"If you want to know the truth I've slept with only two women, well one was a girl I was dating at school when I was sixteen and one was just some women I met after a show"

"But you gave me the come on at the show. Would you have slept with me then if I hadn't walked away?"

Malachi stared down at the ground and put his hands in his jeans pockets

"It's part of the act we have to flirt with the women and be nice and sweet and admittedly some of the lads do go off with one women after another but I can't do that. I was bought up by two women. Who taught me to respect women…..Yep I know I sound like a right limp lettuce, but I can't change what I think is right and what I was taught. My mum and Nan would turn in their graves if I did, and probably haunt me forever. To be totally honest with you I think I would have slept with you though"

Nancy could see Malachi's cheeks blush.

"That's refreshing" Said chatterbox

"My thoughts exactly" Nancy replied her ever annoying voice in her head "But he is a bloke and are blokes really made this way?"

Chatterbox laughed "Who cares! He is gorgeous and could give your chimney a bloody good clean!"

Nancy edged herself back and leaned against the wooden rails of the bridge and began to watch the fast moving stream below

"That's a refreshing thing to hear but let's face it most men would shag anything and anyone that was on offer. Take it from me I know!......... but why would you even want to have sex with me? There were so many young women there that night, I just don't get why you would?"

Malachi joined her watching the water ebb and flow

"Honestly?"

Nancy nodded

"When I looked at you, I saw a woman that was different, how can I put this, sort of strange….No strange is not the right word"

"Thank Christ for that" Nancy laughed

"A woman erm a bit mystical, dark, secretive, and forgive me but so god damn sexy!"

Chatterbox was laughing so hard Nancy could almost envisage her rolling about on the floor holding her stomach muscles, with tears falling down her face, and droplets of wee escaping her bladder.

"He hasn't seen you in your tracksuit pants, bleached t shirt and socks with holes in!"

Nancy replied to her inner voice "For once chatterbox I agree!"

Nancy couldn't help herself and was soon joining her inner voice in rapturous laughter.

"I'm sorry Mal I didn't mean to laugh, but mystical and dark, realllllyyyyyyy?" Nancy swallowed hard and tried to stop another huge guffaw escaping her voice box. "You've got to understand Malachi, most of my life I've been with only one man, who has turned out to be a complete arse hole, but I just don't know if I'm ready to be with someone else just yet. And trust me when I say this, I find you soooooooooooooo (yes she over emphasised the so) attractive and would so like to take you to my bed, but....."

Nancy's mind became swashed in thoughts of betrayal and passion. Mixing together like a chef mixing herbs in a pestle and mortar. But Nancy already knew the answer. She wasn't ready to let another man, see the beauty that lay inside her.

"You're not ready?"

"No, no I'm not I'm so sorry"

Nancy could see the rejection in his face. But what did he expect? She was newly separated and this was only the second time she had ever really spoke to him. Nancy was just not ready to be a one night or day stand. She was 47 for Christ's sake not an 18 year old free loving and spirited female any more.

With one final look into Malachi's smoldering eyes, Nancy took hold of his hand and the pair walked the short distance back to Joes quaint but elegant home.

They had been immersed in the driving rain for such a long time their cheeks were flushed red and stinging and there jeans had stuck to their skin. Nancy being Nancy was prepared for the wet weather and sensibly wore the stripy Wellington boots Joe knew psychically she would need. Malachi on the other hand had a pair of Saint Laurent suede Chelsea boots on his feet. They were nice when he put them on but now bore resemblance to a pair of muddy, soaked foot attire that could have cost a few quid in shoe zone rather than a few hundred when he bought them from Harrods.

Malachi pulled Nancy towards him after they had removed their soaked outer layers of clothing and boots.

"However long it takes, I'm going be waiting"

Nancy gave a disparaging smile, unsure if he was being truthful or just trying to get into her knickers in a very gentlemanly type way.

Chapter 15

The overwhelming feelings and emotions that
Nancy had circulating her tired brain
exhausted her physically. She lay in the bath
trying to regain all her senses. Images of
Ralph, her three times pregnant fat swollen
tummy, her arduous labour, family trips to the
beach, Lurid Lucy with her sagging labia
giving her husband head and now Malachi
with his sun kissed muscular body suffocating
her mind. Panic stated to swell in the pit of her
stomach and adrenalin spread quickly through
her veins. She flushed. A knee trembling, heart
palpitating, mind numbing flush that made
her exit the bath and run to the un-finished
upstairs bathroom. She sat dry retching over
the porcelain bowl. Chatterbox shouted at her.

"For fuck sake Nancy stop this bullshit! You
have done nothing wrong. Breathe woman"

With beads of sweat escaping the pores on her face and her back drenched in the bath water, she expanded her lungs to their fullest capacity.

"But I have done something wrong" she proclaimed answering her internal chatterbox

"NO, no you haven't. If Ralph had never gone with that old slag Lucy, you wouldn't be here now. Which also means you wouldn't be fantasizing about a bloke young enough to be your son!"

Nancy sat down on the untiled floor of the bathroom and run her fingers through her hair.

"But I'm thinking about going to bed with another man, that makes me no better than Ralph!"

Chatterbox shook her head.

A clattering of feet distracted Nancy's thoughts as the ecologist tree hugging mercenaries had arrived back from ye old London town. Their voices were raised with laughter and she heard Joe call her name.

Nancy sat still on the floor her body weak. The cold after flush commenced and Nancy rubbed her bare skin.

The bathroom door flew open and Joe infiltrated her space.

"Oh my darling. What the hell is up?"

Nancy burst out crying holding her-self tight and rocking like a scared child.

Joe bent down and heaved her up. Her naked body tight against his House of Fraser elbow patch wool sweater. His arms were firmly closed around her. Once again Nancy felt secure and her pulse rate slowed.

Joe lowered his head and kissed her tenderly on the forehead.

"Come on princess let's get you back to the boudoir"

Joe placed his arm across her back and around her waist for support as the pair cautiously walked back to the bedroom. The floorboards creaked each step they took and Nancy could not see past the end of her nose as the tears were falling, blinding her vision.

Still holding onto Nancy, Joe threw the fake fur cushions off onto the floor and pulled back the embroidered white cotton cover. He helped Nancy climb onto the pocket sprung mattress and covered her naked skin with the duvet.

Joe stroked the side of her cheek with his well-manicured hands

"I'm just going to get you a cup of sweet tea ok. Then my wild woman of the woods we finally need to have that chat"

Nancy nestled her head against one of the pillows before turning onto her side and curling her body into the foetal position. Her eyes watched Joe leave and fear and uncertainty commenced, gnawing its way through and eating her soul. Even though her body was in some sort of after panic melt down Nancy refused to close her eyes. She wanted Joe to hurry up and return and to feel his loving arms engulfing her menopausal erratic body.

Joe's footsteps could be heard walking up the narrow stairs. Two cups clinking together as he got closer to her room

"OH FUCK!" he screamed as he neared her door

Nancy lifted herself up and rested her head on her hands.

"What's wrong Joe?"

Joe walked closer his arm outstretched so she could take the steaming cup of warm tea from him

"I've just tripped over me own bloody feet! So you now have half a cup of tea......maybe it's an omen"

A confused Nancy shook her head and screwed up her nose

"What? How can spilling a cup of tea be an omen?"

Joe bum shuffled her to move over on the bed so he could sit down beside her. He raised his eyebrows and glanced down at Nancy

"Is your cup half full or half empty Nance?"

Nancy stared down into the cup. The exceptionally sweet liquid rested in the cup motionless and still. The only give away that it was hot was the steamy vapour that eluded the gold rimmed pastel pink tea cup. Nancy blew gently across it cooling it just enough to make that first sip.

"Jesus Joe! How many sugars did you put in this?"

"Three"" he said as he took a mouthful of his home made chamomile and mint tea "I thought you needed a bit of extra energy"

Nancy screwed up her face and she took another gulp. The over sweet beverage made her tongue feel coated and her teeth grimy. Nether the less she finished the drink, placed the cup on the bedside cabinet and sighed as she flopped back into the soft feathery pillows. Joe heaved the duvet up covering her naked body fully and tucked it in firmly around her shoulders. They both sat there staring out of the French doors watching the grey clouds float aimlessly by. Joe turned to look at Nancy with his kind sympathetic eyes staring into hers and with his compassionate loving and reassuring voice asked

"So my princess what the hell is going on with you?"

Nancy run her fingers through her damp hair shut her eyes and swallowed hard.

"I'm just so confused Joe, Mal basically offered himself on a plate to me earlier. I turned him down obviously. Then I just couldn't get Ralph, slut face, and the children out of my head. I just don't know what to do Joe, I'm scared, I'm afraid I'm confused I feel like my whole life has been a lie"

Joe opened his eyes wide and pulled back away from her, his forehead creasing with more lines than a British rail map of the underground

"Oh my dearest Nancy. We both know a lot of your life is a lie don't we. And one day you will have to come clean to those you love about it. But let's not worry about that now let's start with Mal" Joe raised the tone of his voice to sound a little more camp "But before I do I must say I'm highly jealous" he purred "Seriously though, Why worry? The way I see it princess is people come into our lives when we need them. They help us change our prospective on life or may be even to change what we think about ourselves. Ralph has chosen his path, he chose to do what he did with Lucy. Who knows what his reasons are or were? BUT Nance and please listen to what I have to say. I can only sympathise with you and your rampant hot flushes and menopause, I can only imagine how totally awful it is for you or any other woman out there. And I know you are suffering from empty nest syndrome too. But please don't take what I'm about to say the wrong way, try to see how hard all this is on Ralph too." Joe lifted his finger and stroked Nancy's cheek. "He has had to watch you change, he has had to put up with your moaning about the menopause, your mood swings, he has also had to deal with your beautiful children growing up and leaving home and he has also had to learn to accept your colourful past."

Nancy closed her eyes, the one thing she didn't need reminding about was her past.

"So all this is my fault?"

"No Nance that's not what I'm saying but men suffer too you know. They get to a stage in life where they think that's it. They get their middle age spread and salt and pepper hair and something inside their heads snaps. For some reason they have to try and make themselves feel young and virile again. Even if it means poking Mr. pork sausage into some other woman's bap. But you have to follow what your heart is telling you too. There are no right or wrongs in life Nance and there are no mistakes either. There is just two hundred ways to learn how not to do things. Roll with it my little free spirit, just roll with it"

Tears fell from Nancy's eyes as she leaned over and squeezed the dear life out of her, very camp, very lovely and very gay best friend.

Chapter 16

Nancy blinked continuously as she regained consciousness. Her puffy eyes stung as she rubbed them back to life. She lifted her naked body from the bed and noticed resting on the pillow next to her was a note.

My Dearest darling Nancy

You know I love you more than words could ever say. I know   I'm just an old gay highly attractive stupendous man but life has taught me so much. Sometimes, however bad things happen, but there is always a bright side. Life is about the ups and the downs, the good and the bad, the ying and the yang.

BUT it's up to you to decide what you need to do and where you want to take your life. Like many your life has got to a stage where you find it boring and mundane. So enlighten yourself my dear Nancy! Enlighten your heart again and follow those natural instincts. You owe no one anything Nance, but you owe it to yourself to live, live a life free from others expectations of you.

There is only one Queen in our family and that's me but you will always be my princess.

Yours for today tomorrow and eternity

J xxx

p.s But if you do bed our Malachi I will be highly jealous and may never talk to you again......BITCH!

Nancy smiled broadly how she loved Joe. How she loved his arms holding her tight, his reassuring smile, his wise words and his terrible constant way of getting to the point and making her see things so clearly.

"How does he do that?" she said to the emptiness of the room

The room did not answer but her bladder did! She ran out of the bedroom to the bathroom wearing nothing more than her birthday suit. She made it just in time as her bladder bore the undesirable urge to empty. Nancy let out a deep relieving sigh. As she washed her hands and stared at her reflection in the tatty old mirror on the wall she did not see a middle aged menopausal wife or mother. But saw a woman. A women that bore scars of lives traumas, pregnancy and motherhood. Nancy lowered her head and ran her hand over her stomach. No it wasn't toned anymore and did wobble (a little). No her breasts did not hold the firm soldier like position on her chest and were pointing further south than north. Her skin did not hold the suppleness and smoothness of her youth. She may not have the body of Aline Weber the looks of Emilia Clarke or the fun loving personality of Holly Willoughby because she was Nancy Marshal. With sticky up bed hair, laughter lines around her eyes, wobbly boobs, dry skin the odd stretch mark or three and a burning desire to take to bed one of the hottest most divine creatures she had ever seen. She was without a doubt one horny mother that had finally learned that her body with all its issues was a desirable machine that could still be used to turn a man on.

"The only thing is" said chatterbox "You might need a little bit more oiling, as your nuts and bolts creak slightly"

"Fuck off" Nancy answered and headed back to her boudoir.

Dressed in a pair of Levi's and one of Joe's old sweatshirts that swamped Nancy's petite frame she began tidying her room and washing out the bath tub. All she could think about was Mal's rain drenched body, and the way he smelt. God he smelt good! Actually he smelt better than good he smelt divine. Not a Lynx advert divine oh no! A sort of divine that made things move inside her.

Joe shouted up from downstairs interrupting her scrubbing and all the dirty immoral and highly disgusting thoughts her brain was besieging onto her.

"Nance we are having a take away tonight, anything your fancy?"

"Nah I'm easy"

"Well we know that Nance but what do you want to eat"

Nancy whispered quietly

"I will have a two slices of bread, one naked Malachi and a bottle of chocolate sauce please"

Nancy giggled to herself and her profane and totally blasphemous imagination

"Really Joe I don't mind, order whatever" she yelled

Her phone beeped loudly to tell her she had a message through. It was from Poppy

"Hi Mum, are you feeling better? Mum I miss you so much when are you coming home? I know you don't want to and I can understand why. Hell If I was you I would get on a plane and bugger off to somewhere exotic, but I really need you Mum. I'm so scared. I don't like being pregnant and I hate throwing up all the time. You were right about Graham thought you should know that.

I love you, Mum XOXOXO

Nancy didn't bother replying. Instead she went into her contacts box found Poppy's details and pressed call.

"Hello Mum" Poppy sounded depressed and tired

Nancy went into primeval protection mode

"What's he done, has he hurt you, he hasn't hit you has he, if he has by god I..."

"No Mum calm down he hasn't laid a finger on me, but he has walked out on me" Poppy paused and Nancy could hear her sniff and suck back the tears that were now flowing. I just can't do this on my own Mum especially now you aren't here, please Mum come home"

Joe's words rattled around in the corners of her mind 'Live your life without others expectations of you' Does that mean she should forget about being a mother? Slam the door in the faces of her children when they need her the most. Will letting them learn the hard way really make them stronger?

Nancy lifted her head to the heavens and exhaled

"Poppy, I, I, I'm just not ready to come back yet, I can't I need more time" Poppy's sniffles turned in sobs and Nancy felt her heart was being shredded by some old fashioned blunt tailor shears. "Look Pops I will come back tonight, but I'm not staying" she pulled the phone away from her ear, and looked at the time "If I leave now I can be with you at about quarter past seven…….. okay?"

"Thanks Mum, I'll let Willow and Daisy know, I love you mum"

"Love you too Poppy"

Without hesitation Nancy put her phone in her back pocket, put on her converses and raced down the stairs. Joe was sat at the table, Malachi to one side, Walnut to the other. Nancy blushed as she caught Mal gazing longingly at her.

"Joe I have to go, Poppy's in such a state"

A concerned look spread across Joe's face

"It's not the baby is it?"

"No Joe just some other twat of a penis person, present company excluded obviously....have you seen my keys?"

Joe got up and walked over to the rustic painted antique wall mounted key rack. Picked up Nancy's keys and threw them in her direction

"Drive carefully princess, are you coming back?"

Nancy glared at Malachi who was still totally transfixed on her

"Of course"

The dark country roads were quiet with hardly any traffic which made the journey seem quicker than it was. The driving rain had given way to light showers and the air outside seemed to have warmed slightly. The branches of the trees moved in a hypnotic manner and the wind blew through them as if they were speaking, quietly and mystically to all who would listen. Nancy felt serene and tranquil listening to Nirvana and the dulcet tones of Kurt Cobain who sung effortlessly out of her Ipod. She started analysing the lyrics to 'Rape me'......

'Rape me, Rape me my friend, Rape me, Rape me again'

Rape me of what? She thought. Rape me of my feelings, my emotions. Rape me of my life

"I'm not the only one"

"Well Kurt" she said "Your right there! My marriage consists of me and HER!

"And Malachi" said chatterbox

Nancy shouted at her inner voice

"Shut up! I'm having a moment! And if I wish to blame HER I will!

Nancy carried on listening to the song. What is his message in this song she thought? And then it came to her. She spoke allowed.

"He's not singing about rape as in ' I want to be raped he's telling us that no matter who rapes us emotionally or physically we are strong enough to handle it and we can survive it in any capacity…..Oh my god Cobain I lurveeeeeee you"

Whatever epiphany moment that had just happened. Nancy felt strong. Instead of slouching in the chair, she sat up right a stupid 'hell let's rock' smile appeared on her face as she turned the volume up to high. The rest of the journey was spent admiring Cobain's hidden messages in his songs and dreaming

about his succulent blue sapphire
eyes......swoon........

Poppy lived close to town in a newly built
block of flats, sorry apartments. It wasn't big
enough to swing a cat in, not that anyone
should swing cats by their tails! And Christ
knows how she will fit a baby and all the
paraphernalia that comes with one in it but it
was her first rented flat, (apartment!) and after
all size isn't everything is it?..................coughs
clears throat!

Nancy pressed the intercom and it buzzed
loudly

"It's open Mum" Poppy said her voice small
and pathetic.

Poppy was waiting by her front door and
before they could exchange 'hellos' they fell
into each other's arms. Nancy had only left her
children for a few hours before never for days

and the overwhelming motherly love surged through her as she gripped and squeezed her daughter. Poppy looked tired and stressed. Her beautiful clear blue eyes seemed dull and unfeeling. Even though it had only been two weeks since Nancy saw her last, the biggest difference she could see was in her body. She always thought that Poppy was far too skinny and hated the fact that this child worked out at every opportunity and would never dare eat anything that was calorific. But the new pouch that formed around her navel and the slight fullness in her cheeks made Poppy look healthy. Her eyes were very drawn and fatigued but her body seemed to be blossoming.

Nancy went straight to the kitchen after all the hugging and began filling the kettle with water.

"So you going tell me what he's done?"

Poppy rubbed her slightly swollen belly, as all expectant mothers do.

"He said he wasn't ready to be a dad, packed up his stuff and left.....How will I cope? How will I cope alone Mum?"

Nancy plugged in the kettle, flicked the switch and opened her arms to her daughter.

"You're not alone Pop's, you have me and your sisters and your Dad and Uncle Joe...you'll be fine I promise" Nancy tried to hide the uncertainty in her voice. She was no Sally Morgan and really didn't know if she would be fine or not. She hadn't got a clue what was in store for her daughter she just prayed she was right.

Within thirty minutes the door clattered open and her two other off spring were throwing themselves into her arms. After many kisses being placed on cheeks and foreheads and the typical hormonal tears being shed the four women sat on Poppy's Dhs striped fabric sofa. It was only a three seater but somehow they all managed to fit their backsides onto it.

Willow held her mother's hand tightly in her own

"It's so good to have you back Mumma" she smiled showing all her perfect white teeth

Nancy squeezed her hand gently

"I, I'm not back Will's"

"But Mum" Willow gasped "I thought you were" Willows gaze dropped

With her finger tips touching Willows chin she moved her face upwards so their eyes were on each other. Willows eyes had already formed tears and Nancy choked back hers.

"I'm sorry Willow but I need more time" Nancy looked at the demur faces of her daughters "I've only come to check on you lot and pick up some clothes from the house, Joe's bought me some lovely things but to be honest I think he is still trying to dress me like he did all those years ago. I will be going back to Joe's tonight. Please don't hate me!"

"We could never hate you Mum, do what you have to do" answered Daisy and in Daisy's normal format continued "Who wants Pizza I'm buying"

Two hours later with their belly's full of Dominos stuffed crust pepperoni passion, a litre bottle of coke drunk and quite a few hormonal out bursts Nancy got up to leave.

As Nancy reached for her jacket that was laying over one of the arms of the sofa Daisy grabbed her arm

"Mum I'll go and get your clothes, you stay here, I have to pick some of mine up anyway as I'm staying here with Poppy at the moment, so may as well kill two birds with one stone"

Her three daughters looked intently at each other

"Ok," Nancy said and abruptly sat back down "What the hell is it you're not telling me?"

Willow nudged Poppy, Poppy Nudged Daisy, Daisy shrugged.

"Erm its Lucy, she has sort of moved in with dad….. sort of."

Nancy's stomach tightened and she bit down hard on her bottom lip, waves of anger forged through her veins, as she clenched her fists into tight balls

"In my house! I've only been gone for two weeks! How dare she, how dare your father!, And her kids too?" she shouted bitterly

"No Mum" replied Willow "Just the evil witch of the west, her kids are still with their dad, for the time being anyway"

Nancy pulled her car keys out of her back pocket, and picked up her jacket once again.

"Look after each other, I'm only a phone call away remember. I love you girls so very much, don't ever forget that" Nancy headed for the door before anyone of her daughters could stop her, her blood was boiling hotter than the devils fire at the opening to hell.

All it took was five minutes from Poppy's flat to her house. She slowed right down as she drove down the road she had lived in for fifteen long years with Ralph. It felt as if she had never been away. Next doors drive way was still full of rubbish and an old escort that was supposedly being done up was sitting with no wheels, on what was once a nicely trimmed lawn. It had been like this for well over a year and all Nancy had ever seen them do was to jack the front of the car up. Look under it and leave it. It was gathering more rust than a rolling stone gathered moss and the grass was at least two feet high at the sides where the wheels should have been. The people that lived there were a young couple who had recently had their second child. They were friendly enough-when they had to be. However Nancy just couldn't seem to warm to them in any capacity and chose to only give a friendly 'morning or hello when she saw them and always refused the 'pop round for coffee' and 'let's have a gossip' moment. That just wasn't Nancy's scene.

She turned around in the cul de sac at the end of her road unsure if she should pull up onto her drive or park opposite.

"This is still your house" Chatterbox announced

"Yes it is" Nancy said in a defiant way.

The strong 'hell yeah lets rock" feeling that Kurt Cobain had given her started to falter as Nancy noticed Lucy's Range Rover parked on the drive. It was gleaming and shiny and it took all of Nancy's self-control to not carve 'slut' into the paint work with her keys.

"Breathe in deeply, you are strong you are in control and you can handle this" she told herself as she walked the few steps from her car to the front door.

Slowly she opened the door quietly holding the rest of the keys on her key chain tightly in her hand so they didn't clang together. Her heart beat at a rapid pace and a flight or fight moment edged its way through her body. She breathed out through her mouth and inhaled a large quantity of air through her nose. Her head felt light and dizzy but she was determined to see this through.

The floor of the hall was filled with six inch heel neck breaking shoes. Nancy scowled and kicked one ….hard! Childish she thought but who cares! She entered the kitchen. Every available bit of work space was suffused with empty take away boxes, cider cans, wine and beer bottles. She couldn't even see the sink as it was brimming over with dirty plates, glasses and cups. She walked from the kitchen to the living room and spied Lurid Lucy with her loose labia sprawled out on her sofa. She was snoring loudly and her eyes were covered in a silky pink eye mask a cotton t shirt and a pair of French knickers that was being swallowed whole by her anal regions. Nancy looked at her and her dark side took hold.

In her mind's eye she saw herself writing 'slag' in permanent black marker pen across her forehead. Ripping off her semi permanent false eyelashes one by one and epilating her whole body including her perfect blonde, intensely straightened hair. Chatterbox smirked "May be Mal was right you do have a dark side"

Nancy blinked and answered her inner voice

"And you know that's right, so instead of being a sarcastic bitch for once help me get under control"

The conversation in her head and taking revenge on her husband's floozy was cut short by three pairs of eyes looking at her through the French doors. Nancy's heart sunk.

Sitting cold and wet through was her four legged babies.

"What the fuck" she said

Nancy turned the key and opened the door. Her dogs shot through it and encircled their mistress. Their coats were soaked their eyes were sad and they didn't look like they had been groomed in days. Nancy's heart sunk. Lucy stirred on the sofa, as the dogs whined in unison at seeing her. Revengeful Nancy took hold and she had a cunning, slightly warped, plan.

She pointed again to her dogs and gave the command to sit. The dogs sat, but their tails would not stop wagging and made a thumping sound on the floor

"Shh" Nancy said still with a mocking smile on her face

She went to the fridge and removed a one kilo tub of the dog's dinner. A nice mixture of raw minced turkey, bone, carrots, green beans and the inevitable bit of blood. She tip toed back into the living room to where Lucy lay and began scooping out the mixture from the tub with her hands and dropping it all over Lucy's body. Lucy grunted. Nancy stepped back trying to suppress her giggles. She lifted her index finger to the dogs, clicked her fingers again and pointed to Lucy. All three pounded onto her licking chewing and slurping their dinner from Lucy's half naked torso.

Lucy screamed a deafening scream as Nancy fell about laughing and holding her crotch.

The loose labia troll pulled the eye mask off and without even noticing Nancy, raised her right arm to hit Elsa. Nancy moved quicker than Flash Gordon with his jet pack on, clenched her fists, and with gritted teeth punched Lucy clean on her jaw. Lucy's teeth bit down on her top lip and blood spewed from her mouth.

Nancy stood tall, her shoulders were back and her gaze fixated on 'HER'.

"What are you doing here? How dare you hit me" Lucy shouted with venom in her tone "Get out, get out of my house "

Nancy stood not speaking. She looked down at her three dogs who seemed to be enjoying not only their dinner but a slight bit of revenge on this animal hating female. She let her gaze slowly trail back to Lucy's

"This is my house, these are my dogs and you are a middle aged woman whose cunt must have had more passengers than British Rail!.....I should be telling you to leave, but you stay, you and Ralph are obviously made for each other" Nancy turned to walk away as Lucy wiped the blood from her lip with her silky eye mask " By the way, you can tell that husband of mine the dogs will be staying with me for the foreseeable future, and you can also tell him I will be contacting a solicitor to start divorce proceedings........oh and one more thing" Nancy looked down at Lucys groin and her pretty lacy blue French knickers that looked a like a million spiders were trying to escape this dark void "One of the things that grows really fast when a woman gets to your age is the hair around your muff. But don't worry there is a pair of garden shears in the shed and an old lawn mower feel free to borrow them won't you!"

Nancy winked sarcastically, clicked her fingers to her dogs who followed instantly and went upstairs packed as many clothes as she could fit into medium sized suit case. She put the dogs their frozen minced turkey with all the nasty bits and trimmings and their bowls into her car and drove off down the road. The anger had subsided and in its place was a new found freedom, and all the rather daring highly salacious and prurient acts of sexual gratification she wanted to do to Malachi. She grinned from ear to ear, licked her lips and sighed the only way she knew how.....oh so very, very deeply.

Chapter 17

Joe had left the gates open for her, and Nancy drove at a low speed to the house trying to miss the deep holes in the man- made road. She parked the car to the left of the kitchen window by a pile of chopped wood. Nancy felt a pull of anticipation inside. Unsure of if it was related to her bringing the dogs back and what Joe's reaction would be or the fact that Malachi was watching her attentively through the kitchen window. Her heart leaped into her throat. She gulped.

Nancy opened the boot of her car and each bedraggled four legged creature jumped out confused but also curious at their new surroundings. In typical doggie fashion they all squatted and sniffed around. She walked around to the back seat of the car and hauled her suitcase out and placed it down on the ground. She heard a cough.

Malachi stood only a few inches away from her. His hair was pulled back into a low ponytail. His totally beautiful face was smudged down one side with car grease and his T-shirt was torn at the chest revealing a smooth monumental statuesque body……..
and a very small part of his nipple. Nancy hastily moved her gaze.

"Can I give you a hand with anything" Malachi inquired as he stepped closer to her.

Brazen Nancy with her new found ego and determined attitude was speaking loud and clear in her head

"Can he give you a hand with anything? Woooooooohaaaaaa" chatterbox shouted into her frontal lobe

Nancy smiled a teasing grin

"Yes can you take the case please and I'll round up the dogs"

Nancy whistled and all the dogs had gathered by her feet their tongues hanging loosely out of the sides of their mouths. Nancy stared down at them

"Right you guys, you have got to be on your best behaviour, no chewing, no barking, no eating shoes, no stealing food off the table, no drinking out of the toilet and under no circumstances do you pee in the house, okay?"

The dogs tilted their heads from side to side, Malachi laughed and Nancy felt a warm blush travel up the side of her face.

She walked through the open front door just behind Malachi and his oh so wonderfully toned backside. His jeans hugged it tightly and Nancy couldn't help but bite her top lip and envisage sinking her teeth into it.

"SLUT" said chatterbox

The adrenalin began pumping and Nancy knew all too well that a hot flush was brewing and quickly removed her jacket. She rushed to the kitchen sink and began splashing her face with water.

"You okay?" Malachi seemed concerned

Nancy turned to face him, droplets of cold water dribbled down her face onto her neck

"Just old age and the menopause" She tutted

He walked closer, and with the tips of his fingers wiped the excess fluid from her neck. Their eyes bore into each other when Elsa jumped up separating them.

Nancy's heart was fluttering, her pulse racing and her groin begging for attention.

"I'm sorry I'd better dry and groom the dogs and find them somewhere to sleep tonight"

"I'll help you"

"You don't have to"

"But I want to" his voice earnest and sincere

Nancy wasn't used to anyone offering to help her, especially when it came to helping with three very large hairy pointy teeth beings like hers. Nancy smiled gratefully

"Thank you, I'd like that"

With all three dogs dried, brushed and watered and smelling a lot fresher than before she headed off to the boot room with them. It was a small compact room. Where Joe kept all his out-door gear, mops buckets and any other piece of equipment that he didn't want on show in the rest of the house. It was a little too warm for the thick coated beasts so Nancy opened one of the tiny fan light windows. Letting in a nice cool breeze that took the temperature down a few degrees. Joe was very anal when it came to locking up, especially as his cottage was away from any other and isolated in the back of beyond. Nancy so hoped he wouldn't shout at her in the morning for two reasons 1) bringing the dogs 2) for leaving that window open. Nancy crossed her fingers and prayed as there was no way she was going to send them back to Ralph and 'HER'. She kissed them all goodnight before turning off the light and heading back into the kitchen.

When she returned Malachi was washing his hands at the kitchen sink. It was her turn to cough.

"I really appreciated your help then" she said

"The pleasures all mine" he answered grinning with soap suds dripping from his fingers

Nancy smiled ardently at him and walked over to the sink. She opened one of the kitchen drawers and pulled out a 'cooks do it standing up' tea towel

"Do they really?" he teased

"I wouldn't know, I've never been given the opportunity to try" Nancy paused "I think I should possibly go to bed, it's been a very long day"

She threw the tea towel onto the draining board and bent down to pick up her case.

Malachi pushed her hands out of the way

"I'll bring this up for you"

The walk to the boudoir seemed to go on forever. Nancy was tired and drained but something inside her was telling her that tonight she begins living again. She reached out a hand to take the case from Malachi as they stood by her bed, their fingers touched. Enough high voltage currents to light up the whole of London shot deep into her veins. Her skin prickled with expectation. Before she could even grab control of her senses Malachi's sensual lips were on hers. Their lips lingered on each other's for what seemed like an eternity before their mouths opened and their tongues danced in the darkness. Breathlessly Nancy disengaged and bit Malachi's bottom lip. His face was rose red and she could feel his erection touching the side of her leg. Nancy stepped away.

"I'll run a bath" her voice almost a whisper

Nancy was sat on the edge of the bath her hands gently swooshing back and forth in the foaming water. Malachi walked towards Nancy and stopped a few inches away from her. Nancy stood her head tilting up wards, so she could stare into those piercing eyes. Their gaze was locked.

"I just wanted to say" he said

Nancy lifted her finger and placed it on his lips

"Shh, no words, no speaking, and please relax you look so tense, I'm not going to eat you, you know …..Not tonight anyway"

Nancy slid a finger down his arms and across the chest of this power house of a man. Nancy breathed in through her nose as her fingers slipped under the bottom of his t-shirt. She could feel the ridges of his well-toned stomach. Malachi's eyes were staring down on her, he went to touch her breasts. Nancy grabbed his hand.

"No" she said as she returned his arm to his side.

His t-shirt clung to his designer body as Nancy begun walking around him, her finger tips barely touching him. He shivered as she run them down his spine.

"Take off your top" she commanded

Malachi obeyed.

"Take off your jeans"

Malachi obeyed

As he slowly undone the buttons of his jeans Nancy could see the tip of his erect penis. She lifted her arms and placed her left hand on her right shoulder and her right on her left, her head was gently resting on her left hand as she watched him drag down his jeans to reveal his smooth shaved legs and olive tanned skin.

Her eyes examined him closely. She could see his pulse in his jugular beating quickly and her heart began to quicken in time with his.

The long pause made Malachi fidget. He began to feel uncomfortable and nervous. Nancy saw the apprehension in his eyes as she slid off her oversized borrowed baggy sweatshirt and undone the button of her jeans and nonchalantly lowered her zip. Nancy gripped hold of either side of the denim by her hips and without haste pulled them down.

She placed her finger tips on her collar bone and let them slide effortlessly down to her cleavage. She paused, arched her back and moved her arms behind her in one swift movement she undone the clasp of her bra. Her right arm lay across her chest covering her ample breasts whilst her left hand glided the straps down her arm. In one slow action her bra was beneath her feet and her breasts were free from their restraint.

She stood still watching Malachi watching her. His fidgeting had ceased and his eyes were transfixed on this forty something female.

Nancy's right hand began caressing the inside of her thighs. Her fingers stroked her aching and throbbing clitoris. She exhaled as her head tilted backwards and her legs parted. Sedately her fingers rubbed her labia through the pure white laced underwear. Nancy's senses amplified and heightened and she could smell the desideratum that seeped out of Malachi's pores. She stopped abruptly.

"Climb into the bath Malachi"

Malachi obeyed

His muscles flexed as he sat down into the deep filled foam. The water rippled as it hugged his naked body. Nancy sat once again on the edge of the bath. She reached for the natural honeycomb sea sponge, squeezing it in the comforting warm aqua pura. With a full sponge she took her hand out of the water and began compressing it slowly. It trickled down his pectorals. Malachi breathed out heavily. His mouth opened and the tip of his tongue touched the front of his exquisite white teeth. He reached up to touch the inside of her thigh.

"No" Nancy said earnestly

"I want to touch you"

"Not yet" she answered her voice alluring and bewitching.

  Malachi frowned. His voice was deep and rasping

"Why won't you let me touch you?"

"Because I" She paused……..."Please Malachi please stop talking"

Nancy allowed her fingers to travel down the centre of his chest to his cut line. His neatly trimmed man-scaped pubic hair sent her heart racing. She bit her bottom lip as he moaned in pleasure. Her index finger teased the top of his penis in small circular motions. Malachi's hip's tensed lifting him upwards out of the water. Nancy bent down and gently blew across the head of his firm erection. The muscles in his face tightened as she gripped hold of him tightly in her hands. His erection swelled harder than ever before. Nancy squeezed gently. Malachi closed his eyes his body stiffened and constricted, his pleasure zone had been reached.

The light shone brightly through the French doors of the boudoir as Nancy lay hugging her pillow a smug look was spread across her face. No, her cobwebs did not get cleared away, but that brief almost perfect hour of her life, left her with a body that after such a long time had finally began defrosting and waking up again.

Malachi's aftershave lingered in the air. Nancy inhaled so deep that she thought her lungs were about to burst. The self-righteous sentiment she eluded gripped hold of her heart as she hugged her pillow tighter, almost squeezing the stuffing right out of it. Elation spread through her blood stream.

"Well, well, well not so much of a perfect suburbia house wife now are we eh?" said chatterbox

"Will you be quiet, I haven't done anything wrong and to be honest I never actually let him touch me, so my secret wifey place has not yet been disturbed or should I say dismantled or even disrupted!"

Chatterbox, grunted and sealed her rather large mouth closed. Nancy just smiled coyly to herself. In the midst of her rather alternative seduction of Malachi she had totally forgotten about the dogs and Joe!

She would have normally put her forgetful memory down to her age, the menopause or that fact she was just being a typical female with hormones. But she knew it was none of the above as she apprehensively entered the kitchen and took a seat at the table. Joe began pouring her a cup of tea, his face had a stern expression on it! Nancy bit her top lip. She was preparing herself for a scolding from Joe. But Joe said nothing and continued making Nancy a cup of PG tips. He wouldn't even look at her as he added one sugar after another to her tea cup. Nancy had to speak first. Her face contorted as she stumbled on her words

"Jo, joe, I, I ,I," Nancy took a deep breath as Joe slammed down her tea in front of her. She was speaking faster than Lewis Hamilton could drive around Silverstone "Look Joe I can explain, I'm so sorry I couldn't leave the dogs with Ralph, they were such a mess and ...."

"The dogs" Joe interrupted "My dear Nancy, the dogs are fine, I've walked them fed them and now they are sleeping. But I'm highly, highly disappointed in you"

Nancy cradled her cup in her hands

"Well if it's not the dogs what is it, why the stern face and no speaking?"

"I'm disappointed because" Joe hesitated "Because, you couldn't wake me first thing this morning and tell me you accosted our Mal last night"

Joe clapped his hands repetitively together, as an immensely vast smile replaced his scornful expression. Nancy relaxed instantly in her chair as she emanated the tension and fear of being disciplined like a seven year old child.

"Oh Joe, I thought you were going to reprimand me about the dogs" She sipped her tea and spat it straight back into her cup "Oh my god Joe are you trying to poison me! How many sugars went in my tea this time?"

"I lost count after 6, I thought you would need the energy" he sniggered a very camp, childish but highly thoughtful snigger.

Nancy placed the cup down and nudged it to the centre of the table

"Joe how the hell did you know? Have you got secret cameras in my room?

"Well the thought had crossed my mind" He raised his eyebrows and winked, "Of course I haven't you silly woman, I saw Mal this morning, with a smile that went from ear to ear and assumed that something must have occurred. Actually that's a complete lie, I asked him outright. And before you get all pissy he was a total gentleman and didn't kiss and tell. But Princess I want all the gritty details plus I need to know if I should go buy some cystitis relief"

Nancy laughed out loud and told every sordid detail to her very gay, very caring and very nosey best friend.

Chapter 18

The fierce April showers had given way to a mild and sunny start to May. Daisy was sitting on broken step in the back garden of the family home. Sundays were never a quiet time when the sun appeared. As the neighbours children who had been locked up inside for the winter made every effort to disrupt the neighbourhood with their screams and arguments. She sighed as she looked around her garden. The once tidied out door space, that her mother adored, was now a shambolic state of unruly plants and bushes that had grown wild in the early spring months. She struggled to get her head around the fact that for the first time in her life a dog wasn't running up and down the garden chasing a resting pigeon or barking at any person walking past the pathway at the bottom. Her eyes wandered and she gazed at her father sitting on an old rickety bench on the patio. His salt and pepper hair hadn't been cut since

Nancy left and was beginning to become fluffy at the ends. His nicely trimmed beard had grown considerably and his laughter lines around his eyes seemed deeper and darker than usual. Without Nancy, Ralph just didn't know what to do. It was her mother who told him at the right time to get his hair cut and his beard trimmed. It was Nancy who made sure his clothes were clean and pressed. It was Nancy who looked after this middle aged man like she would her own child and it was Nancy who fished that bloody broken rickety old bench out of a skip when a neighbour a few doors down was renovating their house. She had planned to mend, fix, sand and paint it up all ready for this coming summer. But summer was just around the corner and Nancy wasn't there. Daisy's eyes dropped to the ground as the deep realisation that her mum would neither 'make good' that old bench or even quite possibly never be coming home had finally hit her.

"Why did you do it dad?" her voice almost begging him for the truth

Ralph peered over the top of his newspaper, he scanned the garden before answering

"I know what you're thinking Daisy, you think I'm a sad middle aged man who should have known better. But the truth is Daisy I really don't know. I'm not going to make excuses but if I could turn back time" Ralphs voice wavered "You have to know that I have never stopped loving your mother and there isn't a day that goes by that I don't miss her"

Daisy arose from her step and joined her father on the bench. It creaked as she sat down

"Dad you're talking like she's dead! She's not she is alive and well and staying at Joes go tell her dad. If you love her that much tell her and fight for her, she isn't a mind reader. You two were made for each other, you connect like two pieces of a jigsaw puzzle. Forgive me for saying this Dad, but Lucy is, is as fake as that Rolex she wears. She's a moose, I'm never going to like her and nor are Willow and Poppy either, she is just wrong for you and her spray tan makes her look like an Umpa Lumpa"

The father and daughters conversation was rudely interrupted by Lucy and her mint blue feather puff stripper heels. Daisy groaned as Lucy clipped clopped over the patio towards them.

The highly made up Lucy twitched her nose, pouted her mouth and blinked her eyes as the gaze of the sun shone directly into them. A white towel was wrapped around her head, (it should have been her neck but hey this isn't a story about a psychopathic killer....not yet anyway) Her body was covered in a satin baby doll nightie with matching thong. Which seemed to be the only garment that Lucy ever wore irrelevant of what time day or night it was.

"So what are you two talking about?" she asked as she started picking at her nails.

Daisy looked at her father, Ralph looked at his daughter

"Erm" said Ralph, we were actually discussing Umpa Lumpa's from Charlie and the Chocolate Factory if you must know"

Lucy frowned as she watched the father and daughter grin in unison.

"Well seeing as you are not including me into your joke, will one of you please sort out lunch as I have just had my new gel nails done"

Daisy raised her eyebrows, and bit her cheek. Her mouth opened before her brain went into think mode.

"Is there anything that you actually do, do?"

"Daisy!" shouted Ralph

"Sorry dad.....I'll go do lunch, Willow and
Poppy will be here in a minute. May be Lucy
could set the table if that isn't too much for
her, but then again she may over extend those
flabby arms of hers and pull a muscle!"

"How dare you!" shrieked Lucy

Daisy walked over to Lucy who was by now
breathing like a raging bull, and twitching like
a bee had just chewed its way through her
knicker elastic and stung her on a place where
bees just shouldn't go.

"No Lucy how dare you! you may be dads bit
on the side, but this is my home, mine,
Poppy's, Willows, dads and mums. You are
not and never will be able to compete with my
mother, she is worth a million of you. You

treat our home like a hotel and expect everyone to wait on you hand and bloody foot. Well that's not how we do things around here. If you really want to be part of this family, then start getting used to the fact that you have to get down and dirty once in a while! And whilst I'm actually having a go at you, for god's sake do something about your disgusting orange spray tan and shutttttt upppppp, about your tacky buggering gel nails! No one cares! "

Lucy stood mouth open, eyes wide. Lucy was not used to being told to shut up, Lucy was not used to being told what to do, and Lucy was not used to someone referring to her rather expensive tan being described as orange. Lucy had met her match.

Chapter 19

The high pitched beep beep of Nancy's phone distracted her from gawping at Malachi as he was chopping fire wood. He had removed his top as the May sunshine glistened on his skin. The view that day was made even better by his young firm body which eluded strength and vitality. Nancy concluded her thoughts thinking the only thing that was missing was his reticent sexual inexperience, which was an assumption after all as she hadn't let him touch her. But that was something Nancy was more than happy to resolve. She carried on staring at this fine specimen before acknowledging the fact she had a text. It was from Michele.

Hey stranger. I'm so sorry I haven't been in touch. I'm a really crap friend. I know this. Please forgive me .If you have forgiven me please continue to read further. If you haven't then dismiss this text and condemn me to hell (but please read on)....Okay so there is no easy way to say this (hope your sitting down!) but IM GETTING MARRIED!!!!!!!

Sorry sorry sorry again I love you

Mich

Xxx

Nancy almost fell of the pile of uncut logs she was sitting on. She looked over at Malachi, as he wiped beads of sweat off his chest with his t-shirt. She breathed out heavily.

"Erotic, highly illegal thoughts will have to wait" she said out loud and began texting Michele back immediately.

"WTF! Who are you marrying? Stupid question its Simon isn't it? Unless you have had a serendipity moment and found the man of your dreams in Tesco's whilst choosing which winged sanitary attire you should buy?

Xxx

Ps no I haven't forgiven you and yes you are going to hell, but if it's with Simon then who the hell cares lolol (winky face)

Xxx

****

Okay I'm damned to hell, but will go there with a rather satisfying smile on my face (even bigger winky face than yours!) ..... Anyway you need to go buy a great big puffy hat because we are getting married next week. Yes I said next week! Simon wants us to marry before the summer season starts...have to dash now as need to look for a frock. Will phone you tomorrow. OH BTW we are getting married at Joe's!

So excited!

Xxx

P.s .s I sort of invited Ralph eeekkkkkk!!!.... have to dash now as I have so much to do. Will phone you *tomorrow. (Please don't shout at me as I'm a nervous bride to be!)*

Nancy looked at her phone and squeezed it hard. She was going to have to face Ralph for the first time since she walked out on him. She knew that Michele's skittish behaviour was not probably intentional but was she ready to face her husband again. More importantly was she ready to see 'HER', Lurid Lucy with her loose labia, draped over his arm like a dead beaver with her big teeth ready to chomp its way through her newly separated flesh?

Chapter 20

Joe was in his element arranging, hairdressers, beauty therapists and florists in the week before the wedding, and before anyone knew it the big day had arrived.

Michele stood facing the view from the boudoir's open French doors. Her long auburn hair had been put up into a romantic blend of tousled curls and tiny white flowers and hair clips with diamanté centres. Her make-up was subtle and her eyes were accentuated by a full set of semi-permanent eyelashes and she had the glossiest lip gloss on the market. (Joe's touch obviously)

 The hardest job that Joe had this week was to persuade Michele not to wear a pair of Levi 501's on her wedding day. Instead she wore a 1920's fitted off the shoulder White chapel lace tulle dress that fitted her figure perfectly. Much to Joe's disgust but to Michele's pleasure her foot attire did not consist of an embroidered pair of some French designers vintage range, but a pair of white Hunter Wellington boots. Which Joe had said were being forcibly removed from her feet straight after the wedding. Which was to take place in the field adjacent to the house. Michele was only too happy to remove the wellies but she was in her own words

"Never going to fucking wear a pair of shoes that pinched her toes and made her walk like a constipated chicken!"

Willow, Daisy and a growing Poppy, all wore strapless beaded red chiffon dresses. All three women had their hair pinned up into a similar tousled effect of the brides and the obligatory hunter boots covered their feet.

An extremely despondent Poppy stood staring at her reflection in the full length mirror.

"OH MY GOD IM SO FAT!

Joe rubbed her belly before placing a kiss in its centre

"You, are not fat, YOU are a beautiful mother to be who has the miracle of life growing inside her. Now hush your mouth as I need to do your lips again"

"Joe if you put any more gloss on my lips I will probably blind the minister and he will end up marrying me to that man who has been standing outside the door for the last hour. Who is he anyway?"

"OH that's Danny. I made him stand outside guarding the door as I didn't trust Michele to leave the room. She would have only gone and ate a hot dog or something and ended up with tomato sauce all down her dress. ....totally dreamy isn't he?"

"He is okay, not really my sort but I know whose he would be"

Poppy looked over to Daisy who was trying to calm down an apprehensive Michele, who was desperate to pee for the third time in fifteen minutes.

"Reallllyyyyyyyyyyy" Joe's eyes twinkled as he reapplied Poppy's lip gloss "Now you define the true beauty of the female form. Now where is you god damn mother?"

The red satin sleeveless mermaid dress with sweeping train hung to Nancy's figure like a glove to a hand. To the un-trained eye you could have assumed it had been specially crafted to hug her figure in the flawless manner it did. But they only had a week to plan this wedding so an off the peg purchase was all they had time for. The colour, the fit, the design was just perfect for her. Her short blonde hair had been dyed dark brown and cut into a modern pixie style. A tiara in the same shimmering diamantes made the new hair come alive. Nancy looked stunning.

She stood in the upstairs bathroom pulling on the Wellington boots and smoothing down her dress. The last time she had worn anything quite as feminine was at a close friend of the families wedding, when Ralph was best man. Which reminded her in under forty minutes she would come eye to eye with Ralph and 'HER'. The thought of seeing the pair of them together made Nancy's pulse quicken and her throat wretch on its own accord.

"Oh look at little miss fearful pants" said chatterbox "You are such a hypocrite"

"What do you mean!?" Answered Nancy to Nancy

"I mean" came her annoying alter ego " You are getting all high and mighty thinking 'woe is me' but you have actually molested a man young enough to be your son, so in my book that actually makes you as bad as him!"

Nancy felt confused as Joe opened the bathroom door.

"Wwwwwwell I never, you scrub up very well, you look fabulous"

"I don't feel it Joe, I will have to face Ralph soon and I'm actually scared shitless, but I just don't know if I'm scared of seeing him or scared of him finding out what I done with Malachi. I don't think I can go down there Joe"

Joe took Nancy's hands in his.

"Look princess when the warm spring sunshine beats down on a lonely daisy, the daisy opens its petals and smiles. When the dark storm clouds of spring come and the rain drops fall, the daisy closes up its petals to protect itself. Don't let those dark clouds force you to hide yourself away shielding your beauty from others."

"But Joe"

"There are no if's, no may be's and there are certainly no but's. You are not a goat. You are a middle aged women in the prime of your life. You are my Nancy whom I love, adore and if you don't get your arse downstairs now I will slap you on the back side with a brillo pad. Understand?"

Nancy re arranged her dress once more and those awful pull you in highly un -sexy pants and made her way downstairs to a jittery Michele. Her beautiful daughters and a congregation of fifty which included the wonderfully moulded and pumped cast of 'let them rip'......oh and Ralph and HER.

Nancy bent down to straighten Michele's dress which had got caught on the back of her Wellington boots. Sitting not two feet away from her she saw her husband. He was suited and booted but his hair was unkempt and his beard looked like it had become home to a few nesting sparrows. Ralphs eyes were transfixed on his wife's. Nancy's on her husbands. A dig in the ribs by Lurid Lucy soon bought Ralphs attention back to 'Her'

Nancy swallowed hard and continued fluffing around with Michele's dress.

"Nance, I need to pee" whispered Michele

"Tuff, you will have to hold it. Just promise not to sneeze, or cough, look just promise not to piss yourself okay"

"Oh my god Nance I'm getting married, it's really happening isn't it, this isn't a dream is it? Pinch me or something"

"If you don't shut up I'm going to punch you not pinch you. Now stop fidgeting, take your dads arm and go get married!"

The old Story and Clarke piano had been carefully carried out from the living room and placed on a hired stage next to the seated guests. Joe nodded to the piano player aka Kevin the compare. His short stumpy fingers hit each key in turn as Nancy's Joe began singing.

'You are so beautiful, to me, you are so beautiful, to me, can't you seeeeeeeeeee'

Michele was going down the aisle to her favourite Joe cocker's song. This was her gift from Nancy.

"Thank you" mouthed Michele

"Pleasure" answered a smiling Nancy

Joe's raspy voice continued to sing out the words to the song as Michele and her father walked past the standing guests admiring this perfect, albeit fidgety bride. As she reached Simon, the minister ushered the wedding party to take their seats. A few giggles could be heard as some of the guests sat down. The old wooden benches Danny had made in the week prior to the wedding where a few inches smaller than they should have been. The cast of let them rip were over 6ft tall their knees where bent into their chests and they resembled Will Farell in Elf (but it has to be said were a lot better looking and dressed in designer suits rather than an Elf one) The mild May weather was perfect, The wooden arch that was draped in red and white ribbon billowed gently in the breeze. The white and red roses that cascaded over each side of the arch smelt like a warm summer's breeze dancing through the sky like unicorns and fairy dust. The day couldn't have been more perfect.......well almost perfect.

You see Lucy would not listen when Willow explained to her that the field in which the ceremony was to take place had not fully dried out after the early spring rain. Even though Joe had covered most of it in dry straw, there were still a few bits that were a bit boggy. Well Lucy was having none of it and instead of a 'safe' pair of wellies she donned her feet with a pair of highly sequined Louis Vuitton four and a half inch heels. Ceremony complete, all guests moved to the large marquee in the field next door. To get to this field all guests young and old had to climb over a small sty. Obviously Lucy wore a tight fitting abnormally short dress that left nothing to the imagination. As she lifted one of her legs up to step on the sty her Louis Vuitton's got stuck in the half dried mud. Her dress ripped, her old thong snapped and she ended up face down in the cold brown slush.........maybe it was a perfect day after all.

The three course dinner was scrumptious, the live music flawless even when a slightly tipsy Joe, Malachi and Danny sang Lady in Red to a profoundly crimson Nancy. The rest of the evening turned into a karaoke showdown and it wasn't long before Nancy had the microphone thrust into her hands. She stared out into the crowd and found her waiting target. Ralph. The music played and Nancy never lost eye contact with her husband as she serenaded all who could hear with her rendition of Randy Vanwarmer's 'Just when I needed you most'. You couldn't hear a pin drop when she sang out the final note but Nancy graciously handed the microphone back to Joe and with her head held high walked over to Ralph and Lucy picked up the fullest glass of red wine she could and poured it slowly over Ralphs head. A very drunk Sasha alias walnut laughed so loud and so hard she choked on an olive that was floating around her Martini. Simon had to give her the Heimlich manoeuvre, and then slipped on the regurgitated olive twisted his ankle and ended up spending the last few hours of his wedding in the local accident and emergency department. Finally once his ankle was bandaged and crutches were given to him, Michele and Simon were on their way to France. To spend four gratifying days and nights in an idyllic Chateau in Chantilly. Which was kind heartedly paid for by the rest of the cast.

Nancy was scolded by Joe, in his typical 'oh my god why didn't I think of that manner" before she retreated to the kitchen where an open shirted Malachi stood.

"You still love him don't you" he asked

"Of course I do Mal, it's only been a few weeks"

"So what about us….Is there an us?"

Nancy walked closer to Malachi gripping hold of the sides of his unbuttoned shirt

"Can we not just enjoy whatever this is and not worry about the rules of how things should be?"

Her satin dress touched his naked chest as her lips kissed his bare skin. Malachi lowered his head smelling her hair. His hands slid down her dress, he ruched it up and gripped it tight. Their lips touched. Nancy reached for Malachi's hands as they travelled up the inner sides of her thighs.

"No Mal"

Malachi pulled away, turning in the opposite direction to Nancy. He took a sharp intake of breath as he ran his hands through his hair. Frustration was set on his chiseled face.

"Are you ever going to let me touch you?" he asked his voice sardonic and disparaging.

Nancy edged closer and lay her head on his back, tears where forming in her eyes

"I'm so sorry Mal, I'm just not ready to let another man touch me…please don't hate me"

Malachi turned to face her. He lifted her face with his well-manicured hands.

"I could never hate you Nancy, never"

"Oh Mal" the falling tears glided down her face as once again her lips searched for his.

Chapter 21

Everyone was poised waiting with curiosity as to why Joe had called an emergency meeting. The demonstration was to take place in under four days and he never pulled everyone together so close to it unless there was something really urgent that needed to be addressed.

Idle chit chat was taking place, except for Nancy and Malachi who were sitting opposite each other playing footsie under the table. Their eyes were locked, both mentally undressing the other and watching for that raised eyebrow, smirk or the unforgettable 'wide eyed syndrome' better known as 'have you really just put your toe there?' There somewhat teenage behaviour was interrupted by Walnut slamming down a six cup mocha coffee maker in between the pair of them. Jolting them back to the issues of the day and some rather obtuse glares from the other seated members.

Joe arrived carrying a wad of papers and a map of London. Nancy hated London. She hated the busyness. She hated the constant smell of petrol and diesel, and even though she was a country bumpkin she hated darting in and out of the pooping pigeons. But what really made her dislike good old London town so much was 'the people'. Oh don't get me wrong she loved Londoners, she loved the way they spoke with their cockney twang, she loved their tom foolery and witty one liners she even liked the fact that so many different Londoners came from all walks of life and different ethnic origins. Nancy just couldn't stand people in general. The thought of so many people in one place made her want to elope to the moon. Obviously her first choice would have been Malachi but she would have gone with chunk from the Goonies if it meant she had to spend longer than half a day there.

"Are you two going stop giggling now" Walnut asked, her eyes unable to make contact with neither Nancy nor Mal

Nancy rubbed Walnuts arm

"Are you okay?"

Walnut was curt in her response as she pulled out Joe's chair for him to sit down

"I'm fine"

Mal shrugged his shoulders and mouthed 'Hormones'. Nancy gave him a 'just don't go there look'

"Right is everyone here" inquired Joe

A tall lanky man with a bald head, dressed in combat trousers and Doctor Marten boots answered. Nancy had never met him before and she instantly took a dislike to him. His lip twitched and turned at the ends. He spoke in a broad London accent and smelt of cheese and old socks. A Union Jack had been tattooed on his fore arm and a swastika on the inside of his left wrist.

"Danny's missing" he answered in a gruff voice

"Oh" said Nancy her gaze being distracted from the new cheesy smelling man "I think he is outside with Daisy, they are supposed to be mending the gate to the driveway. Shall I go get them?"

"We haven't got time for that!" Cheesy man snapped "I would have thought you would have been a lot more organised than this, my time is money you know"

Joe could see that the disparaging way he had spoken to Nancy, made her feel uncomfortable and he could see those hormones bubbling ready to explode under the surface.

"Yes Smithy we do know" Joe exclaimed "You came to us though remember and I will not be paying you a penny. Because it is your fault we are having to now rearrange our whole demonstration"

Huge sighs travelled round the table and everybody began asking why all at the same time. Joe shook his head and puffed his cheeks before exhaling the trapped air and the reason.

"SSH, ssh calm down everyone and I will tell you. It would appear that our original date of the demo for the 1st June has been, double booked with, his, sorry Smithy's organisation. So we have two choices, we postpone or we find another route"

"What the fuck" Shouted Danny as he entered the kitchen, with Daisy hanging of his arm "We've been planning this for months, why can't they move their demo, why should we have to?"

Cheers and here, here's bellowed from every person in the room.

Smithy strutted over to Danny pushing his head forward as he got closer like some demented turkey,

"Look son"

"I'm not your son"

Smithy shock his head and sucked his teeth

"You are my son and don't you ever forget it! Your demo is not as important as ours. Ours is a march of over five thousand very pissed of British tax payers , and yours is, well yours is a march of about five hundred cripples in wheelchairs"

Nancy could take no more, she pushed her chair backwards walked over to Smithy and his cock sure attitude, and punched him square on the chin. Did it do any damage, no nothing, Smithy didn't flinch. He didn't mark, bleed or bruise. Instead he stood laughing at her.

"You pathetic woman! You really think you or these poofs could do any damage to me. Mad dog Smithy. I could knock the whole fucking lot of you out just by breathing on you"

Nancy could feel her past tearing away at her soul. She bit the inside of her cheek, flared her nostrils and stared around the room full of gawking people. Her gaze was met by a nodding Joe, who mouthed "No Nance" Nancy blinked and looked Smithy straight in the eye.

"Some people's mothers should have so kept their kids as a wank or a blow job! Otherwise we end up with a fucked up ejaculation like you!"

Joe rose from his chair and stood between Smithy and an outraged Nancy. His fifty plus years and broad shoulders squaring up to Smithy in size and stature. The tonality of Joe's voice had deepened he glared into Smithy's bloodshot eyes.

"Don't you ever come into my home threaten my guests, my friends and don't you ever call me a poof again. I my dear sir am not a poof, I am a Queen "Joe puckered his lips, twitched his nose and in a very camp manner minced back to his chair at the table.

Screams and bellowing laughter transmitted from everyone in the room. Everyone except mad Dog Smithy who once again sucked his teeth, moved his neck in a demented turkey fashion and strutted to the kitchen door

"Change your dates gay boy" Smithy extended his arm and pointed a skinny thin finger at Joe "This....This aint over!"

"Yes it is" replied a red faced Danny "Yes it is"

Chapter 22

The start to summer was absolutely atrocious. The rain lashed down every day since the meeting to cancel the demonstration had taken place. Joe had been in foul mood for days. Which even caused him to shout at Nancy on more than one occasion as the dogs were constantly damp and that god awful wet dog smell lingered around the house like some steaming old rancid kippers. Nancy's mood wasn't much better especially as she just found out Lucy kept asking when Ralph was going to file for divorce as Nancy hadn't bothered even though she said she would.

The boys and Kevin from 'let them rip' had just started their summer tour but before they left Daisy moved in to be closer to Danny. She was in love and no one or nothing was going to brake her swooning around the house like a love struck teenager. Nancy still revoked Malachi's advances after their first explicit meeting but she missed him terribly. She desired him like children do haribo, but her brain would not let him get further than her shoe lace.

Walnuts mood hadn't got much better either and each time Nancy tried to ask her what was up. Walnuts response was the same as all the time's before 'I'm fine'. Which was preceded with the same icy cold shoulder.

Nancy tided the magazines for the fifteenth time before standing at the double French doors in the living room. The rain was relentless and the dark clouds above didn't look like the weather would change any time soon.

Joe picked up a magazine and sat on the handmade leather chesterfield couch. It creaked as he sat down and sent a smell of almond leather shine spray floating around the room. The smell was truly remarkable well it had to be, it was yet another of Joe's own recipes. There wasn't anything in the house that was shop bought. Everything from washing up liquid to insect bite cream was formed and fashioned in the boot room where Nancy's dogs stayed at night, or when they were wet, or when they smelt a bit funky, basically when Joe had had enough of them drooling and dribbling all over his pristine home.

"Joseph"

"Joseph" called Nancy again

"Joseph, you miserable old fart. What the hell is up with you? This is so not like you?"

Joe put his magazine on the empty seat next to him and took a rather large sigh.

"It's Smithy"

"What about him?"

"Your find out sooner than later so I may as well be the one to tell you" Joe bit his top lip and gave Nancy the are you ready to hear this look

"Well. Danny as you know is his son"

Nancy nodded

"Well" Joe fidgeted "Well he actually isn't his son he is mine"

"WHAT!" screamed Nancy "Fucking hell Joe you kept that a bit secret? But I thought you only had eyes for men's bits not women's gaping orifices!"

"I don't, I mean I do. Oh my god can I start again"

Nancy nodded her head in quick succession

"Okay so it was long after you had left us. I had just met Taylor at an anti- badger baiting demo. But Taylor was with another young chap, whose name I just can't remember. Anyway to cut a long story short I was trying to make Taylor jealous and started getting a bit fresh with a young lady called Sophie. In all honesty it made me feel so sick each time I kissed her. Don't get me wrong she was beautiful but there were no other gay men around and I so wanted Taylor to want me that I was willing to try anything to get his attention. My plan didn't quiet go to my plan and I ended up sleeping with Sophie. Next thing I know is she is pregnant"

"Well I never, you dirty old rogue" Nancy sniggered

"Actually Nance that's not the whole story. Sophie was with Smithy at the time but both of us thought it best to keep our night of passion a secret, and we were doing really well until

Sophie wanted another baby. The long and short of it is Smithy can only fire blanks. She denied knowing who Danny's father was and told Smithy it was just some random bloke she had met in a pub. For the last twenty or so years I have paid a fair bit of money into a secret bank account for Danny and Sophie. And to be honest this money has kept the whole family going. Smithy spends his money on beer, football, Mary Jane and crack. He also likes to throw his weight around and Sophie has been in hospital on more than one occasion. Anyway last spring, I got a phone call from Sophie, she was in accident and emergency after Smithy came home drunk one night. He broke her nose and threatened to kick Danny out of the house and beat the living shit out of him if she didn't open up and tell him who Danny's father was. And the rest is history"

"Well I'll be, you're more of a king rather than a gay old queen now Joe" Nancy's laughter echoed around the room "So tell me what happened next"

"Well after Sophie admitted to Smithy that I'm Danny's dad. Smithy kicked him out anyway and that's why he lives here. Danny knows the whole truth because I told him and he seems more than happy with it. Actually he was ecstatic, and now Daisy is here I don't think I have ever seen him smile so much. But poor Sophie has been left with that animal. I have offered her a bed here it's not like I haven't got the room is it? But she refuses…..I just don't know what is going through her mind"

Nancy's face dropped as the memories of her early life flashed before her eyes

"I do…….She's probably so afraid that leaving will be worse than staying. It's weird Joe but my mum, Sophie, know deep down inside that all this is wrong but a mixture of fear, helplessness and a sense that they deserve what they are all getting plays a part. They feel ashamed and paralysed. Sometimes they are more comfortable with what they know rather than what is outside their own front door. Unless Sophie can find that bit of strength inside her to make that decision then the chances are she will end up like my mum….. Accidentally falling out of the loft hatch."

Joe pulled Nancy close into his arms, and kissed her tenderly on the forehead

"We make a right old pair don't we"

"Yep" answered Nancy "One very hormonal, menopausal woman whose lady bits get a bit too hot when a certain young stallion is about and one old but exceptionally handsome very gay, very camp, very house proud poof"

Chapter 23

The torrential down pours that had nearly but drowned the whole country left all the boys with an unexpected week off. The last show that month had to be cancelled when the theatre they had booked became flooded with water. It was visible to everyone that the damp weather, the demo's cancellation had left a bitter after taste in Joe's mouth. But Joe was never a person to be defeated that easily and put all his energy into re-booking the demonstration. The new date was organised for Saturday August the 16th.

Joe had thought seeing as the boys were back for a few days he could kill two birds with one stone. Arrange yet another of his meetings, put the final check list in place for the demo and also audition some females for a new erotic dance troop he was putting together.

The idea for forming a female group wasn't actually his but Michele's. When Michele and Simon arrived back from their honeymoon in France, Joe had offered a PA role to her. She had spent the last ten years of her life working as a PA, sales person, tea maker and general dog's body to a local Estate Agents. She hated it, but she hated her fat balding leach of a boss even more. He asked her to stay late on more than one occasion. Let's just say her course in self- defense got her out of more than one sticky situation with her bald headed bully of an employer. Whereby her knee accidentally on purpose ended up making him sing higher than a choir boys before maturity set in.

She accepted Joe's offer without any hesitation and had great pleasure in going into work the day after she arrived back from her honeymoon. She pushed open her boss's door, picking up an indelible black marker pen and drawing a huge cock on his forehead which included the sprays of semen too. For a brief few moments she stood back admiring her art work before holding a middle finger high in the air and shouting

"FUCK YOU" In her loudest voice.

She loved her new job and she loved the fact that wherever her husband went so did she. It's not that she didn't trust him at the after show drinks. Actually that's a total lie she didn't trust him, or the raving nymphomaniacs that came to see the shows! So this new job meant she could keep a close eye on all the sexual tension that built up during and after show time. Simon was on a short leash but in all honesty he seemed to enjoy being Michele's lap dog. As for Michele well she seemed to enjoy being his dominant other half. Her nickname was and will be until the end of time 'the dominatrix (whips and handcuffs essential!)

Anyway back to the story. The old barn had been newly spread with dry straw and a sound and lighting system. Twenty or so women had turned up that day to bump and grind and 'do their thing' in front of all the members of 'let them rip'. The audition table had four seats on it. Joe's, Nancy's, Michele's and Kevin's. The rest of the group sat on bales of straw around the barn. After much discussion with Michele, Joe had decided that they needed six acts for their new troop. Which was going to be called Midnight Masquerades. Midnight after one of Michele's cats and Masquerades as Joe said most people were false and couldn't keep up the masquerade for too long.

The first few auditions were totally awful. The girls could shake it, move it and grind it but their erotic dancing resembled what you would see in the local kebab shop after the clubs shut on a Saturday night. Joe wanted the full package, looks, legs and the ability to be provocative without looking like they had just stepped out of a porn movie, oooooing and rrrrinnnnng with every pulse of their hips. And why did they all have to twerk every second of their routine. Joe hit his head on the table as a five foot six brunette took to the stage. The other girls in the audition laughed and whispered behind their hands to each other, as this dark haired beauty removed her coat. A black pair of knee high boots led your eyes up towards sheer black stockings. Her torso was being covered by a highly sequined very short black flapper dress, her hands covered by three quarter length gloves. She stood nervously before nodding her head to Simon who clicked play on the Ipod. Her shoulders twitched back and forth as the backing track played. Her mouth opened and she started to sing 'all that Jazz from Chicago. Her voice was demur but when she moved her body every person in that barns jaw dropped to the floor. Her hands slid with ease up her thighs, her legs kicked high, she lay provocatively on the straw ground and teased the audience with her ample bust. As she hit the final note she effortlessly slid down (which wasn't easy on straw) into the splits. Everyone in that barn stood and applauded. Nobody could believe what they had just witnessed, not one twerk was in her routine she was outstanding. And she was also a size 18.

Joe, Nancy, Michele and Kevin shouted in accord

"YOU'RE HIRED"

By the end of the day they were still one act down and had no one left to audition.

"Well" Said Kevin "We will just have to use five acts instead of six. With Little Miss Chicago over there I'm sure we could put together something spectacular"

"I need six" Joe answered "It always has to be six"

As the two men began arguing between themselves a timid Sasha stepped forward

"I'll do it"

It was now Sasha's time to bring silence to the room.

"Don't be silly Walnut" said Joe "You can't dance......can you?"

Sasha handed her Ipod to Shawn

"Track three"

Shawn pressed play as the deep rooted lung action of Christina Aguilera sung out Dirty. Walnut twisted her hips, grinded, danced and removed her top. Okay so it wasn't polished but that girl could move. Walnut finished by blowing a kiss. A kiss to Malachi. Who stood at the far corner of the barn. He smiled as he caught it mid-air. Nancy now had her reason for Walnuts cold shoulder. She choked back her tears and closed her eyes tight before standing with the rest of the team applauding this miss-fit woman she had grown to love.

The newly formed female dance troop were ready and booked up for their first show. Let them rip were back on the open road and Poppy had also moved into Joe's as her baby was due second week in July. Nancy hadn't seen a lot of Mal or Walnut before the tour started, as every spare second was spent rehearsing, rehearsing and rehearsing some more. Walnut seemed to have gotten out of her foul mood, but as she had Malachi teaching her the new routines it was no wonder really, was it?

The rain was still unyielding and instead of scantily clad bodies roaming around in shorts and flip flops they were wearing wellies and jeans. Joe had turned the barn into an in-door exercise room for the dogs, as his OCD and their muddy footprints was causing him great distress. But he seemed to have mellowed somewhat with them because in the middle of the night someone had crept into one of the other outbuildings and set fire to it. It didn't take Einstein to guess who the guilty party was. But for Danny's sake Joe blamed it on a dis-guarded cigarette even though he hadn't smoked for over twenty years. The dogs that night barked continuously and if it wasn't for them raising the alarm then it could have been more than just an old wooden shed that burnt to the ground.

Nancy spent most of her time sitting in this old barn with her dogs. The imminent birth of her grand- child going round and round in her mind. Her own memories of all the times that her and Ralph used to joke about having grand-children and all the amazing things they were going to do with them. Waves of depression flowed through Nancy as it would not be her sharing the grand-parent role with Ralph now but Lucy. Ralph did get in touch regarding the divorce but both agreed they would leave it till after the baby was born and after Poppy was settled. Much to Lucy's disgust. It was obvious to everyone Lucy wasn't child friendly, especially Nancy. The ties that bound around Ralph and Nancy's heart were going to be the hardest bonds to break. But Nancy knew sooner rather than later she was going to have to succumb and let him go…..Just not yet.

Nancy gathered up her trailing thoughts and walked into the house her three dogs running behind her. Joe made her jump as she removed her boots and coat.

"You okay Princess?"

"I think so Joe, just got one of them messed up brain moments"

"I'll put the kettle on shall I?" he asked as he headed into the kitchen.

Nancy stood in front of the lit aga watching as Joe poured her a fresh cup of PG Tips. The aroma in the kitchen was prodigious and Nancy breathed in the extraordinarily fabulous scent. Crisp tones of citrus and coconut engulfed her senses.

"Joe what is that smell, it is divine"

"That is my new sugar scrub, lemon lime and coconut"…totally fabulous isn't it" he twitched his nose "Here you go Princess, Tea and an old fashioned homemade flap jack with a pinch of cinnamon, just to warm the cockles of your heart"

Nancy gave Joe a pleasing grin.

"So what s up?" he asked in his normally mother hen approach

"I dunno Joe...I think I'm just feeling my age"

"Then feel someone younger Princess" Joe winked "Malachi thinks an awful lot of you, you know, but if you're not careful that ship could sale away without you?"

"I know Joe, but I'm just not ready. Don't get me wrong what we done that night moved more than just the earth, but." Nancy broke of her sentence

"But" said Joe "You are still in love with Ralph. But Ralph is with Lucy, Nance"

Nancy snapped back her response

"I know but that still doesn't stop me loving him does it"

"No Nance it doesn't but as Forest Gump says, 'life is like a box of chocolates', but men are more like them than life. You see, your eyes light up when you first spy them, you have great pleasure ripping open their shiny cover, but then you taste them. Some are sweet, some make you want more, some leave a bitter after taste in your mouth and some you throw straight in the bin without even tasting"

"And your point is Joe?"

"My point is Princess, is too many chocolates make you fat" Joe laughed…"No, no,no that's not what I meant. What I mean is my point is there is a lot more to most men than what you see on the surface. They are not all a hard shell of scrumptious chocolate, if you look a bit further and are brave enough to take that first bite you may be surprised at what you find."

"So you're saying I should fuck him"

"No Nance, I'm not saying you should fuck him, you have gotta do what feels right. But nobody should go through life without tasting something different once in a while. But remember Nancy sometimes what we think we want tastes different to what we expect."

"So now it sounds like your saying I shouldn't fuck him"

"Nancy, Nancy, Nancy you are such an idiot sometimes! What I'm saying is don't go through life without at least trying new things. You may like it you may hate it but you are never going to know what you really want unless you're brave enough to try"

Chapter 24

"MUMMM" Poppy's voice echoed around the house. Joe and Nancy rushed to the kitchen, and found her crouching on all fours on the floor.

"Mum my waters have broken"

Joe began waving his arms around like a windmill, "Right we need towels, hot water and erm towels...shouldn't we call the paramedics too?" Joe screamed out as he began pacing the room.

Nancy was smiling away to herself as she watched this erratic gay man dressed in a pair of silk pajama trousers and matching top prancing around the room with sheer panic on his face. Good old reliable Joe had turned into a fretful mess of confused testosterone. Nancy handed him a banana.

"Joe, it's her first baby and could take hours, sit down eat your banana"

"Why have I got to eat a banana at 1am in the morning?"

"Cos I said so" answered a sniggering Nancy

A phone call to the hospital reiterated what Nancy already knew. When Poppy could take no more pain or when the contractions where five minutes apart lasting around 90 seconds each time, they were to bring her over. It was going to be a long night. But nobody expected what would happen next.

By 4am Poppy's contractions were exactly five minutes apart. Poppy had done so well with the pain. Her mind had been distracted for over an hour as Joe had fainted, after Nancy lifted Poppy's nightdress, to see if she could catch sight of anything happening. It was all too much for Joe he fell flat on his face into the dog water bowl by his feet. Nancy called the paramedics shortly after but it had been nearly forty five minutes since she made the call and they still hadn't arrived.

Just as she was about to call again, her mobile phone rung. It was one of the paramedic's team.

"Oh hi, yeah, erm, I don't know how to say this, but we are sort of stuck. Don't know how it happened but there's a tree blocking the entrance to your house. We can't even go around it. But don't worry, the fire service are here now and working hard to move the tree. Is…" the line went dead.

"Fuck it" Nancy said as calmly as she could

Poppy was crouching again on all fours as Nancy lifted her nightdress she could see Poppy was crowning.

"JOEEEEE! Oh my god she's crowning"

"What do you mean she's crowning!" shouted an agitated Joe

Nancy pulled down Poppy's nightdress and grabbed Joe by the arm and dragged him outside the room

"I mean this baby doesn't want to wait any longer you are going to have to give me a hand because in all honesty I don't know what the hell I'm doing Joe"

"What do you mean you don't know what the hell you're doing, you've had three, woman!"

"Joe I was sort of the one pushing not catching you prat!"

Beads of sweat were falling from Joe's head and his hands were shaking

"Okay okay" said an edgy Joe "I've delivered kittens, it can't be much different can it!"

"Kittens Joe? Oh my god give me strength…..right you reassure her I will catch okay"

"Deal" Joe answered feeling highly relieved he wasn't going to be down the messy end.

Twenty minutes later and a few highly obscene words shouted, (which mainly came from Joe) Poppy and her new baby daughter lay cradled together on Joe's Kitchen floor. Five minutes after two very out of breathe paramedics came clambering through the door. Mother and baby were doing fine. The same couldn't be said for Joe. He had a huge bump on his head where he face planted the floor and was now in total shock as the full after effects of watching just what a woman's lady place could do had finally hit him.

Chapter 25

Poppy and her daughter Lilly stayed at Joe's for the next two weeks, and then moved into Willows house with her. It's not that she didn't want to stay with her mother and Joe would have never asked her to leave. But the house now had to cater for two sets of erotic dancers and seeing that the demonstration was just around the corner, the house heaved at the seams.

In typical Joe fashion he had arranged for a BBQ to take place. Which was the norm before any sort of demonstration. Joe was in the living room going over the route with some of the parents of the disabled children who after a bit of persuasion had agreed to take part. The whole demonstration had been planned after Joe saw an old school friend's son. He had a severely disabled daughter and the conversation got onto how difficult it was getting the necessary equipment for his daughter, and how the cost of the equipment was four times as high as an able bodied child's.

"Take a typical garden swing" said Liam "It costs what thirty quid in any high street store? But you want the same piece of equipment for a special needs child and you're looking at around 300. But do you know what the most sickening thing is? It's the fact that the special needs swing only has an extra couple of Velcro straps attached to it. And don't even get me started on essential bits of equipment we need. We have to beg and fight for everything. Then just as you think you're getting somewhere they drop the bomb shell. We've run out of money'. It doesn't matter where you live, it's the same all over the country. Kids with special needs are having to wait months for equipment, they are having to make do with some old second hand shit and go without the one thing they all deserve, a quality of life"

Well that was enough for Joe to set the cogs in motion. This demo was to show the 'people in power' that whatever policy they had written, whatever promises they have made nothing has ever changed. Joe wanted this march to show them all that profit over the quality of life for a child was not going to be stood for any longer. Five hundred people were expected to walk the streets of London, all armed with the one thing that no government could ignore. The love every parent has for their child.

Finally the weather had taken a turn for the better and the BBQ was in full swing. The humid air and dry heat meant most were still dressed in shorts and t shirts. Leanne or Miss Chicago as she was now called slotted in well with her new friends and was standing by the old piano, which had again been bought out from the living room, and was singing out other songs from well-known musicals accompanied by none other than Kev.

Joe stood on a straw bale and he shouted for everyone to listen to him

"Can I have your attention please?" he commanded

Miss Chicago instantly stopped singing and nudged Kev on the piano to stop playing. Silence was now bestowed on the party goers.

Joe smiled and continued his speech

"Right everyone, the day we have all been so patiently waiting for has finally arrived. I know a few of you are a little apprehensive about tomorrow. For those of you who have never done anything like this before, don't worry. We do not and I'm going to say again DO NOT go in for violent demonstrations. I'm not going to lie, occasionally tempers get a bit torn but if you feel like you are getting a little angry take yourself away, take a few deep breathes have a drink of water and re-join the demo when you feel you can. The march is to be in total silence only speak to each other in a whisper. I have found these sort of demonstrations work well than a group of people angrily shouting their mouths off. But please take it from me, once you get into your stride it's a piece of cake. You should have all by now seen the route we are going to take. We will be leaving Hyde Park at 10am on the dot. So make sure you give yourself plenty of time to get there. There is a list of those who are driving, those who are going by train and those who are coming with us in the hired coach. Check and double check where your name is on the lists. If everything goes to plan we should be back home by around 10pm. Let's go kick some ass"

Cheers, high fives and clinking of plastic glasses echoed around. Nancy stared around the field looking at the smiling faces. Her eyes stopped when she saw Malachi sitting on a stacked bale of straw. His cut off denim shorts, long trim muscular legs and timberland boots made him look like he was the most perfect vision of beauty. Right at that moment in time she was sure there really was a god in heaven. Salacious thoughts entered her mind.

She began pushing her way through the revelers as Miss Chicago belted out Cher's, you haven't seen the last of me, from Burlesque. She was only a few feet away from Malachi when she spotted a highly excited Sasha throw her arms around his neck and kiss him. Nancy's heart felt like it had stopped beating and try as hard as she might the tears in her eyes fell freely. She swallowed and ran through the crowd into the house and into her boudoir.

As Nancy lay on the bed holding a faux pillow to her chest the door opened.

"Joe go away I don't need a pep talk right now"

A hand stroked her hair

"It's not Joe it's me" Malachi whispered

Nancy held her breath and gulped back her tears

"Well I don't need you either" she answered trying her hardest not to sound like a wailing cat who had just caught its tail in a mousetrap

" Malachi lifted his bare legs onto the bed and began to spoon her.

"Tough, cos I'm staying right here"

He rested his head on her shoulder and kissed her neck. Her heart pounded away inside her chest as she began to finally come to life again. Carnal urges moved beneath her skin. A red eyed smudged make up Nancy turned to face him. Malachi wiped away a lose strand of hair on her face before kissing away one solitary tear from her cheek.

"Malachi" she muttered

"Shush, no talking" he said

Malachi slid his body up effortlessly into a seated position and ran his fingers through Nancy's hair. She sat up and stared longingly into his eyes. Their heads moved closer as their lips touched. Their tongues danced like snakes, massaging every corner of their mouths. Nancy took hold of Malachi's disheveled hair in her hands and tugged gently. Slowly guiding his head down onto her collar bone. He kissed it tenderly. Nancy pulled away.

"Nance please don't do this to me again" he moaned

Nancy placed her finger tips onto his lips

"SSH"

She clasped hold of the edge of her cream laced vintage baby doll dress and lifted it over her head. Her chest was flushed and imbued with droplets of moisture. Her hands reached round and un- done the clasp of her bra. Malachi watched as his concupiscent passion grew. He lent his head forward and affectionately kissed her breasts. Nancy sighed deeply and tilted her head backwards. Malachi's finger trailed down over her abdomen to the top of her shorts. Attentively he undid her button as his fingers slid into her liquid pool of desire. Nancy gasped.

She clawed at his clothes as her mouth found his once again. Malachi removed his finger and lifted it up to their mouths. The amatory scent fueled their desire as Nancy removed Malachi's top. Beads of sweat poured down his chest and his body glistened like snowflakes at dawn. Nancy coerced Malachi to lay down on the bed, as she removed his washed out denim shorts.

Nonchalantly Nancy removed her own shorts

"Turn over" she asked

As Malachi turned Nancy could see the muscles of his neck and shoulders flexing through is olive skin. Her excitement was growing as she manipulated his flesh with her hands. Moving slowly up the centre of his back and with smooth precise strokes she glided her hands over the deep tissue in his shoulders. Malachi groaned. She replaced her hands with her mouth, and gently kissed every inch of his Adonis body.

With one swift movement Malachi was now hovering over Nancy. His toned body leaning over hers.

"You are so beautiful" he purred as his lips kissed the inside of her thigh

Gently and with precision his tongue moved smoothly caressing her soft smooth flesh. Nancy languished in his touch as her hips moved effortlessly in time with his mouth.

"I need you" she begged

Chapter 26

Nancy reached for Malachi as her eyes opened. But he had already left. She picked up her mobile phone it read 6.30am.

"Shit" she screamed realising that she was supposed to be up, washed dressed and ready to leave by 7am. In record time she showered, there was no time for blow drying her hair or applying make-up. Nancy dressed quickly and reached for her Brixton Coventry snap back cap and grabbed her bottle of Joe's hot flush cooling spray before running downstairs.

People were rushing in every direction as she clambered her way through to the kitchen.

"You're leaving it a bit fine aren't you? Joe said

Nancy opened the fridge pretending not to hear him

"Joe, have we got any cranberry juice?"

Joe's mouth dropped open, as he took hold of Nancy's arm dragging her into the boot room

"You done it didn't you?"

Nancy giggled

"Yep Joe, I done it"

"Oh my gawd…..well?"

Nancy blushed

"Well, it was erm, sort of fantastic!" Oh my bejessus Joe, it was the best sex I have had in years, and it went on for hours"

Joe clapped his hands in consecutive movements (which had become his 'I'm so happy trade mark)

"Okay so do we need Uncle Joe's Spritzer of tea tree to help things heal?"

"Joe I don't need a spritzer I need fireman's hose full of it"

"I think you've had enough hoses for a while" laughed Joe as the pair of them walked back into the bustling kitchen full of eager freedom fighters.

The sun cream was being passed from person to person and unopened bottles of Avian handed round to all who were taking part in the demonstration. The weather man said a few showers later in the day but these were going to be few and far between. Even so, Joe had gone out the day before and bought everyone an umbrella just in case.

Joe shouted his voice full of excitement and eagerness

"Let's go to London"

Everyone was poised and ready for Joe to give
the go ahead and for the demonstration to
begin. Joe had ordered Nancy, Michele, Shawn
and Malachi to walk ahead of the others to
check no unfortunate circumstance could halt
proceedings. Nancy may have been
approaching her 48th birthday but inside she
felt younger than she had done in years, albeit
suffering from a slight case of honeymooner's
disease and an even more desperate urge to
pee than normal. But her face showed true
contentment and her smile and up beat
manner even shocked Michele. Who was
trying her hardest to guess why Nancy's mood
had suddenly changed, especially as she hated
London so much.

Malachi and Nancy were giggling like two
teenagers in love when Michele tapped her on
the shoulder

"Nance, Nance"

"Huh"

"Look, over there. Is that Smithy?"

"Where?"

"Over there, by Nelsons column"

Nancy gazed over in the direction Michele's finger was pointing to.

"Fucking hell" exclaimed Nancy "Why is he here? I don't like the look of this Chele. There are about twenty of the other neo Nazi boot boys with him too"

Shawn rubbed Michele's arm

"Wasup chick"

Nancy stared at Michele and swallowed hard sucking in her top lip

"Chele, you Mal and Shawn go tell Joe, I will stay here and see just what they are up too"

"I'm not leaving you" said Malachi

"Mal I will be fine, look the place is surrounded by tourists…… go! Joe will probably need your help more than me"

The trio set off re-tracing their steps as Nancy stood watching Smithy and his boot boys alienate some poor Chinese tourist. It didn't take long before he caught a glimpse of Nancy watching his every move. He whispered into some man's ear who had a Union Jack draped over his shoulders, before strutting his way towards her.

Nancy looked around her praying that Mal and the others were soon going to return. But she couldn't see anyone as a coach load of tourists had just disseminated over the hole square. Frantically Nancy began pushing her way through the crowd and further away from Smithy. She spied Joe heading in her direction. But he was on his own.

"Oh my god where are the others" Nancy said out loud

"W'er ere love"

Smithy was by her side.

"Don't touch me" she said swallowing hard

His voice mocked hers

"Nah love you got it all wrong I ain't going touch you, I'm just going to have a little fun that's all" Smithy ran his fingers down Nancy's bare arm

Joe walked in-between them and tersely pushed his hand away

"Oh Look if it ain't the old poof himself" Smithy sniggered

Joe grabbed hold of Nancy's arm and tried pulling her away from Smithy's leering advances

"Oi oi oi" Said smithy "Not so fast, the lady wants to stay with us, in that right boys"

The other men nodded in agreement and smirked. Nancy lifted her arm and slapped Smithy across the face

"Go away you nasty evil little man!"

Smithy reached out and forcibly took hold of Nancy's wrists again

"You've hit me one to many times love"

Before anyone could gauge any form of reaction Smithy punched Nancy in the face.

She fell to the ground as the onlookers gathered around her.

"Joe" she screeched as a size 11 boot crushed its way down on her arm "Arrgghhhhhh" Nancy screamed.

More tourists came over to her and Nancy's vision was blocked by the marauding crowd. Joe was nowhere to be seen. Nancy wiped the tears of pain from her eyes and then she saw him. Joe was lying face down on the ground, blood was seeping from his nose. Nancy watched helpless as another black Doctor Marten boot landed on his head.

Nancy sat in silence with Michelle, Malachi and Shawn in the front entrance of the police station. They had all given their statements and were waiting to be told they could leave by the desk sergeant. Nancy's arm was broken in two places and she had six stitches to her head. But no pain could compete with the agony she was feeling inside knowing the love of her life, was now laying in a cold mortuary somewhere in London. Malachi tried to take hold of her hand but Nancy pushed him away. She didn't want his touch, she didn't want anyone's touch.

The old brown fire door opened and a grinning Smithy walked out followed by an unshaven suited police officer. Nancy jumped to her feet

"Why you letting him go?" she demanded

"We don't have enough evidence" The officer shrugged his shoulders

"I don't understand" begged Nancy "He assaulted me"

"But you assaulted him first"

Smithy sucked his teeth

"But, But, he killed Joe"

"I'm Sorry, according to witness statements Joe fell and hit his head. In all the commotion he got just got trampled on. I'm sorry, I really am, why don't you go home, there is nothing more you can do here"

Nancy cried into her hands and ran outside. Her stomach heaved as she vomited its contents over the black tarmacked path. Michele rubbed her back as Nancy's stomach wretched on nothing but bile.

"Better luck next time love" a condescending Smithy barked as he walked past her

Nancy wiped the vomit from her mouth and ran after him. Grabbing hold of the back of his shirt. She stared right into his eyes, and spat the last bitter mouthful of stomach acid at his feet

"You really don't know who I am do you? But what I will tell you is always look behind you Smithy, because one day very soon you will find out." Nancy patronizingly slapped Smithy on the cheek before walking back to her friends.

Chapter 27

In typical Joe fashion his funeral was very
camp, very loud and very over the top. He left
strict orders that everyone had to wear a fancy
dress costume suited to ones that were worn at
gay pride. Nobody let him down. Even Lilly
was dressed in a sequined fluorescent pink
baby-grow and matching tutu. Nancy's dogs
all had the same pink bows tied around their
collars and the boys from Let them rip wore
four inch platform boxer boots, with gold lama
shorts and enough chains hanging over their
chests to tie up King Kong.

Nancy hadn't spoken much to anyone since
Joe's death. Malachi had tried, so had Michele
and her daughters but Nancy was in a place
no one could enter. Her mind was dark, her
heart was frozen.

"Mum" said Daisy

"What" Nancy answered as she began folding Joe's clothes for the umpteenth time.

"I really need to talk to you"

"Talk then"

"Mum, I'm, I'm pregnant"

Nancy turned to face her youngest daughter

"Why didn't you use contraception? For god's sake child!"

Daisy edged closer to her mother holding out her hand for reassurance. Nancy just shook her head and carried on folding Joe's clothes

"Mum please don't be mad, I did, I mean we did use a rubber but it sort of broke"

Nancy bit the flesh inside her cheek

"Daisy I don't need this today, its Joe's funeral and to be honest I'm struggling to hold it altogether I don't need your drama right now!"

"Mum it's not a drama it's a baby….and like it or not Joe isn't here but I am and I need you" Daisy began sobbing into her hands

Nancy rubbed her forehead with the palm of her hand, before her sobs joined with her daughters. She reached out for her daughter and pulled her close.

"I'm sorry Daisy I'm so sorry. I didn't mean, when is the baby due?"

"It's okay Mum, Its due end of January. Danny and I sort of had a bit of a fumble not long after you moved here. As my periods are so erratic I didn't even know I was pregnant, till I saw the Doctor yesterday. I'm sorry I told you today I just thought what with everything that's happened it may cheer you up a bit. I really didn't mean to make things worse"

Nancy sniffed, swallowed and took her youngest daughters face into her hands.

"Well you certainly don't hang about do you? Look, I'm sorry. Let's get today out of the way shall we and we can discuss everything tomorrow. Deal?"

"Deal Mum"

Joe's service was not to take place inside a church or any other room of religious etiquette. But in his field close to the house. His casket was carried by Danny, Mal, Shawn, Kev, and Ralph and was placed on a bier surrounded by candles. As the four men stepped away, Leanne began singing I won't last a Day without you by Karen Carpenter. The sorrow that could be heard in Leanne's voice percolated around each person standing in that field. Nancy took her place in front of the on looking congregation.

"Joe always used to say that wherever we go, whatever pain and suffering we feel and whatever footsteps we chose to follow we always have to blame someone else for how terrible we are feeling, and we always look up and shout to the sky. And that's the only time we really look up, that's the only time we really study the clouds see the beauty that is above our heads. Well. Now we have a reason to look up" Nancy swallowed back the lump that had formed in her throat.

"It's time to move on Joe, where no one else
has gone before,
To infinity and beyond by some still and
tranquil shore,
To a place where imagination is everything
and a place where dreams are made,

Where strong foundations are built, where
strong foundations are always laid,
Where the wind blows freely through your
hair and through the corners of your mind,
Where people know only love and where
people are so very kind,
To a place you no longer have to hide the
torment in your heart,
To a place you belong where you're not split
in two and falling apart,
You cannot change this world any more Joe or
take away others pain,
Even though I know you will try over and
over again,
You've searched a life time for the keys that
undo the lock,
But everything has to end Joe, because life is
nothing more than the ticking of a clock.

Joe's Casket was carried to the waiting hearse
as Kevin played Ludovico Einaudi, Reverie.
Not one person held in their sorrow as Joe's

body travelled for the last time through the gates to his home.

Chapter 28

The solicitor's office was strewn with papers, folders, books, stained and empty coffee mugs. A heavy musky smell lingered through the room, as Nancy, Danny and Daisy sat waiting for the solicitor to enter. The open sash window let in a welcoming breeze as the Indian summer the weather men had said would come, came with full force. The temperature on the barometer read twenty nine degrees which made sitting in that room abnormally uncomfortable for a flushing menopausal woman. Nancy began fanning herself with the letter that the solicitor had sent her.

"You alright mum?" asked a concerned Daisy

"Yeah I'm fine, just wish he would bloody hurry up that's all"

Danny tugged on Nancy's full length broderie anglaise peasant skirt like a four year old would his mothers.

"Nance, I can understand why you are here but why am I here?"

"I don't know Danny, I don't even know why I am here to be honest. Joe hated Solicitors at the best of time." Nancy rubbed his hand "But we will find out soon wont we, hopefully!"

The door flew open as an out of breath man entered. He was short, very short. He couldn't have stood much taller than four foot eleven in his bare feet. And much to everyone's surprise was not dressed in the typical Marks and Spencer off the peg suit but a pair of jeans and a black Kurta top.

"I'm so sorry I'm late I got caught up in court." He held out his hand to Nancy "My names Rashir, Rashir Peterson"

Nancy shook his hand

"Pleased to meet you" she said

Rashir stood behind his rather cluttered desk, moving around some of the tan coloured folders.

"Ah here it is. Firstly I am so sorry for your loss. Joe was an exceptional man. I first met him about ten years ago. He came to see me asking me to help a young Muslim family gain residence in the UK. Sadly we lost that battle but since then I am honoured to say Joe became a close friend"

Nancy fidgeted, re-arranged her skirt and shook her head

"That's lovely" she said in a confused tone "But why are we here? I'm sorry I don't mean to sound impatient but I don't understand why?"

"I'm sorry, I know this must be a difficult time for you all and I was just as shocked when I heard the news" Rashir opened the tan folder and smiled at Danny

"When you were born your father, opened an insurance policy for you. It has matured greatly since your birth. He has also put money away for you in an off shore bank account which is regulated by FINMA, Swiss Financial Market Supervisory Authority. As we all know Joe didn't trust UK banks so the majority of his wealth is hidden from the Inland Revenue" Rashir chortled and handed Danny a slip of paper

"I can't read" said Danny

Daisy took it from him. Her mouth dropped open and her eyes widened

"Danny, I think you should take a deep breathe. This says that you have 4.2 million pounds, in a Swiss bank account. It also gives details of account numbers, cards and all the paraphernalia that you need to access these funds"

"What the fuck!.....I don't understand?" Danny was totally perplexed and overwhelmed by the whole situation

Rashir smiled

"Basically, Danny, you don't mind if I call you Danny do you?"

Danny nodded

Rashir continued

"It means Danny, you are a very, very rich man"

Danny sat in total shock, not knowing if he should laugh cry, scream or do all three.

Instead he just sat staring at the piece of paper in front of him.

"But" Rashir concluded, "There is a condition, you need to use some of the money to go back to school and learn how to read. If Miss Daisy would like to look at these" He handed Daisy a glossy folder. Inside it gave details of a private college, that would not only teach Danny the three 'R's' but also teach him a trade or skill. "It is expensive mind, but you can afford it. Now on to you Nancy" Rashir picked up another of the tan folders "Joe has left you his house, his 15 acres, his business and yet another considerable amount of money. All of which is in another Swiss account. The final amount has not yet been calculated but it is estimated to be in the region of 6.7 million. Oh and this" he handed a leather bound book, titled The Complete poems of Emily Dickenson.

As Nancy took the book from Rashir the book opened and a tiny white pressed daisy fell from its pages. Nancy bent down to pick it up. She remembered.

Two weeks after she first met Ralph, Joe had taken her to Pooh-sticks Bridge, in the heart of Ashdown forest. For hours they played together, each taking it in turn to throw there sticks into the water then race to the other side to see which one had won. Joe may have been the kindest sweetest man she had ever met but when it came to pooh-sticks he was a Spartan, a gladiator that would never lose! After Joe had won for the millionth time they ventured deeper into this ancient forest. Nancy's feet hurt so she made Joe stop for a rest by a fallen down tree stump. As Joe picked bits of bracken out of Nancy's hair he noticed one solitary daisy growing out of the trunk of a tree. He picked it, handed it to her and spoke the timeless words of Emily Dickenson

Escape is such a thankful Word

I often in the Night Consider it unto myself

No spectacle in sight

Escape – it is the Basket

In which the Heart is caught

When down some awful Battlement

The rest of Life is dropt –

'Tis not to sight the savior –

It is to be the saved –

And that is why

I lay my Head Upon this trusty word -

Nancy became consumed with her memories, as she recalled the events of that day. She never realised Joe had kept that daisy.

"Always the romantic" she said as her mournful tears fell

Daisy reached over and took her mother's hand

"Mum, you okay?"

Nancy nodded

"I will take the book Rashir and the flower but I don't want his money"

"Hmmmm" said Rashir as he inhaled sharply "He thought you would say that and if you did I was to read this out to you" Rashir picked up a crumpled piece of paper.

My little lady of the woods,

If this is being read to you, then it will mean you have refused your inheritance. My dearest Nancy that is not going to happen!! When I first met you all those years ago I instantly fell in love with you. You were a cheeky teenager who made my heart skip a beat each time I saw you. Even first thing in the morning when we had camped out for days. You're unruly sticking up bed hair, dirty sun kissed cheeks and your inability to put on lip stick made me love you more than I did already.

If I had been graced with a daughter, then I would have wanted her to be just like you. You are truly the most totally fabulous person I have ever known and loved. This little offering that I bestow on you, is no more than you deserve.

If there is indeed a heaven then from my rather pink cloud I will be watching you and taking care of you. Nancy I adore you. I always have and always will.

You are my little Nancy

I love you, for today, tomorrow and for the rest of eternity

You're highly camp, extraordinarily gay,

Joe

Ps. now take the money or I will haunt you, hide your knickers and

make you recite the complete oxford
English dictionary....backwards!!!!

Nancy smiled through tear stained cheeks

"I love you Joe"

Chapter 29

Let them rip and Midnight masquerades where coming to the end of their summer tour. Apart from the total wash out flooding cancellation all shows had gone according to plan. Only two more Hen Parties and three private shows were booked for the rest of the year. Midnight Masquerades had been a total success and Miss Chicago took the top spot at every show, she was fast becoming a head-liner and Michele had fears that she would soon move on to pastures new. It took five bottles of wine, six bags of Doritos with dip, about a ton of pistachio nuts and three boxes of after eight mints, for Leanne to reassure Michele, she wasn't going anywhere.

Since Joe's death Nancy had changed. Gone was stuttering Nancy, gone was her erratic hormonal outbursts, gone was her nervous anxious worrying self. Even her constant thoughts about Lurid Lucy and her Loose Labia was nothing more than a memory. Nancy was slowly becoming who she was born to be. Nancy had become a woman who took no crap from anyone.

Poppy, Willow and Lilly had stayed since Joe's funeral, just to make sure she was coping with all that had just happened. Nancy was coping. They had planned to leave the day after the solicitor's meeting but Willows car had broken down and she had called her dad to see if he could have a look at it. Well Lucy obviously came with him. Ralph couldn't so much as sneeze or fart without her being close by.

Anyway, when Nancy, Daisy and Danny pulled up into the driveway, Ralph had already lifted the bonnet of Willow's car and was tinkering with the engine beneath. Lucy was standing by his side picking at those fake nails of hers. As soon as she saw Nancy she edged closer to Ralph and began rubbing his backside through his overalls.

Nancy just rolled her eyes, not really taking much notice of Lucy or Ralph come to that. She went straight into the house to try and absorb everything Rashir had told her. But all Nancy was really interested in was reading the poetry of Emily Dickinson in a bid to ignite yet more memories that were hidden away in the sub conscious part of her mind.

Nancy stood by the aga waiting for the kettle to boil when Ralph entered the kitchen.

"Hi"

Nancy turned to face him

"Hi" Nancy replied

"I was wondering if you were okay."

Just as Nancy was about to answer him Lucy
walked in clip clopping on the stone tiled
floor. She went right over to Ralph and forced
her arm through his. Nancy turned back to
watch and wait for the kettle. Sighing as she
did so.

"So" said Lucy "When are you planning on
filling in those divorce papers then?"

Nancy's tone was indignant as once again she
turned to face her visitors

"What!"

Lucy answered sarcastically, whilst gripping
tighter on Ralphs overalls

"Well it has been a while since you first got
them"

Nancy walked towards her totally ignoring
the kettle that had just started whistling.

"You really are an un-fucking-believable bitch aren't you? I have just buried my best friend in the whole wide world and you have the cheek to waltz into my house and ask this now! You really are a contemptuous whore!"

Lucy flicked her hair and sucked in her lips

"This is not your house, and as for contemptuous…..I don't actually know what it means"

"It means dis-respectful! You total brainless, open legged disgustingly stinky blue waffled vagina! Oh as for this house not being mine, yes it is."

Ralph could not suppress his laughter any longer and almost chocked on his own spit as his vocal chords went into spasm

"Are you going to let her talk to me like that" an incensed Lucy asked

Ralph cleared his throat.

"One thing I've learned being surrounded by four women is you don't get in their way, when they are arguing"

Nancy poked Ralph in the shoulder

"You can shut it too!, trouble with you Ralph is you don't get involved in anything that doesn't include a game of rugby a can of cider or some cheap little tarts open legs!....What happened to you? Look at you, your hair looks like you could fry chips in it, your beard makes you look like the dawning of the Aquarius is fast approaching and you must be at least a stone heavier......Oh and one more thing, if you are so happy with this trollop then why the fuck do you never smile?"

Lucy's jaw dropped, Ralph just started into open space. And Nancy picked up her book and walked right out of the kitchen to her boudoir leaving a confused Ralph and an ostentatious Lucy arguing.

Chapter 30

Nancy's word's hung in Ralph's ears and within a day of the head to head he had packed Lucy's bags, and ended their sordid affair. Lucy skulked back to her dupe of a husband begging forgiveness. He forgave. Men are pathetic (well he is anyway)

As for Ralph, he threw away every last bit of alcohol in his house. Apart from one sad lonely Guinness he was saving for the match between Harlequins and Wasps. He had his hair and beard cut and was trying hard to lose the stone he had gained. He had also started doing all the jobs he had promised Nancy he was going to do before she left him. Was he actually thinking with his brain now rather than his genitals?

Nancy had made arrangements for an architect to design all three of her daughters their own house on her fifteen acres and had also bought Michele and Shawn a brand spanking new four bedroomed detached property, complete with chickens and pygmy goat. Something Michele had always wanted.

Danny had enrolled on a course in the private college and Daisy had begun planning a December wedding. Malachi had taken it upon himself to make sure the Midnight masquerades, learnt their new routines, and if he didn't have a show himself he would drive, escort and make sure they got to and from theirs safely. This left very little time for Nancy and Mal to spend quality time together. Nancy didn't seem to care. Having any sort of romantic fumbling was far from her mind. She wanted revenge on the man that killed her Joe.

"Danny" Nancy called him into the living room

He followed leaving a curious Daisy sitting in the kitchen

"Yes mother in law to be, how can I be of assistance"

Nancy looked at Danny over her glasses

"Why the hell are you talking like that?"

"Because it's how one speaks at college Madam"

"Well you aren't at college right now so stop playing games I need to talk to you, sit down"

Danny sat in the armchair close to the roaring open fire. Nancy sat on the chair opposite

"How's your Mum" Nancy enquired

Danny looked into the crackling flames, watching them change hypnotically from gold to amber to red.

"Not good, she was at A & E last week Smithy hit her over the head with a bottle. He had been on one of his binges and was out of his head on ketamine. I've tried telling her that I can help her now but she is either just too thick or too scared to leave him. I fucking hate that man Nance. Hate him"

"Good, I'm glad you hate him. But the question is how much"

"I don't understand what do you mean how much?"

Nancy sat back in her chair.

"Do you hate him enough to kill him?"

Danny stared at Nancy not speaking but thinking deeply. After a few moments he replied.

"Yes"

Nancy smiled.

Daisy sat crying into her pillow as Danny put the last of his clothes into a scruffy old rucksack.

"I don't understand why are you going back home, you said you loved me, you said you would never go back to that horrible house, you said"

"SSH" Danny screamed at his pregnant girlfriend "I do love you but I I .."

Nancy walked into the bedroom and gave Danny a harsh glare.

"Enough Daisy "She demanded "If Danny wants to go home then he has the right to do so."

Daisy pulled a fresh tissue from its box and blew her nose. She was totally perplexed by the events that were taking place.

"Mum what's happened to you? You have never been such a hard faced cow. Something is going on I know it is. Danny I know you love me and I know you don't want to go back to Smithy and your Mum and I know there is something deeper to this than either of you are telling me. So if someone doesn't tell me the truth soon by God I will do something stupid!"

Danny looked hard at Nancy as Nancy walked over to the bedroom door and shut it tight.

"You really want to know?" Nancy asked her daughter

"Nance NO" shouted Danny as he walked between her and daisy

"Yes, for fuck sake tell me!"

Nancy sat down on the edge of Daisy's bed picking up yet another tissue to wipe the dripping snot from her daughter's nose.

"We, meaning Danny and I are going to kill Smithy. I want that man to suffer, I want him to hurt, and I want Sophie to be free from his fists. I want revenge for Joe"

Daisy instantaneously stopped crying. She looked at Danny, she looked at her mother she blew her nose and threw the used tissue across the room into an already over flowing waste paper basket.

"Awesome" she smiled "How and when are we going to kill the mother fucker"

"Well that went better than I thought" said Danny

"She's hormonal" Nancy replied" But it is in her blood"

Daisy gave Nancy a questioning glare

"Eh"

Nancy kissed Daisy on the forehead and dried the last of her tears that were falling down her cheeks

"One day I will tell you, just not yet" Nancy gave her daughter a half-baked smile and left the room.

Chapter 31

It was typical for Joe to put on an end of season party and Nancy was not going to break with tradition. It may have been her house now but she knew Joe lurked around every corner. She could sense him and more often than not could smell him. Well his home made concoctions and lotions and potions.

The house was decorated with tombstones spiders and inflatable ghosts. Pumpkins with their insides scooped out and a tea light now glowing inside them shone at every downstairs window. The living room had been cleared of all the furniture except for one small wooden table with a bowl in the middle of it which was filled with spogs (the aniseed jelly button sweet covered in a candy ball coating) and sherbet. The game wasn't dissimilar to apple bobbing, except there was no water, no apples and you didn't bob. You dived. Straight into the sherbet. Childish but fun.

Trick or Treaters never ventured this far away from the beaten track but Malachi and Simon had bought enough sweets, chocolates and candy to make even Willy Wonker feel less than adequate. Everybody was in such high spirits. Everybody except Danny. Because Danny wasn't even at the party, but stuck in some back street boozer in East Grinstead high street.

He left Nancy's house at the beginning of October. And for all pretense and purposes, and as far as everyone knew, Daisy and him had split up. He had gone back home to be with his mother who was still recovering from her latest trip to Redhill hospital. Only the three of them knew the real truth as to why Danny had gone back home. The stage was set.

Danny was sitting in the corner of the pub surrounded by middle aged boot boys. Most of them didn't have hair. Not because they had shaved it off to look the part, but age had caught up on them and they were balder than Shawn the sheep at the height of summer. Draft lager was a must, so was the strut, the ug's, grunts and manly pats on the backs. Danny could have won an Oscar that night. He could have actually won, one for the last few weeks. He had joined Smithy's group of neo nazi reprobates and had even started working for Smithy in his Tarmacking business. I say business what I actually mean is screwing people over, doing a shit job and charging an arm and a leg for his lack of workmanship. Danny kept his rather substantial inheritance a secret too. It beggars to think about what could or would happen if Smithy ever found out that his step son was a multi -millionaire.

"Dad, D'you want another pint" Danny asked as Smithy groped yet another under age female drinker's arse.

Smithy nodded his head as his lecherous advances caused him to have yet another smack round the face "D'you really have to ask boy"

The bartender was just like everyone else in that pub that evening. A total prat. He was tall with dark hair, and used to pick his nose roll his bogies in his fingers then proceed to eat them when he thought nobody was looking. He used to admire Smithy too and thought he was the hardest nut in town. But the bartender was nothing more than a twenty eight year old dick head. Who thought he was god's gift to women. But all the women who had been with him either turned into a raving lesbian or realised that when they moved on to a new partner men's penis's are larger than 3 inch's when erect. Poor unfortunate bar tender (sad face)

"Two pints of San Miguel please" He asked the complete mindless prick who stood behind the bar.

"Glad to see your back where you belong son" the bartender said

"Don't call me son mate, just do your job and fill the glasses. If I wanted small talk I would go down to mega-bites" Danny responded

Mega bites was the only place to get your after drinking burger and chips with special sauce. As long as you didn't mind having to queue for a while or if you were female didn't mind getting touched up or propositioned. It has to be said though that you had to mind your footing after leaving Mega bites at 3am in the morning or you could very well find yourself treading in regurgitated burger and chips and enough beer to sink the titanic.

Danny took the drinks and went to take his seat back at the table in the far corner. He placed his pint on the table but before calling Smithy over to get his, he took a small brown bottle out of his trouser pocket. He looked round the room to make sure no one was watching and poured the contents into the pint. Four diazepam fizzed as they mixed with Smithy's drink.

"Dad" he called "Drink"

Smithy walked over to him, chest pointing out, neck doing his famous turkey impression and lips turned at the edges.

"Cheers boy"

The two clinked the glasses together and Danny watched as he downed half of it in one mouthful.

"Dad, do you remember telling me the story of how you used to jump off the viaduct into Cook's pond every Halloween to scare the girls?"

"Hell yeah boy, I've gotta tell the lads this one. Oi boys come ere got a story to tell ya"

The rest of the neo nazi's all walked over to Smithy and Danny in the same pompous manner, and so did Mr Bogie picker bartender of the year. They gathered round him like flies swarming shit.

"So lads you're going to fucking love this. So every Halloween we used to go down the woods, and stand on the viaduct. When the girlies where close enough we used to jump off it screaming. Fuck me it was the funniest thing ever. Mind you it was fucking cold swimming in there at this time of year and your bollocks went right up inside ya, but fucking hell is was a laugh. We will 'ave to do it one year boys. Such a crack......Ooo I dun half feel woozie that last pints fucking dun me"

Danny tried to take the half- drunk pint away from Smithy.

"Not so fast boy, don't wanna' get that tipped down the drain do we? Smithy swigged back the last of the drink "Right that's me done, time to go home and poke the Mrs"

Danny swallowed hard and began heading for the door. Smithy raised his arm and shouted.

"Rule Britannia"

A chorus of God Save the Queen echoed around the bar as Smithy nodded his head and walked out the door.

The wind was blowing and it was a dry night for October. A slight chill in the air but not one that needed gloves, scarf's and insulated boots. Which is exactly what Nancy was wearing. Her car was parked a few streets away from the pub, down a dark alley that only had one street lamp in it. The good thing about this lamp is it was either never turned on or didn't work anyway. Nancy was hidden in the darkness, when she heard Danny and Smithy sauntering down the road. In fact it's a wonder the whole town didn't hear them as Smithy was still singing God Save the Queen. The only time he stopped was to spit out a phlegm ball that he hacked up.

Nancy stepped out from behind her car, her face lowered and her head covered by an M&S Faux fur trapper hat.

"Fuck me woman" Shouted Smithy "You nearly gave me a art attack"

Perfect thought Nancy, the alcohol, the diazepam and the darkness all mixed together meant Smithy didn't have a clue who the woman standing before him was.

Nancy looked at Danny and mouthed

"Ready"

Danny nodded

"Ere Dad this woman's offered us a lift home"

"Result" answered Smithy "Just got piss first"

Smithy urinated into open space, as Nancy opened the car door.

"Hey dad why don't you sit in the back, lay down and catch forty winks"

"Good call boy, converse some energy for poking the old woman"

Nancy bit the sides of her cheek

"I think you mean conserve" she said sarcastically

"That's what I fucking said woman" Smithy answered as he clambered in the back seat.

The drive to the opening of the woods took no longer than seven minutes. Smithy had in that short time fallen into a semi- comatose state. Nancy and Danny climbed out of the car at the same time and walked round to the back passenger door. Smithy lay with his face stuck to the seat and dribble oozing out of the corners of his mouth.

"How many did you give him Danny?"

"Four, I thought if he can handle ketamine then four diazepam ain't going to have much effect"

"We've gotta walk a good mile so let's hope we can at least get his feet to move" Nancy responded

Danny poked his dad in the chest

"Oi dad wake up"

Smithy grunted and wiped the drool from his mouth

"Are we home boy"

"No, not yet dad, but come on won't be long, swing your legs round"

Smithy swung his legs round and Nancy placed his feet onto the ground. Danny hoisted his father up and put Smithy's arm around his neck to stabilize him. Danny and Nancy had walked the route through the woods half a dozen times in the last couple of weeks. Nancy even made Danny down four cans of Magners cider so she could see how long it would be walking with someone slightly inebriated. What she didn't take into consideration was the fact that as well as being drunk, Smithy would also have slower reactions due to the diazepam.

"So how did you get away from the party?" Danny asked as he helped Smithy climb over some bracken

"Oh that was easy, everyone was so engrossed in the party and pleased that the tour had finished that when Miss Chicago started belting out 'Take That' songs everyone joined her. I just sneaked out then. If anyone should ask Daisy's just going to say I had to pop out for a bit. But no one will don't worry"

Nancy and Danny followed the exact same route as all the times before. The final hurdle they needed was to get Smithy up the muddy bank to the Viaduct. Nancy slipped a few times and mumbled The Lords Prayer. For three reasons.

one: she didn't want to slip and die.

two: she didn't want to slip, fall into Cook's pond and drown.

three: she didn't want to get caught.

Danny's stomach had begun gurgling and turning over as they reached the top of the viaduct and making some rather obtuse noises.

"Oh Nancy I think I need a pooh"

"Eh"

"My stomach feels like I have the whole terracotta army marching through it"

"Danny really, can you not just clench" Nancy said breathing deeply

"No I don't think I can Nance, I always get a bit of irritable bowel when I get nervous"

"Oh heavens above!" Nancy said with sarcasm "Well hurry up then, and just make sure you do it far enough away from me that I don't have to smell it!"

They reached the edge of the viaduct and luckily enough Danny only needed to sit and drop once. Precariously they sat Smithy resting on the thin ledge of the steel that went right across the whole vertical bridge. He had started singing God Save the Queen again and moving his head from side to side like a cobra exiting a wicker basket.

Danny grabbed hold of Nancy's arm

"Nance"

"Yes"

"I don't think I can do this.

Nancy exhaled loudly,

"Bit late for that son"

Danny stood with his arms raised and his hands resting on his head. He wanted to run as panic and fear toyed with his insides.

"Don't get me wrong Nance I hate him, I hate him more than I have ever hated anyone in my life but I just don't think I can go through with it"

Nancy leaned in and gave Danny a hug

"Well something has to be done Dan or you can just spend the rest of your life watching Sophie spending more time in the hospital. Plus I want revenge Dan"

"Maybe we could just go to the police" Danny asked as Nancy threw a stick over her shoulder.

"But would Sophie have the courage and be brave enough to tell the police everything this vile piece of shit has done to her Dan?" Nancy raised her eyebrows "I think we both know the answer to that one don't we?"

Danny and Nancy stared over at Smithy who was by now on the third chorus of God Save the Queen.

"Thy choicest gifts in store
On her be pleased to pour
Long may she reign
May she defend our laws…"

Nancy brushed some mud of her jeans and frowned at the site of the fat balding man she hated with every ounce of her body

"Right let's get his over and done with cos I cannot hear one more line of God Save the Queen, in fact I never want to hear this song again!"

Danny froze on the spot as Nancy turned and began walking into Smithy's direction. She was no more than two foot away from him when….

SPLASH

Smithy had fallen off the ledge straight into Cook's pond. Nancy calmly peered over the edge.

"Oops" she said unable to stop the biggest grin appear on her face.

Danny walked to Nancy's side shocked at how amused she was. His heart was pounding, his mouth dry and fear eluded from his pores.

"Please can we get out of here now" he begged

They both descended the bank of the Viaduct. Nancy slipped a few more times and spoke the Lord's Prayer out loud this time with quite a lot of 'effing and geffing thrown in for good measure. They both stood by the edge of the deep murky water. Danny shone his flexi torch into it. But they saw nothing except a few ripples.

"Look what's that over there?" Nancy pointed to a floating mound that couldn't have been more than a six feet from them. Danny walked attentively into the water and started dragging the water towards him in a bid to get the mound to do the same. It Did. It was Smithy.

And there they were. Nancy, Danny and the body of Smithy.

"Is he, is he dead?" asked Danny

"I don't know, poke him"

"But I don't want to touch him," Danny answered

"Then poke him with a stick"

Danny reached down and picked up a rather rotten stick and began poking Smithy in the stomach with it. He didn't move or make a sound

Danny looked over into Nancy's direction

"I think he is dead Nance"

She walked over and bent down over Smithy's body and placed her hand on his stomach. It wasn't moving.

"Well if he isn't dead he is a heavy sleeper" she said, but smacked him hard across the face just too be sure "Right job done, I'm just going for a wee before we leave, back in a Minute"

Danny was still so shocked at Nancy's calm state as he clambered back up the bank onto firmer ground. "Nance, you can't do that, have you never watched Silent witness. Your pheromones will be all over the place and then they will be traced back to you"

Nancy began fidgeting, holding her crotch and dancing on the same spot

"Don't be so fucking stupid Danny!"

"Well they take samples of everything so they may pick up a leaf with your piss on"

Nancy just shook her head dropped her trousers and let her bladder empty.

"Yeah and you shit behind a tree remember?"

Panic was rising in Danny's voice.

"Oh my god I did didn't I"

Nancy zipped up her trousers.

"Amateurs" she said under her breath and re-joined Danny watching the body of his step dad float back out into the cold, dark water of Cook's pond.

Nancy slapped Danny across the back

"Right job done, onto stage two of our plan"

The smile on Nancy's face could not express the feelings of sheer jubilation she was feeling inside. Danny's on the other hand showed concern and dismay at how cheerful and buoyant Nancy actually was.

Danny was silent walking back to Nancy's car. Nancy on the other hand began singing out the chorus to Destiny's Child Independent women, and even when Nancy shook her ass in front of him, Danny still couldn't shake the remorse he was feeling. He felt sick to the pits of his stomach, his face was pale and his hands were shaking.

As they reached Nancy's car, she took his face into her hands.

"Danny, just stick to the plan okay?" Get your phone out of your pocket and call the old bill. Tell them to come quick, tell them your dad has fallen into the pond, and you will meet them at the opening of the woods. As far as everyone in the pub is concerned Smithy wanted to come back here. Tell them he forced you to go with him. No one will question that, cos they know what he is like. Say you didn't think he would really jump and you thought he was just mucking around. Stick to the story

Dan and everything will be okay. And to be totally honest with you that really isn't far from the truth is it?"

Danny nodded

"But Nance, what about the place you done a wee, and where I done a pooh and all our muddy footprints we left behind? What about Silent witness Nance?"

"Danny man the fuck up! There are a million sticks in that wood, there are loads of footprints on that bank, people fish there and as for my wee and your shit, do you really think they are going to waste police time, tax payers money picking up every single leaf and testing it for my, what did you call it, oh yeah pheromones! ….. Danny just make that phone call and go back to where you are meeting the police. It's all going to be fine trust me.

As the days past by Danny waited nervously for the coroner's report. The police had questioned Danny for hours. But Danny stuck to his story and by the end of it he could have won not only an Oscar but also An Emmy, A Bafta, The Peoples Choose Award and an MTV one too. He played his part remarkably well and even had one of the female police officers who was questioning him in tears by the end of his interview. But it had been nearly four weeks and still no one had heard the verdict of the coroner.

Danny had moved back in with Nancy and Daisy but this time he bought his mum with him. There was no way he was going to leave her in that tiny two up two down house. That had vomit, urine, and blood stains on the carpet. A kitchen whose doors had been punched so many times they were hanging off their hinges and a bedroom full of so many bad memories.

Kevin had taken quite a shine to Sophie, and she seemed to come out of her shell a little when he was about. She even laughed at his Dick Van Dyke impersonation. But Nancy put that down to the fact she has had one to many blows on the head over the years. Everyone still questioned why Smithy had Danny as his next of kin on all his personal paper work, but everyone came to the same conclusion that Smithy probably didn't think Sophie would live long enough to take on this responsibility. May be one day he thought he would probably take it too far and kill her. But the only fact that anyone could now be sure of was Smithy was gone, Sophie was safe and Nancy had fueled her passion for revenge.

Nancy was outside in the field throwing a ball for the dogs when she saw the postman walk up the drive. She walked towards him, dogs following at her heels.

"I'll take them" she said smiling sweetly at the rather fearful postman. You can't blame him for being a bit on the hesitant side. As the three dogs had all jumped the fence and were circling him, and doing what dogs do best, sniffing his crutch.

Nancy toyed with the letters in her hand as she trudged towards the house. A brown envelope with Mr. D Armstrong stood out from all the others.

Nancy called his name as she entered the boot room at the back of the house.

"I think this is it" she said as she handed him the brown envelope.

Danny raised his eyebrows and bit his bottom lip

"Read it to me Nance"

Nancy tore open the envelope and conscientiously began to examine the contents of the letter

"Well…It says here that death was by accidental drowning. But it also says that this was helped along by substance abuse. Fuck me Danny it's a wonder he didn't die of a heart attack sooner. He had alcohol, diazepam, ketamine, hash and MDMA in his system"

Danny took the letter from Nancy

"So does that mean we are in the clear?"

Nancy smiled

"Yep I think it does Danny boy, I think it does"

Chapter 32

Nancy was looking over the final plans with her builders for converting the old barn into an in-door rehearsal room for the dancers. She had decided to project manage the conversion herself. After all she had been married to a builder for years so knew a lot about what goes on behind the scenes. Nancy had thought about getting Ralph to do it but still didn't feel totally comfortable around him. Plus he was working day and night, knocking down walls, taking out the old bathroom suite and doing all the jobs he had promised her for years in their marital home.

Malachi and Danny were helping with the construction. It was good practice for Danny as he was not only at college once a week learning his A B C's but was also doing an evening course in carpentry. Walnut was sort of doing her bit too, sweeping, clearing up and making tea. She appeared to be in much more of a mellow mood with Nancy of late. But that may have been because Nancy was now her boss and her land lady.

By mid-November, Kevin had taken Sophie on a three day excursion to Texas to meet his one surviving member of his family. His Mum. For the first time in an age .Sophie walked with her head held high and a constant smile stretching literally from ear to ear. Nancy had promised her that when she got home from her holiday she would employ her to help Michele run both exotic dance troops. Nancy just couldn't get her head round all that paperwork and being stuck in an office all day was driving her crazy. She needed to be out in the open, doing and making stuff not imprisoned in a stuffy old room every day six days a week.

Michele and Simon had now moved into their new home but not just with the chickens and pygmy goat but also with a horse, a Shetland pony a donkey and a rescued tea cup pig who had not actually stayed a micro pig but had grown to be a full sized porker.

Willow and Poppy had chosen their new kitchens, door handles, flooring and furnishings for their new homes. Which were now up to roof level. Nancy had hoped that by her shoving a few extra grand in the builder's hands would have meant they would have at least been on the second fix by now. However the builders still said they will both be in their new homes before Christmas. A couple of local people were quite concerned and confused as to how Nancy had been granted planning permission so quickly. But when Nancy was asked she just told the truth

"The council and councilors are as bent as a five bob note, how do you think a new housing estate got built on pasture land and so near to the forest? Money talks and it's not what you know but who you know"

Life for everyone right now had seemed to be running smoother than it had for months. Well if truth be known it was, until ….

Danny had the bright idea that he wanted to do something different for Daisy on their wedding day. Something a little out of the ordinary.

Danny's plan was sweet, romantic and meant that Nancy had to spend many nights around Ralph's. Thankfully Willow, Poppy and Danny were there too. Nancy felt her heart strings pull heavy inside her chest each time she drove down that same road she drove down for fifteen consecutive years. Her brain was on repeat with memory after memory flooding her conscious mind. At least the bitch known as Lucy wasn't anywhere in sight any more, otherwise Nancy would not have probably gone along with Danny's plan.

Three nights a week they practised until they were almost word perfect. The only issue was Nancy's poor sad decrepit menopausal brain found it hard to remember all her lines. But she tried. Much to the amusement of the rest of them.

"So will the barn be ready for the wedding" asked Ralph as he handed Nancy her coat

"Yeah should be" the plumbing, electrics, and heating should be done by the end of the week. Joe had put a new roof on last year so at least that saves us a lot of work"

"So are you leaving the mirrors and all the partitions till after the wedding?"

"Yeah, I have told them that can wait until the New Year. Just really want the internal bits done so at least it's usable"

Ralph reached for the latch of the front door as his other two daughters came out of the kitchen.

"Right well, erm, I will see you all in a couple of days then" He said as he kissed each daughter on the cheek

"See ya' dad", they said in unison

Nancy pulled up the zip on her jacket

"Bye Ralph" she said holding her hand out for him to shake

Ralph took hold of her hand and stared into her eyes. Their gazes locked.

"Bye Nance"

When Nancy arrived home that night the house was silent, apart from the dog's tails banging against the cupboard doors when she entered. Silence was the one thing Nancy missed since moving into and actually owning Joe's house. She didn't mind the hustle and bustle of the day time hours but it was her evenings where she could pick up a good book and sprawl out on the sofa with a blanket that she never seemed to be able to do any more.

"Let's make the most of it" chatterbox said

"Agreed" Nancy answered

With dogs in toe and armed with a pot of tea, a whole packet of her favourite rich tea finger biscuits and her Emily Dickenson's complete book of poetry she snuggled under a handmade crochet blanket in the living room. It wasn't long before her eyes were shut and she had drifted into a slightly fidgety sleep.

Elsa growled a low growl in the back of her throat, as a key turned in the door. Childish giggling accompanied by two highly excited voices walked into the hall outside the living room. Nancy stirred, yawned and rubbed her eyes.

"I had a lovely time tonight Mal" Said walnut

"Yeah it was good fun, but did you really have to throw popcorn down the back of that man's shirt?"

Walnut laughed

"Well he deserved it, telling me to shut up. The film hadn't even started. Miserable old goat" Walnut paused "Erm well I s'pose I should be getting to bed. Can't have you workers going without your tea on the morrow can I"

"I don't know what we would do without you"

"If only that was true Mal"

"What's that supposed to mean" Questioned Malachi

"It's nothing, forget I even said anything" replied Walnut

Nancy tired not to move under her blanket, she didn't want that old chesterfield squeaking and letting the two people in the hall know she was awake and eves dropping on their conversation.

"You wouldn't have said anything if it was nothing Sasha, tell me what did you mean?"

Nancy could hear Walnut taking a large intake of breathe

"It's just, I mean, oh hell!....Mal I think I'm in love with you, there I've said it but..."She stopped talking

"But what?"

"But you are with Nancy, and I just don't know if I can be around you two any longer. I've got to be honest I find it a little weird. She's nearly twenty years older than you"

"Age is only a number Sasha. But me and Nance we are, well different. There are no ties, no strings. For god sake Sash, Nancy doesn't want to spend the rest of her life with me, Christ anyone with half a brain knows she still loves Ralph. Me and her well, we are just, me and her. I love her to bits, but she has never said we are going to be a lifelong thing. She's just good Old Nance. And to be honest one day I want children lots and lots of children. Six I think would be good" Malachi laughed

"Six sounds amazing" replied Walnut "Right well I will see you in the morrow, night Mal"

"Night hun…and Sash I'm really fond of you too….see you in the morning"

Nancy sucked in her lips and silently let the tears fall down her cheeks. Reality had finally hit her. How could she, a nearly 48 year old menopausal woman and a grand -mother at that, make a man half her age really happy?. Nancy pulled the blanket up to her mouth to silence her crying.

"Do you love him" came a voice in the dark

"Joe" Nancy answered, unsure if she was sleeping or had overdosed on rich tea fingers

"Well who else would it be, I'll ask you again, do you love him?"

"Yes, I mean no, I mean yes, I mean I don't know!"

"Oh my little Princess always confused. You may have found your feet again and turned into one hell of a business woman but when it comes to love you are a complete novice. What am I going to do with you? My dear little Nancy, don't let others take you for granted any more, follow your heart and Nancy remember I love you"

Nancy was left alone with an ache in her heart, a tear in her eye and a desire to go smash the bathroom mirror so she could never see 'just good old Nance' ever again.

Chapter 33

Nancy stayed on that old chesterfield all night, crying herself to sleep. Did she want Ralph, or did she want Malachi. If the truth be known she loved both of them equally. Ralph was her husband (still). The father to her three daughters and the man she fell hook line and sinker for all those years ago. Okay so he had changed. But so had she. Okay he had an affair with the awful Lucy. But she had bedded Malachi, so what's the difference? And he was changing again, back to the man she first fell in love with. But what about Malachi? He was young, so very young. Youth was on his side. He was an amazing lover with a kind heart. His body was one of an Adonis, but he was young enough to be her son. Who wanted six kids, and last time Nancy looked her lady bits had stopped working years ago. Would it really be fair on him not to let him go and be with a woman his own age? A woman who could give him six kids, a woman who he could grow old with and go through all the things Nancy had with Ralph. Ever since she had met Ralph Nancy had always been the nurturer, Nancy had always been the quiet suburban house wife and done all that was expected of her. Was it time for her to make a choice or was it now time to change back into the person her birth dictated her to be?

As the morning sun shone through the gap in the living room curtains Nancy walked into the kitchen her dogs at her heels. She took their bowls out of the cupboard and emptied their breakfast into each one. Danny was sitting at the table reading his first ever book Cecil Le Plop. He was chuckling away to himself as he turned the pages. Nancy smiled. Malachi was frying two eight ounce steaks and mixing together a protein shake with four raw eggs. One for him and one for Danny. Just the thought of it made her stomach churn.

"Can I get you anything Nance?" he asked as he took the first gulp of his high protein drink.

"Erm no you're alright, I'll just stick to a cup of tea thanks" she answered trying her hardest not wretch as an egg yolk slid down his throat

"Oh the post is on the table, just a lot of pamphlets, but there is an official looking letter addressed to Mrs. N Marshal, I've left it on the top of the pile."

Nancy sauntered over to the post and examined the envelope, like most people do before ripping it open.

"What the fuck!" she shrieked "Mal, Danny hurry up and eat your breakfast, we have to go out"

"Why what's happened?" asked a curious Danny, a little scared it had something to do with Smithy

"Just go and get dressed" Nancy replied "Oh and make sure your suited and booted"

"But I've only got my wedding suit Nance"

Nancy put her cup in the sink and sighed

"Then borrow one of Malachi's Dan, with all those protein shakes, steaks and work outs you've been doing your biceps must be nearly a similar size by now. Now hurry you two"

Nancy stood staring into the open wardrobe doors hoping and praying that amongst all those clothes Joe had bought her there was going to be at least one business suit. Because almost certainly and without a shadow of a doubt a pair of River Island Four way stretch super skinny jeans, SuperDry Lumber Jack twill shirt and a pair of timberlands, would not suffice today. Joe hadn't let her down....but when did he ever?

Nancy smoothed out her sheer tights and for the first time ever admired the transformation a designer suit could actually do for her middle aged figure. It was a little too short for her taste, but the beige Ted Baker, snake effect one button blazer and matching skirt, certainly made her look like the educated business woman she needed to be. Now all she had to do was to make sure she didn't fall arse over tit in the matching high court shoes.

"Relax and breath" Nancy told her reflection before heading downstairs to a waiting Malachi and Danny.

"Twit twwwwwwwoooooooo" Said Malachi as he stared at the tastefully dressed Nancy

Nancy winked at him.

"Mal we are taking your car, the four by four is covered in dog hair, and the Fiat Ebath just won't be right"

"Nance you okay" asked Danny "What's all this about?"

"You'll see" Nancy answered as she picked up the keys to Malachi's silver Audi A4 Saloon

Malachi reversed his car into one of the only spaces left in the car park of the local council offices. Nancy couldn't help but watch as the muscles grew taught in his neck.

"God he is gorgeous" said chatterbox

Nancy couldn't help but agree with her. He was stunning. His hair had grown over the last couple of months and he had taken to wearing it loose rather than tied back in a low pony tail. The natural waves cascaded down the sides of his face highlighting his square jaw. If Danny wasn't in that car she may have taken him there and then but he was, and more important matters needed to be dealt with.

"Right boys" she said "When we get into reception I want you Malachi to take the lead, tell the woman behind the desk you have an appointment with Mr. Bulldock, flirt with her, give her those come to bed eyes of yours. Danny just look official, and hold this in your hand" Nancy handed him an empty black leather folder. "I will just stand there trying not to need a pee. Are we ready?"

"Yes Nance" the boys said in harmony

Malachi's charm worked a treat and the receptionist was putty in his hands. As usual like most women do she handed him a piece of paper with her telephone number on it. Malachi winked at her as he put it in his pocket, and headed for the lift, Nancy and Danny following.

"Right" said Nancy "I will take over when we get to the third floor, just follow my lead okay"

"Yes Nance" the boys answered.

Nancy exhaled and rearranged her skirt before heading out onto a packed third floor. The office had over thirty desks positioned close to each other and all eyes were on Nancy and her boys as they walked, shoulders back, chest out, eyes front through the cramped office suite. Most of the woman had stopped clicking away on their computers to ogle these two suited and devilishly handsome young men. But most of the men also stopped to glance at Nancy too.

The trio reached the office near the end of the suite but instead of knocking on the door Nancy just pulled down the handle and entered. Mr. Bulldock was sitting behind a teak veneered desk talking to someone on the telephone. Nancy walked straight up to him, took the phone out of his hands and placed it back down onto the receiver.

"Excuse me!" said an irate Mr. Bulldock "How dare you walk into my office an.."

"SSH please" Said Nancy as she sat down in the seat the other side of his desk.

She crossed her legs and smoothed down her skirt as Malachi and Danny stood either side of her chair

"Mr. Bullshit, sorry, cock, sorry dock, Mr. Bulldock. I received a letter from you this morning, claiming I have to stop work immediately on the two timber framed houses that are being built on my land. Can you explain why? Nancy handed him the letter

"Well Mrs. Marshal the letter is self-explanatory. We have had a considerable amount of objection letters and a number of people complaining about how quick planning was granted"

Nancy smiled sarcastically

"Yes Mr. Bullshit, I can see that. But you see I don't really understand, as you and Mr. Chudley each received from me a little bonus of ten thousand pounds each to get planning through, how shall we say, erm immediately."

"It's Mr. Bulldock"

"I know what I said" replied Nancy as she continued to stare into his eyes "I would appreciate an explanation. Now." Her tone was adamant

"People have complained, and as head of planning I have to look into all complaints. Your original plans showed two timber framed houses, but they didn't show the two garages. So I have to authorise you to stop work until you have provided me with the revised plans. But I do have to point out to you this could take months for these to even get past the paper work stage....Unless..." he paused

Nancy cleared her throat

"Unless, I write a cheque out for you here and now?"

"Well I think if that happened Mrs. Marshal then we could say, it would be pushed through rather sooner" Mr. Bulldock smiled smugly

Nancy took her cheque book out of her handbag. Malachi looked at her questioning what she was doing. Nancy winked at him, as she reached for Mr. Bulldock's engraved silver pen. She began filling in the cheque, and held her hand out for him to take it from her. Mr. Bulldock took it and Nancy tried her hardest to suppress her laughter as he read the contents of the cheque

He stuttered his response back to her

"I, I don't understand, how dare you!"

Nancy had wrote in the amount section 'FUCK YOU'

"Let me explain Mr. Bullshit" she said as she lifted up a cheap pound shop silver framed photo on his desk and examined it "Oh is this you and your brother" she asked

"It's my wife"

Nancy placed the photo back down on the desk "MMm nice beard, anyway, where was I, Oh yes. You see Mr. Bullshit, when a woman gets to a certain age our brains work a little differently. We have a terrible tendency to think ahead and think of the 'what ifs in situations. When I first came to see you about planning and gave you and the other money gabbing sponger the back hander. I took out a few insurances. Firstly, my accountant, has kept all documentation regarding the twenty thousand that got paid to the pair of you via automatic transfer."

"But that money was not paid into our banks accounts" he interrupted

"I'm aware of that Mr. Bullshit, my accountant opened two completely new ones for you both, and if my memory serves me correctly, both accounts were in your wife's maiden names. But if I recollect accurately both your wives, removed half the contents of the accounts at exactly the same time on exactly the same day. Five thousand pounds is a lot of money to be withdrawn in one go. And what I don't think you realise is banks have cameras everywhere. I'm sure on one of their tapes we will be able to see, both your wives clearly withdrawing the funds. That's unless your wife had a wax beforehand and removed her beard, making it a little harder to recognise her?"

Malachi coughed holding in his laughter. A red faced pursed lipped Mr. Bulldock began fidgeting in his seat

"I will deny, all knowledge, you can't prove anything, and anyway you will be in just as much trouble as me. It would be fraudulent activities on your behalf"

"Hmmmmm" said Nancy "Yes it would, but like I said we women of a certain age think ahead. If you remember I had a gentleman with me that day I came here before. One that in all honesty you should have recognised. His name was Rashir Peterson. Do you remember him Mr. Bullshit?"

"Vaguely" he answered

"Well, you should remember him. You see he was the solicitor who took this authority to court, after evicting ten families from their homes. This council had claimed the house's they were living in was suffering a bad dose of subsidence, and the houses were unfit for human occupation. This council then proceeded to sell off the houses and land to a developer. But for a change the developer had a heart and thought more of the evicted people than he did money. And the rest as they say is history"

"What is your point Mrs Marshal"

""My point is this, Mr. Peterson won the court case against this authority claiming it had lied to the occupants. Sold their homes in order for your council to make an awful lot of money. Your council then had to reimburse all ten families involved. Now, you see Mr Peterson is not only a very good friend but is also a witness to the back hander I paid you. We wouldn't want it to be a Panorama moment would we? It would be highly easy for me to claim that this was nothing more than a test to see if you had all learned your lessons, and changed your ways"

"What do you want? "Said a nervous Mr. Bulldock

"What I want Mr. Bullshit. Is simple. You will call your secretary in right now, and dictate an apology letter to my good self, saying to ignore the previous letter as it was nothing more than a misunderstanding. I will then watch as you sign it and will then take my leave, whereby I will bid you a very good day"

"And what if I just refuse and call the police now?"

Nancy reached into her handbag again and pulled out her mobile phone.

"I don't really think you want to do that, do you? You see it will take me seconds to phone both my accountant and Mr. Peterson. But it would only take me a few seconds more to phone some friends of mine. They are, how can I put this in a terminology you would understand, they are first degree pykies. And would love the chance to camp out in your nice tidy well pruned garden. I'm sure your middle class suburbia housewife with a beard, wouldn't mind them shitting a few times on your lawn after all they do bury it. "Nancy licked her lips and raised her eyebrows at Mr. Bulldock.

"Fine" he answered through gritted teeth and pressed the intercom on his desk.

He handed the newly wrote and signed letter to Nancy who folded it carefully before putting it into her handbag and walking out of Mr. Bulldocks office, her boys following. Once at the lift Nancy puffed out her cheeks and pressed the button for the lift doors to open

"Nance" laughed Danny "that was amaze balls!"

Nancy just exhaled looked at both Malachi and Danny, and in a grinning Cheshire cat sort of way smiled and said

"Yes, yes it was"

 Malachi put his arm around Nancy's waist

"Nancy Marshal I must say I' m rather impressed, but where the hell did that come from?"

Nancy looked up at him as she removed her shoes (her feet were killing her!)

"Let's just say it's in the blood"

Chapter 34

A nervous Daisy was trying on her wedding dress for the hundredth time. Checking that it still fit her growing bump. The sweetheart neck, long line dress with a broderie anglaise bodice looked totally divine on Daisy. Walnut was an amazing seamstress and had altered the dress to fit her growing stomach. An organised Nancy had everything under control.

The old barn had been decorated with ribbons and bows, and an ornate hired glass chandelier hung from the centre of the room. Each table had been dressed with the finest white linen and exquisite china. In the centre stood a glass candlestick adorned with a wild and relaxed arrangement of white Lillies and amaranthus. The tables were simple yet opulent. The chairs had been covered in the same white linen and tied at the back in a luxury flower tie to match the table arrangement. In the far corner of the barn Nancy had transformed a bare wall into a space any bride would have been proud of. The back drop consisted of long flowing silk pale pink curtains. In front of these were four white pillars all strategically placed each draped with white silk and on top of them were bowls of Lillies and trailing amaranthus. The barn not only looked palatial but smelt wonderful.

Willow and Poppy were Daisy's bridesmaids and in typical Daisy style could not be dressed in the normal dusky pink, purple or yellow dresses. Their dresses were A-Line, temperament Black Satin with Wide Straps, pleated natural waist and finished off with a three quarter sleeves bolero style jacket. Daisy had wanted her sisters to wear a pair of Black matching Doctor Marten boots but Nancy had refused her daughter this one thing. Instead they wore a pair of Jasper Conran toe high court shoes. Which not only accentuated their perfect legs but set off the full style of their dresses. Their hair was delicately curled and a single white lily was pinned to one side.

Lilly was dressed in a black tutu dress which had been adorned with Swarovski crystals, which shone like stars in the sky when the light caught it in a certain way. Each crystal had been sewn on by hand by the ever talented Walnut. Nancy's dress was simple and elegant. A black (to match her daughters) classic, v.neck line chiffon gown with three quarter length sleeves and floor length hemline. Everything was set and ready.

Ralph stood outside the boudoir waiting to take the arm of his daughter and walk her down to the alluringly decorated barn where her marriage to Danny was to take place.

Nancy lent out of the door

"She won't be a minute" she told him "Why don't come in everyone is decent"

Ralph followed Nancy into the room and stood with his mouth open staring at his three daughters, wife and the cheeky little face of his grand daughter

"I don't know what to say" he said "You all look stunning"

"Yes they do" said Nancy as she picked up Lilly ready to carry her down to the barn

"I did mean you too Nance" Ralph said blushing ever so slightly

Nancy smiled and graciously said

"Thank you.......Come on girls we have a wedding to get started." Nancy leaned in and air kissed Daisy on the cheek" "See you down stairs in five" She said

As she began to walk away a de ja vu moment flew into her conscious mind. Three second rule, if I turn and he is looking, he is interested in me. She reached the door and couldn't help but look behind her. Ralph was looking. Nancy felt those butterflies from all those years ago return. But did she really want them to return?

All the men were wearing double breasted dinner suits, much to Daisy's disgust. But Danny wanted them and Danny put his foot well and truly down to get them.

Daisy had the biggest grin on her face as she took hold of her father's arm and walked to her future husband in total silence. Danny was standing watching her. He was a little fidgety but soon calmed down as Daisy joined him by his side. Ralph did not move away from his daughter, but instead walked forward with Nancy, Willow, Poppy and Danny. The five of them stood in front of a curious Daisy. Danny nodded his head to Kev who flicked play on his Ipod. The backing track to Boyz II Mens I swear echoed round the barn as the quintet all sang to a giggling Daisy.

Nancy had remembered all her lines which was fortunate and as soon as the applause died down the registrar began the service.

"I now pronounce you husband and Wife, you may kiss the bride"

Danny bent down on one knee and kissed her tiny baby bump, before scooping Daisy up into his arms and rather passionately kissing her. Nancy was crying, Ralph was smiling and the congregation where letting out rather obscene gestures and remarks about getting Daisy knocked up already. The celebration had begun.

Nancy watched as the highly excited crowd all began to relax. She stood by the barn door. Walnut was leaning up against one of the pillars, Malachi stood in front of her, He reached for a lose strand of hair and tucked it behind her ear. She looked elegant and alluring in a black gold full length backless evening dress. Her long auburn hair flowing gently over her shoulders. Nancy stood watching the two of them, clink their glasses and smile longingly into each other's eyes. Before she even realised what she was doing she was by Malachi's side.

"Oh hi Nance" he said placing a kiss on her cheek

"Can I have a word please Mal"

"Yeah sure what it is?"

"Alone please" she said as she turned and walked to the barn door

Malachi followed as Walnut just watched with jealous eyes. Nancy led Malachi into the kitchen of the main house and instantly she filled up the kettle and placed it onto the aga to boil.

"What's up Nance" Malachi asked a concerned tone in his voice

Nancy sighed

""Mal, over the last few months I have grown to love you so much. You have given me a new life, a life where I feel more confident than before. But I have to finish this between us"

Malachi walked over to her gripping her tight around her waist

"No Nance, NO! You can't I mean we can't end. Nance I love you more than anything, why are you doing this, why are you torturing me like this?"

"DON'T CRY" shouted chatter box

Nancy swallowed back her tears and tersely pushed Malachi's grasp away from her waist

"Mal, I have a confession to make. The other night I heard your conversation with Walnut. I heard you say I was just 'good old Nance' and in all honesty you hit the nail on the head. I am old, okay I'm not needing to be spoon fed old and I'm not sitting in some home watching countdown old. But I am old enough to be your mother. You need to be with someone like Sasha. Someone who can give you the six kids you so desperately want. I can't give you that Mal, and let's look at this with our eyes open shall we. If I'm still here in thirty years you are only going to be fifty eight, whereas I'm going to be seventy eight. If I'm lucky I may still be able to walk and have complete control of my bladder but you, you, will be in the prime of your life. Hopefully bouncing your first or second grand child on your knee. Mal I can't thank you enough for all you've done for me. But you need to go have a life, a life with someone you can grow old with and make loads of babies with. You just can't have that with me."

"But Nancy I, I love you"

Nancy hated seeing men cry but Malachi was doing just that. She pulled some kitchen roll of its holder and wiped his falling tears.

"Malachi please don't, don't cry"

"The thing is Nance, I do actually understand, but I want to make you happy"

"And you will, if you go sweep that beautiful girl out there up into your arms and tell her just how much you really do love her"

"How do you know I love her Nance?"

"Woman's intuition"

Malachi bent down and for the very last time lifted Nancy into his strong arms. He kissed her devotedly. With one last lingering look Malachi stood by the kitchen door and watched Nancy pour the boiling water into her cup.

"I will always love you Nancy Marshal"

"Ditto" she answered.

Nancy could hear the music playing as she sat alone at her table crying into her own hands.

"You're going to miss that boy" said chatterbox

"I know"

"I'm going to miss his body" chatterbox sighed

"Shut up and go back in your box"

"How long are you going to sit here wallowing in self-pity for?"asked chatterbox

"I'm not, I'm going to go upstairs, get out of this god forsaking dress put on my skinny's, one of Joe's old sweatshirts, my timberlands re-do my face then I'm going back to the celebration. Good old Nancy Marshal has gone. It's time for me to take control of the rest of my life"

Chatterbox grunted "What about Ralph?"

"I love him I'm not going to lie, I've loved him since the moment we met all those years ago. And if he wants to come back to me, I will probably let him. But it will be with new Nancy not the old one."

Nancy walked up to her boudoir and sat on the edge of her bed staring at a picture of Joe.

"Time to kick some arse Joe, and as much as I sort of like being a girl, I can't change who I am" she leaned forward and kissed him "I will always be your Nancy, you will always be my Joe"

As Nancy entered the barn all eyes were on her. Gone was her designer dress and heels instead she was wearing her skinnys, Joe's sweatshirt and her timberlands.

A frowning Willow tapped her mother on the shoulder.

"Mum what the hell are you wearing?"

"I'm wearing clothes I'm comfortable in Will's. I can't enjoy myself in that frock or any frock, and please don't start, not tonight"

Ralph was standing by her side a glass of fizzy mineral water with ice and a slice in his hand.

"I think your mother looks stunning" he said as he handed the glass to Nancy.

"Thank you" she answered as Kevin grabbed the microphone and began addressing the crowd

"As it appears to be somewhat of a tradition Danny would like to sing to his new wife. Daisy please could you come join us up here"

Daisy walked over to Kevin and Danny, who had already started to blush.

For the second time that day Kevin hit play on his Ipod. The backing track this time was to Ed Sheeran's, Thinking Out Loud.

"When your legs don't work like they used to before, and I can't sweep you off of your feet, will your mouth still remember the taste of my love, will your eyes still smile from your cheek"

 Everyone in that barn joined Danny in the chorus

"Darling I will be loving you till were seventy......"

Ralph took Nancy's glass out of her hand and led her onto an already packed dance floor. She rested her head into his firm chest and inhaled his scent. How she missed the smell of him. How she missed his arms holding her close. How she missed feeling his touch and the security she had being close to him. How she loved him.

All of the revelers had disappeared and Nancy and Ralph were sat leaning up against the long pink drapes. Nancy was in total shock as Ralph did not have his usual pint of cider in his hands but a glass of fresh fizzing spring water. He wasn't even tipsy.

"Have you stopped drinking now?" she asked

"No not totally, but I'm quite liking, being sober most of the time. Plus I've lost all the weight I gained and more"

Nancy rubbed Ralph's stomach

"It suits you"

Both sat staring out at the mess of the barn.

"Nance"

"Yup" she answered

"Is there, I mean would you consider taking me back?"

"Yes Ralph I would consider it, but you have to know I'm not the same Nancy that I was"

Ralph took hold of Nancy's hand and kissed it tenderly

"I think I've gathered that Nance"

Ralph lent forward and kissed her lovingly on the lips. Nancy did not pull away and affectionately kissed him back.

"Ralph" she said as she edged her face away from his "I don't want you to move in with me straight away. I want, I want, you to date me, I want us to go back to the beginning. Start again, start afresh"

Ralph brushed her cheek with the back of his hand

"Anything you want Nance, we have all the time in the world"

His lips touched hers once more as his hand, slid slowly up her rather baggy old and thread bare sweatshirt. Nancy instantly relaxed and, moved her body down under his. She could feel his erection touching her thigh and her excitement just grew beyond measure. They kissed like it was the very first time. He lifted her sweatshirt over her head and stared at her white lace balconette bra.

"Joe's touch I assume" he asked

"Are you complaining?"

"Why not at all" Ralph smiled "Do the knickers match?"

"Well if you take off my jeans you will find out won't you" Nancy answered

Without losing eye contact with her Ralph pulled down Nancy's jeans showing that the knickers did indeed match. He kissed the front of them, before his fingers attentively moved them down her legs. Fervently Nancy unbuttoned his shirt and kissed his chest. Ralph eased his body on top of hers. Nancy began unzipping his trousers. She cupped his buttocks in her hands as she guided him inside her. Spiritedly their bodies ground together in a methodical motion. Everything felt almost right, but something inside Nancy just didn't quite connect.

Chapter 35

Ralph knocked on Nancy's door a bunch of white lily's in his hands. Tonight was their first date. He knew Nancy didn't go in for posh French restaurants and fine wine, but he would not tell her where they were going. All he told her was to dress casual, but make sure she was dressed warm. That wasn't hard for Nancy, Jeans, sweatshirt, long thermal socks, timberlands, trapper hat, gloves and scarf.

Nancy was delighted with her flowers and put them in a vase on the kitchen window sill. Walnut was sitting on Malachi's lap putting small tiny braids in his hair. She looked so happy and content. They looked remarkable together and Malachi seemed to be captivated by her. He had told Nancy that if Ralph ever hurt her again, he would make him sing higher than Aled Jones singing the snowman. But she assured him that if Ralph ever did wander again, she would castrate him with two bricks and a skipping rope. Both of them had made this known to Ralph and in not to dissimilar words, so had Danny, Kev, Simon, Poppy, Willow and Daisy. Let's hope he can keep his promise.

"So where are we going" Nancy asked him as she shut the car door

"We are going to the fair"

"Eh" she asked removing her gloves as her hands were getting a little too hot "It's the middle of winter, no fairs are open at this time of year"

Ralph answered her smugly with a stupid childish grin on his face

"Nance, it's not what you know but who you know"

Ralph drove down a quiet country lane that was dimly lit. It wasn't unlike the road Nancy lives down but instead of a quaint cottage being at the end, stood a carousel and fully working bumper cars. The smell of candy floss and hot dogs filled the air and Nancy began clapping her hands together like an excited child. She couldn't get out the car quick enough and ran straight towards the carousel. Jumping on the first horse she came too.

"Come on Ralph make it work, make it work" an enthusiastic and excited Nancy screeched

Ralph nodded to a rather obese looking man wearing a flat cap. The carousel began spinning round and round as Nancy began singing supercalifragilisticexpialidocious from Mary Poppins. After going round at least a dozen times, and after Nancy sung nearly every song from Mary P, the two middle aged love birds sat on an old tartan checked blanket. Eating hot dogs and candy floss.

Their teeth had become so sticky and full of sugar that they both had a job to open their mouths.

"I've had a lovely time Ralph" Nancy said as she used her finger as a make shift toothbrush

"So have I Nance, to be honest I forgot just how childish, you could be"

"Me childish, how very dare you" she laughed "I'm only a child on a day of the week ending in 'y'"

Ralph kissed her on the lips a little bit too passionately. Mr. Flat Cap coughed rather loudly to try and end this moment of monumental intensity.

"I think we better leave" Ralph said as he hoisted Nancy to her feet

"Would you, I mean could you stay at mine tonight Ralph" she asked as she bit her bottom lip waiting for his response

"I thought you would never ask" he answered

"But Ralph"

"Yes"

"I'm not sleeping on the wet patch"

"Nance"

"Yes"

"You won't be sleeping at all"

Ralph turned the car heater on full as they started there thirty minute journey home. Even though Nancy had come prepared and dressed for a blizzard she was shivering so much her rather sticky teeth made more noise than Ralph's angle grinder sawing through a 32mm York stone paving slab.

They turned onto the main A road. The frost had already started to gather on the abundant flora. Nancy moved over in her seat and rested her head on Ralph's shoulder. She reached down and turned up the volume on Ralph's cd player. Randy Crawford sung out One day I'll fly away as Ralph whistled. For that split second his eyes left the road and he was staring into those dark eyes of his wife.

"Eyes front sir" Nancy said

Ralph raised his eyebrows and tried to straighten the car up, but the steering wheel would not turn. He slammed his foot hard down on the brakes and the car came to a complete standstill in the middle of the road. Nancy shook her head in a disapproving manner, Ralph exhaled slowly, angled his head and pouted his lips. Nancy couldn't resist those full lips and kissed them devotedly.

"Let's just get home in one piece shall we?"

As the final word escaped her mouth the gritter lorry collided with their car. Ralph twisted his body and held Nancy tight, as the car veered on the glacial surface. The car swung violently to the left and with a forcible impact crashed into a mighty oak tree. The smell of diesel was strong and drifted through the air like stale cigarette smoke. Ralph opened his eyes and lifted his body away from her.

"Nancy"

But Nancy was still and unmoving, blood was trickling down the side of her face. He called her name again before falling into an unconscious state

Chapter 36

The icy conditions had meant the accident and
emergency unit was heaving with blooded
and broken bodies. The nurses were running
around like headless chickens, the reception
staff were trying to remain calm with angry
patients who had been waiting for three hours
plus to be seen.

Ralph was in a small cubical his privacy being
protected by a blue curtain. He had a few
bumps and bruises and a dislocated shoulder,
which had been put back into place by a junior
Doctor and a large volume of gas and air.
Poppy and Willow were standing by their
fathers bedside and a heavily pregnant Daisy
was seated on an uncomfortable plastic orange
chair. She was dissecting what was left of a
tear filled tissue.

"Poppy" Ralph said in a faint voice "Where's
your Mum?"

Poppy swallowed hard as her two sisters
began crying once more. She rubbed Ralph's

forehead unable to stop her own from falling again.

"Mum's not good dad. She has a swelling on the brain and they are putting her into an induced coma. She has been transferred to ITU. The Doctors have said that it's a waiting game. They can't tell us if she is going to be okay or not. We just have to hope mum is strong enough Dad." Poppy paused and wiped her eyes with her fingertips. "Dad the police are waiting outside they want to talk to you, do you feel you can?"

Ralph nodded his head.

Willow pulled back the curtain ushering the two police officers into the cubical.

"Can you please wait outside ladies" they asked

The girls all headed back to the overcrowded waiting room where Malachi, Danny, Michele, Simon and Kevin were. Walnut and Sophie had stayed at the house to look after Lilly and the dogs. Michele got up from her chair and placed her arms around a still crying Daisy's shoulder's

"How's he doing?"

"He's fine, sore and in a bit of pain but apart from that he's okay" Daisy answered

"Has he said what happened" inquired Kevin

Willow answered him as she looked for change in her pocket to get a rancid cup of tea from the vending machine.

"He just said the steering wouldn't work on the car, then the gritter lorry hit them. He can't remember much after that except seeing Mums face covered in blood and waking up here"

Danny scratched his forehead

"But the car only had a service last week, I know cos I was the one who took it and picked it up. They said the car was in perfect nick, not a bloody thing wrong with it."

"I'm only saying what Dad said Dan, the steering wheel wouldn't turn" Willow answered adamantly

Their conversation was halted by the two police officers.

"Ladies, gentlemen, we have everything we need for the time being. We will be keeping the car for a while and running a few checks on it. If your mother wakes up can you please call this number on the card" The officer who spoke handed Poppy the card.

"If" Willow said bitingly "You mean when. Our mother will wake up, she's stronger than she looks"

"We know just how tough Nancy Buckland is" said the other officer

Willow frowned confused by the name change

"My mother's name is Marshal, not Buckland"

The two police officers stared at each other questioning their own words

"Just call the number on the card when your mother wakes. Okay"

"They will call" answered Malachi

For three day's Nancy's children stayed by their mother's bedside. Only leaving to eat, shower or when the Doctor's needed to examine her. Malachi had to be forcibly told by Willow.

"To go home" after day two.

Ralph stayed for the first day but was collected from the hospital by none other than Lucy. Who relished in telling Poppy

"She will take good care of her father"

None of the girls could understand why he had called her, when there was more than enough people to take care of him back at Nancy's. But neither daughter had the energy or the desire to fight and argue with their dad. There only concern was for Nancy.

On day four an unshaven specialist registrar Doctor who looked like he had not slept for months asked the daughters to accompany him into his office. His desk was filled with random post it stickers and blue folders. A sports bag full of clothes and a toiletries bag sat at the far corner of the room beneath a silver filling cabinet and an empty Dominos pizza box rested on top of an over filled waste paper basket.

"I'm so sorry the room looks like disorganised chaos" the young doctor said "We are just so busy right now"

Willow answered him with a snigger in her voice

"You don't need to explain, I'm an ODP. Overworked and underpaid "

The young registrar smiled back at her

"Anyway" he said "We have some news about your mother. Please don't look all so scared. Its good news. The swelling on her brain is going down nicely and we are going to reduce the amount of medication we are giving her. We are hoping in a couple of days we will be able to stop it all together."

"Oh my god that is brilliant" shouted Daisy

Willow bit on her top lip

"There's a but coming, isn't there?"

The Doctor played with a Biro on his desk pulling the lid off and putting it back on again.

"Yes, at this moment in time we are not sure if your mother will make a full recovery. It's a little too soon to say if she will suffer any long term consequences. Like……."

Willow interrupted him.

"Like brain damage"

The registrar nodded

"But she is a strong woman, all her vitals are normal…… Look why don't you all go home and get some sleep. You all look worn out." He looked over at Daisy "Especially you, how much longer have you got to go?"

"Four weeks" she answered

"I promise if there is any change I will call you personally, you have my word on it"

Chapter 37

The cottage, surrounding fields and woodland looked alluring in the summer but in winter it was transformed it into a deep mystical place that resembled a fairy tale scene. The harsh frost lay on the ground like a million diamonds and the air smelled fresh and clean. The daughters arrived back at Nancy's house a little after 2pm. They all were emotionally and physically worn out. Malachi was first to greet them. He hadn't shaved since the accident and the new beard looked exceptionally fetching on him.

"How is she doing" he asked his voice full of desperation

Poppy looked up at him with tired eyes

"They are reducing the medication, but she's hanging in there, we have just got to hope and pray there is no long term damage. They are going to call if anything changes. Is dad here?"

"No" Mal answered with a slight embarrassment in his voice "Erm Lucy phoned and said she was staying with him at Ralph's, and for no one to worry as she will sort him out"

"Yeah I bet she fucking will" Daisy said venomously as they walked through the solid oak door into the kitchen. "Where's Dan?"

Malachi reached for the kettle and began walking towards the sink to fill it.

"Where's Dan?" Daisy asked again

"Tea or coffee ladies?"

"Oh for fuck sake Mal where is my husband!"

Malachi turned to face the three curious women, his arms folded tight across his chest as if he was trying to protect himself from the full force of their icy glares.

"He's taking Sophie back to her house"

"Why?" Daisy demanded

"Look, I don't know all the ins and out's but Sophie and Danny had a huge row after he came home the night of the accident. Danny mentioned some bloke called Pilot and then Sophie said she was leaving. Kevin is heartbroken and yesterday he booked himself a ticket and jumped on the first flight back to America. I really don't know what the hell is going on around here right now. The police have been here every day, searched the house, the barns and even the woods. I don't know if you noticed when you drove up the drive but there is an unmarked police car sitting at the gates."

Malachi shrugged his shoulders and returned to making the daughters a hot beverage.

"Oh and one more thing" he said "They keep referring to Nancy as 'Buckland', who the hell is Buckland?"

Poppy held her tea cup in both hands and blew gently across the top of it.

"I haven't got a clue, but the police officer in the hospital called her that too"

"May be Mums an escaped criminal" Daisy said growling through gritted teeth

Willow laughed loudly

"Yeah and may be your pregnancy hormones are making you deranged"

The laughing subsided and the four of them all sat in total silence for the next ten minutes. The only noise heard was that of the dripping tap and the occasional snore or grunt from one of the dogs. Malachi had taken it upon himself to be in charge of these three beasts and every morning since the accident he had run with them in the woods. But dog pooh just wasn't his thing and he point blankly refused to clean it up. This job he left for Walnut. She didn't seem to mind at all as she just couldn't watch Malachi gag and wretch to the point of his mouth being full of spit and his eyes watering like a volcano leaking lava. Even though she did find it highly amusing watching him shovel shit onto a spade and nearly puking each time he did. If the truth be known Walnut liked the fact that she was the woman of the house. She liked that Malachi was not distracted by Nancy every time she entered the room and she liked having his undivided and total attention. Don't get me wrong she loved Nancy liked the mother she never had. But somewhere in the back of her mind she could not help but be a little afraid of the power this woman had over Malachi. But maybe it wasn't the power she had on him that should concern her, but the power she had at the tips of her fingers.

Chapter 38

Five days after the accident Nancy began slowly opening her eyes. All her medication had now been withdrawn and it was time for her to see the world again. It took a full twenty minutes for her full sight to be restored. And looking straight back at her were her three stunningly beautiful daughters. There was however, an even bigger surprise awaiting her. In Daisy's arms was a brand new, perfect baby boy. It could have been the stress of Nancy's accident that caused him to be born three weeks early. Or even the fact that this bundle of joy just didn't want to stay in Daisy's womb any longer. Either way, Nancy was now a mother to three and a grandmother to, two gorgeous creations.

Daisy walked closer to her mother's bed and placed her new son down beside her.

"Wyatt I would like to meet your Nana" Daisy said her face beaming

Nancy licked her lips and tried to speak, but her mouth was drier than the bottom of a parrot's cage. She mouthed 'water' to the Doctor who was standing the opposite side of the bed to her children.

He reached for a lidded tumbler and told her to sip slowly.

"I just want a check a few things Nancy" he said as he ushered Daisy to pick up her son.

The junior registrar, shone a light into her eyes.

"Everything looks fine there. Nancy I want you to squeeze my hand"

Nancy squeezed.

"Now the other one"

She squeezed again.

"Can you feel this" he asked as he pricked her thighs with a pin

Nancy nodded

"Now wiggle your toes"

Nancy wiggled

The Doctor smiled.

"I think you are going to be just fine. I will leave you alone with your family" He looked at Poppy "Not to long though, your Mother needs her rest, any problems just shout"

Daisy placed Wyatt once again beside his grandmother. Nancy gazed at him with admiration. He was practically perfect in every way. In a weak voice but with her gaze still on her new grandson Nancy spoke for the first time.

"I'm so sorry I wasn't there for you Daisy"

Daisy shook her head.

"Mum its fine, Danny was remarkable. Poppy and Willow were there too. We were told one of them had to leave when I was about to pop, but hey rules are there for breaking, isn't that what you always say?"

Nancy scanned the room. The machines that had checked her vitals were still attached to her skin and beeped every so often.

Nancy licked her dry lips once more.

"Where's your father?"

The girls knew this question would arise sooner or later. But how could they tell their mother he was at home being taken care of by the voracious predator, known as Lucy.

"He's at home resting Mum, but is going to be fine, don't worry about Dad right now, just concentrate on getting better" Daisy answered her and stared into the stern faces of her sisters.

Poppy and Willow had visited him the day before. In typical Lucy format she was marauding around Ralph's house dressed in nothing more than a chemise, a pair of French knickers and her annoying clip clopping heeled slippers. The house though, it had to be said was clean and tidy, and as much as each daughter hated her, she was doing a rather good job taking care of their father.

Ralph was sat on the shiny brown leather sofa, his daily tabloid newspaper on his lap. Apart from a black eye and his arm still in a sling he looked well considering what he had just been through.

"Would anyone like a cup of tea" Lucy asked her voice softer than it ever has been before. With no sarcasm or intent lingering in it.

Shocked at how polite she was, neither girl refused.

"How ya' feeling dad?" Willow asked as she took a seat beside him

"I'm okay, still a bit sore but Lucy is taking good care of me"

"Course she is" Poppy said her voice edged in cynicism

Ralph folded his newspaper and threw it down onto the oak laminated floor. He shuffled slightly in his seat and rearranged his foam sling.

"She's not all bad ya' know. And before you ask, yes she has left her husband, and no we haven't had sex, and yes I do still love your Mum. How is she doing anyway?"

"Well if you would come to the hospital you would know, wouldn't you" Willow replied

"Willow I can't. I hate being in those places and I just can't handle it when someone is sick. Christ I couldn't even visit you, when you had your tonsils out"

Lucy re-entered the room carrying a tray with four cups of tea and a packet of digestive biscuits. Poppy raised her eyebrows at her and walked to the window overlooking the back garden. She was stunned at how much work

Ralph had done to it in the last couple of months. A new patio had been laid, a play area for Lilly had been built and hanging baskets and troughs full of ivy, viola and flowering winter heathers had been planted. Poppy turned back to face her father.

"But she is still your wife Dad and right now none of us know if she is going to recover fully"

Lucy picked at the edge of her chemise and dunked her digestive in her tea.

"But she isn't his legal wife" she said in a monochrome way

"LUCY!" shouted Ralph

Lucy jumped in her seat as her soggy biscuit fell into her tea.

"What does she mean?" demanded Willow

Ralph pursed his lips and rubbed his hands through his greying hair

"Fucking hell, I knew this day was going to come sooner or later. Look Nancy, I mean your mum wanted to tell you herself. If and I mean IF, she doesn't wake up or there is something wrong with her, I will tell you the whole fucking story. But right now don't push me for answers. All I'm going say is some of your mums history is not quite what it appears to be."

No persuasion, shouting or begging from his daughters would get Ralph to open up and in a typically hormonal fashion both girls left their fathers home in a foul temperamental mood.

Chapter 39

Nancy discharged herself a little over two weeks later. As far as she was concerned no one ever again was going to wipe her backside, tell her what time to eat or take complete control of her life. Her movements were a bit slow but her own stubbornness to get back on her feet and back to her family as quickly as possible meant she pushed her body to its limits. The doctors wanted her to leave with a zimmer frame and a wheelchair but Nancy was having none of it. Was this the menopause that was causing her to harden up or was this the true Nancy appearing for the first time in over 30 years?

The unmarked black Vauxhall Insignia was still parked outside the gates to Nancy's home. Two plain clothes officers sat inside. Nancy's eyes were fixed on its occupants and theirs on hers.

"They've been here since the accident" Mal said as he drove the car up the drive way "We have had a few visits from the old bill too, searching the house, the woods, the barns even the dance studio. Did Willow tell you they wanted to speak to you?"

Nancy blinked hard and bit her top lip

"Yeah she told me, but they can wait"

Malachi reversed the car close to the pile of chopped logs and turned off the engine.

"Nance, before we go in I need to tell you a few things. First Kev has left and gone back to America. Sophie has moved back to her house after a huge row with Danny. I still don't know the full reason why as Danny won't even tell Daisy, all I know is the name Pilot keeps being mentioned and the police" he paused "The police keep calling you Nancy Buckland not Marshal."

Malachi stroked Nancy's leg

"What the fuck is going on Nance?"

Nancy reached for the door handle and gingerly stepped outside. She glanced once more at the Insignia before linking arms with Malachi and heading for her front door. Ignoring Malachi's questions for answers.

A white sheet which had been artistically decorated by Daisy saying 'WELCOME HOME MUM' was hung from one side of the kitchen to the other. The quaint farmhouse kitchen was full to bursting point with helium filled balloons and enough flowers that even the Chelsea flower show would have been envious of. The smell flooded Nancy's senses and she inhaled their scent deeply. Poppy, Willow, Daisy, Danny and Walnut all stood from their seated position at the table when Nancy entered the room.

She laughed out loud as they looked like regimented soldiers on a parade ground.

"What are you all waiting for?" Nancy asked "Someone either speak or hug me for Christ's sake!"

No one needed to be told twice and each one went in for a mammoth group hug! Nancy kissed all the happy smiling faces in turn before declaring

"Oh my god it's so good to be home, someone make me a cup of tea in a china cup pleaseeeeeeeeeeeeeeeeee"

Walnut already had the kettle simmering on the aga, and a tray set out with Nancy's favourite pink china tea cup and her rich tea finger biscuits. She must have drunk at least six cups and consumed all but two of the biscuits before anyone tried to start up a conversation. Nancy could see and feel the tension rise in the room and she was the first to break the silence.

"I had such a weird dream when I was sleeping" She said as she gazed around each questioning face in the room. "It was such a lovely spring day and I was walking through the woods. The sun was shining brightly without a cloud in the sky. I was walking on a carpet of bluebells, their smell was intoxicating. My Dad was sitting on a fallen tree and when I got just inches from him he got up, reached out and hugged me. The last time I remember him doing that was when I was about twelve, before…..before. "Nancy hesitated "Anyway Uncle Joe appeared from behind a sycamore tree. I had almost forgot how handsome he was. Now he knew how to hug. He squeezed me so hard I thought my bowels would rupture. He then said to me, 'My little lady of the woods, you have to go back to your roots' the sun disappeared then and the rain began to fall. And that was when I woke up."

Nancy reached for the last two rich tea fingers and watched the audience in front of intently. She broke one of the biscuits in half and nibbled at the edges of it.

"I'm shocked your dad isn't here" she continued "Is he at home still recovering?"

No one wanted to answer that question and everyone looked to the other for moral support. Nancy could see their trepidation and uneasiness at answering her. She wasn't going to push for answers.

"Never mind, your dad never could handle a bit of blood or sickness" she concluded. "I suppose…..I suppose it's time to tell you all the truth, because somehow I don't think I'm going to be able to keep everything secret for much longer" Nancy breathed in and exhaled through pouting lips. "My Name is Nancy Buckland. And before anyone asks, no I'm not married in the legal sort of way. You see me and Ralph were married in the middle of Ashdown forest by Joe. I then, for all intense and purposes took his name. But legally I am still Nancy Buckland, and not really married. Joe called me the lady of the woods not just because I loved being in them but because I was born in them. You see my family travelled from place to place…."

"So you're a pykie?" Willow asked

"No I'm not a pykie, a tinker or a diddicoy and my family are not really like those in big fat gypsy wedding either. The head of my family are always female. The men are there for two purposes muscle and procreation. It's the women who rule the roost and take charge. And yes I have shit in the woods, yes we did travel with wagons, and no we never made a mess wherever we went. Because we believed in nature first. We believed that nature had to be protected and taken care of. Anyway, as time moved on the work and hatred for the gypsy and travelling community grew. Nobody wanted to employ 'our type' to work the lands any more, harvest the fruit or take care of livestock. So many of my family went into protection. We were basically hired muscle. But as time moved on so did what we were asked to do. What I mean by that is we done things for money that others just wouldn't do." Nancy sighed "There are no excuses for what we done but we needed to survive. And before long our family had a reputation, a reputation that no one messed with." Nancy raised her eyebrows and for a moment was lost in the memories of her past. "Anyway, the head of my family is who I am named after, Grammie Buckland. I know she is still alive because if she wasn't then I would have been contacted by now, because I'm next in line to take her place. But I haven't seen her for years. Another pot of tea please Walnut, if you don't mind?"

Walnut left her seated position from the table, filled the kettle, rinsed out the pot and never once questioned the authoritarian, albeit, rather bossy order from Nancy. Daisy began undoing her shirt ready for the imminent breast feeding session and Willow and Poppy just looked dismayed at what they were hearing.

"So" Poppy said "What the hell happened next?"

Walnut returned with the steaming pot of the burnished liquid and played mother by pouring it into every person's cup who wanted a refill. Nancy thanked her as she once again began telling all, of her jaded history.

"Well, like I said our family went into the protection business. And your grandfather, my dad, was paid a huge sum of money to.....how shall I put it, to remove a certain person from civilisation. Pereguin, done what was asked of him. He torched a person's house with him still inside. But what he didn't know was there were two other people in the house that night, who were not supposed to be there. The man's wife and his six month old baby daughter."

"Oh my god that is awful" Willow bellowed

"Yeah it was. That's why your grandfather turned to drink. You see the one thing that is sacred to our family is women. We get treated like royalty and irrelevant of how we are or what we do the men in our family will never raise a hand or a fist to us. Things changed after dad started drinking. He couldn't live with what he had done and each glass or can of alcohol he consumed, turned him into some form of wild animal. He forgot his roots and used mum as a punch bag. Never hit me though" Nancy gulped down another mouthful of tea "So, when I was twelve or thirteen can't quite remember exactly. Me, mum and dad moved away from our camp site and left our tribe. But I did go back and visit Grammie from time to time. Your Grammie was and still is I think a Shuvvanis and used to earn money reading peoples fortunes."

Malachi giggled

"Don't laugh Mal, she was the real deal, and became very well known for her gift." She gave Malachi an icy glare "Right, let's move on or we will be here all day. When I was born I was betrothed to another traveler who followed the same beliefs as our family. His name was Jibben but we all called him Henry. We were inseparable as kids. And it broke my heart leaving him and Grammie. I was supposed to marry him a short time after my sixteenth birthday but Mum wouldn't allow it. Then I met your dad and like I said before we got married in a non-marriage sort of way."

Daisy removed Wyatt from her breast and placed him over her shoulder to wind. She had learned the one swoop technique of getting her boob out of his mouth, and covering her exposed breast in record time, so as to not embarrass the people around her. But the people around this table were neither embarrassed nor ashamed at seeing her use, her body for what nature intended. Daisy was just a natural, she took to motherhood like an ice cream to a cornet. Deliciously.

Once Nancy finished observing the remarkable sight of mother and child she resumed her life's history to her curious listeners.

"Percival was the eldest of the three brothers and his wife died from influenza early on in their marriage. He never married again as most men didn't after their betrothed died. Pereguin obviously married mum and they had me. But it was Pethius's daughter who then went on to marry Henry after I left. She died in childbirth along with her unborn son. And so that's why I am next in line to be head of the family. And that's it, that's my history and yours too........Now that's out of the way I'm feeling a little tired so if you have any questions can you ask me later cos right now

I'm more tired than a prostitute doing the late shift"

"But Mum you can't leave it there" Demanded Daisy,

"Yes I can Daisy"

Nancy arose from the table, pushed her chair under it and walked straight out the door in to the lounge to rest on that old squeaky chesterfield. Unsure if her daughters and the other assemblage could accept just what she and her family really were. Will they ever accept their past, their present or even their future? Time will tell.

Chapter 40

The one good thing to come out of the accident was Nancy had not had a hot flush, a cold flush or the desperate urge to pee like a race horse, since she woke up from that induced coma. She was feeling different. Her mind felt clear, her body stronger than it had for years and she had an uncontrollable urge to finally break down the barriers and chains that had held her prisoner for so long.

Her attitude had already started to change after Daisy's wedding but now, now she was more assertive than ever before. She had one final hurdle to jump and one void to fill and that was the emptiness in her heart.

Nancy sat on Joe's old bed. His room had not been touched since he had died. His re-cycled tin cans where still filled with pens on his desk, his clothes still hung in the wardrobe and the smell of his favourite aftershave lingered through the air. Nancy could hear his rapturous laughter bellowing around the room and bouncing of the walls. She was procrastinating and putting of the inevitable. She knew she had to get around to sorting Joe's personal possessions out. Just not yet.

Nancy bit her top lip and let the memories of her time spent with Joe disentangle themselves from the barren parts of her mind. Joe still captivated her heart and not one day went by without her feeling resentful about his death. Rightly or wrongly, Nancy smiled with cold eyes as she recollected watching Smithy floating in that water. But something was not quite right. She knew Smithy was a rogue, a tyrant and in all honesty a cold hearted bastard. But he didn't have the brains to concoct the brutal attack on Joe. In Nancy's mind something just didn't add up. Her thoughts were interrupted by a gentle knock on Joe's door.

"Can I come in?"

It was Ralph. His arm still being held in place by the foam sling. His face held trepidation and embarrassment. He blushed as he sat down next to Nancy on Joe's bed. He took hold of her hand in his and stared straight into her tired brown eyes.

"I'm so sorry I wasn't here when you came home. You don't need to say it I'm an awful husband"

"Yeah you are" Nancy said snatching her hand out of his

"Oh Nance please don't be like that, you know what I'm like in those sort of situations."

Nancy was curt in her response

"Yeah I do, and you're not actually my husband so we can drop that lie now"

Nancy rose from the bed and went over to the window. She gazed out at the open fields.

"So how is Lucy?"

Ralph exhaled and rubbed his good hand through his hair

"What?"

"Oh Ralph stop being such a dick head! Do you really think I was born yesterday? The kids always change the subject when I ask how you are, and I know you too well. There is not a fucking chance of you taking care of yourself when you're healthy, let alone when you're sick!" Nancy blinked hard as she turned to face him.

Ralph sat uneasy on the bed, he wanted to look at her but he felt shamed at realising Nancy knew, before anyone had the heart to tell her.

He walked towards her and run his fingers down the side of her face

"Nancy nothing happened, I promise you"

"And you expect me to believe that?"

"But it's the truth Nance. She stayed over yes, she helped me out, she cleaned. Cooked and to be honest she was really good at it"

"Oh so that makes it alright then does it?" De ja vu. Nancy hesitated waiting for him to respond. But all he done was to stare vacantly at her

"Look Ralph, look at this from my perspective. You destroy what we had by fucking another woman, and when I'm close to deaths door you go back to said woman. To be honest Ralph if you loved me like you say you do, you wouldn't have left my bedside irrelevant of how much you hate hospitals and situations like this. If.......If you really loved me you would have been here when I got home. But you wasn't, you didn't even call or text me."

"But Nance I do love you"

The tone in Nancy's voice grew abrupt and stern

"Do you, do you really? Look Ralph, love is about being there for someone through thick and thin, sickness and in health love is about sitting listening to someone even though you have no interest in what they are saying, love is about lifting a person up when they feel low, love is about them not you. And if you can't think about them, then love just isn't for you" Nancy began to falter as the realisation that may be Ralph just didn't love her enough to stay by her side grew strong in her stomach "Maybe….maybe the love you once had for me is more one of habit than one of commitment"

It was breaking Nancy's heart further to think that after spending the majority of her adult life with this man was just nothing more than an addiction.

"So Ralph, answer me honestly, do you really love me?"

Ralphs eyes were bloodshot as he sniffed back his tears, he took Nancy in his arms and held her tight

"I do love you Nance, but…."

"But you just don't love me enough to be all the things I want, do you?

The security she once felt was just not there any longer. Her unbridled passion for this man did not heat up. She felt numb in his grasp. Whatever they had, whatever these two consenting adults needed from each other had disintegrated into dust. Leaving nothing more than memories in its place.

They stared meaningfully at each other. Nancy leaned forward and kissed Ralph softly on the lips. Piece by piece her disorganised mind knew just what she had to do next.

"Ralph, it's time to let each other go. What we had was so special, but what we want is just too different. Let's not waste any more of what little time we have feeling trapped. I love you Ralph, I always will, but sometimes it's better to carry on moving rather than going back to what we thought we wanted. Things can never be the same for us, no matter how hard we try. If something is broken there is no point in constantly gluing it back together is there?"

Ralph took Nancy in his arms and held her tight. Both of them knew they needed to let go. They had to find the strength inside them to walk away now and begin their new journey into the unknown.

Ralph released his hold on her. With his eyes brimming over with tears he placed one final kiss on her cheek.

"I will always love you Nance"

He turned and walked out of Joe's room this time he didn't look back.

Chapter 41

Nancy lay in her bed, the duvet pulled tight under her chin. She reached for her phone, the clock read 6.15am. She had been lying awake since 3.30am as her over thinking part of her mind had kept her awake. Nancy was questioning everything that had happened over the past few months. Joe's death, Smithy, Ralph, Lucy, Malachi, the accident, Sophie, and Kevin leaving and why wouldn't Danny tell her the reason? She knew she had done the right thing with Ralph. She was even beginning to tolerate Lucy. No, she would never like her but for the sake of family harmony she would endure her. Or try to anyway.

The restless empty feeling in Nancy's heart was growing each day. She observed Malachi closely, and not even his muscular Adonis form made her groin ache and her desire build. Was this just another stage of the dreaded menopause eating away at her? Making her body dull and without feeling or did it go much deeper. No matter how hard she tried nothing was tempting her into doing obscure, rather passionate and highly immoral acts of sexual gratification. Even her little box of tricks that buzz and whir, which at least one in three woman owns were gathering dust in her knickers draw. Her lady bits were more hostile than the Gobi Desert without the excessive heat build-up occurring between her legs.

"May be you're just a dried up old prune" shouted chatterbox

"Oh I wondered when you would rear your ugly head again. Just go back into your box will ya'!" Nancy replied bitterly.

Chatterbox tutted and vanished into the abyss of Nancy's mind like some scolded child who had been sent to their room.

Nancy took a deep breathe, kicked off her duvet and reached for her dressing gown. She winced as she stood on the cold oak floor. Her slippers were nowhere to be seen so she just put on her socks she had worn the day before and headed for the door.

The lights of the insignia shone down her drive as Nancy stood at the kitchen sink filling the kettle.

"Well if nothing else, at least they are dedicated" She said as she placed the kettle onto the aga "But what the hell do they want and why are they here?

"Well" said the voice inside her head, who crept cautiously out of the back of her mind, not wanting to be scolded again "There is only one way to find out, go ask them?"

Chatterbox was right. Nancy went into the boot room and donned a pair of wellies and grabbed Malachi's Trialmaster wax cotton jacket. She headed for the front door and with her three dogs in tow she walked to the un-marked police car.

Elsa jumped up at the window as the driver of the vehicle opened it. A blast of stale cigarette smoke exited the space

"Well, well, well" Nancy said as she observed the passenger "If it isn't the biggest and bent pestilential and mephitic piece of shit that was ever born"

"I've missed you to Nance" he answered as he inhaled deeply on his cigarette

Nancy gave him a sarcastic grin.

"So" she said as she pulled Malachi's jacket tighter "Why are you here Jonesy, and what the hell do you want?"

The driver of the car looked uneasy as he saw the look of resentment spread across Nancy's face "May be we could talk inside the house" he said, hoping that he could remain neutral in this obvious awkward and hostile conversation.

Jonesy undone his window and threw his cigarette out of it onto the ground "I think that may be a good idea Buckland, after all we wouldn't want you to end up back into hospital with hypothermia now would we" he answered mordantly

Nancy held her gaze on his as Jonesy took another cigarette from its packet. She stepped away from the car and whistled for her dogs.

"Okay, but you're not fucking smoking in my house, the stench of your odour alone is going to be more than enough to bare without you poisoning my lungs as well"

Jonesy reached for the door handle and stepped into the crisp morning air.

"Always the lady, eh Buckland? I see money hasn't changed your gutter mouth"

"Always the prick eh Jonesy? I see time hasn't changed you from being a cunt"

Jonesy and his counterpart sat watching Nancy as she filled her dog's food bowls with the dissected and butchered turkeys. She was trying her hardest to look respectable, but as she had only just got out of bed, her hair was all over the place and her lime green novelty socks with monster faces made her look exceedingly childish. It didn't help that dog drool was now dribbling down her bare legs. And she was sure that a boob had escaped the confinements of her robe when she bent down to feed her dogs.

"So if you've finally finished gawking at my breasts, can you tell me why the fuck you are here? Nancy questioned as she sat at the head of the oak table, pulling her dressing gown as tight as it would go across her chest.

She observed her unwanted guests. The young officer was well groomed. Obviously he had a bit of stubble, after all he had been parked outside her house all night. But his hair was neat, his finger nails and clothes were clean. He couldn't have been no more than twenty and looked very wet behind the ears. Jonesy on the other hand had not aged well. His face had deep lines and she could still see the scar down his left cheek. The scar that she had put there.

Nancy was fourteen years old when it happened. She had gone back to visit Grammie Buckland. It was a balmy humid August night she had fallen asleep to the sound of the nightingales and was lying beneath the branches of an old oak tree about five hundred yards from their camp-site. Jonesy and umpteen other officers raided their encampment. It was true to say the police and Nancy's family never did see eye to eye, and Jonesy seemed to take every opportunity he could at getting their names on his arrest sheets. Everybody knew that Jonesy was a bent copper who topped up his pension working alongside the Rufus brothers. They were not dissimilar to Nancy's family and had moved to Sussex from Manchester around the 1890's. Some say they moved here to escape the poverty but most believed it was because they were running from the horrendous acts of violence they bestowed onto others. Power was their desire and fear was not allowed.

Nancy did not hear all the commotion at first but was woken with a start as the hand of a complete stranger entered her top. Her eyes remained tightly closed as he fumbled for her breasts. She felt him undo the button of her jeans and just as he went to kiss her, she bit the side of his cheek. Her assailant fell backwards clutching his face and with the taste of his blood in her mouth Nancy began running back to the camp-site. It wasn't long before he had caught up with her and rugby tackled her to the ground. With his fist clenched he punched her clean in the mouth, blood spewed from her lips. Nancy screamed, but her screams could not be heard over the pandemonium that was occurring. Her aggressor resumed his stance over her. Nancy stopped fighting and calmed her body. She lay still on the wooded ground and smiled at her attacker. Just as he began un-zipping his trousers Nancy thrust a stick into his eye. He rolled off her body. It was now his turn to scream and writhe in pain. With her clothes covered in blood and her heart beating uncontrollably inside her chest Nancy stood, only to see Jonesy standing before her. He had witnessed the whole scene and did nothing to stop one of his officers from attempting to rape her. Jonesy started to walk closer towards her and for a split second Nancy froze. But then she remembered. Tucked in-between her socks and her boots was her Charade automatic knife, she used for hunting and gutting fish. Nancy bent down and took the shiny blade out of her socks. Jonesy was only inches away from her. Without thinking or hesitating, Nancy swung the blade. Her mouth was still oozing blood, her assailant was still lying on the ground and now Jonesy had a gaping wound from just below his eye to the top of his lip. Nancy still to this day does not know if Jonesy was going to help her or continue what his colleague had started. But as neither he nor the other officer pressed charges against her, she would like to think it was the later.

She continued to recall the events of that night as Jonesy removed his black woollen beanie hat and placed it onto the table. His balding head had beads of sweet sticking to its surface. His teeth were stained and his hands shook ever so slightly as he leaned back in his chair.

"You've aged rather well, Miss Buckland"

Nancy folded her arms across her chest to try and cover more of her dignity.

"Stop with the small talk Jonesy, and just tell me why the fuck you are here?"

Jonesy scratched the top of his head and rubbed his hand down the back of his neck

"Well it's like this, a few months ago I happened to see a file. A file that contained details of Joe's death. Then I saw another file, this time it was regarding Mr Smith's death. Both these files had one similarity. Can you guess what that was?"

Nancy just continued to stare at him.

"You're going to tell me anyway aren't you?"

"Indeed I am, the similarity was you. But to make my curiosity a little bit stronger I then hear that you and Mr. Marshal were in a car accident. For a car that had just had a recent service there was an awful lot wrong with it. Quite a lot under that bonnet had been loosened and in a nut shell your car was not road worthy. In fact I wouldn't have even driven it myself"

Nancy leaned forward and didn't give one more thought as to the fact her robe had loosened once again and the top part of her breast could be seen.

"So what are you saying? My accident was not actually an accident?"

"In all honesty Buckland I don't think it was. Tell me what do you know about Mr. Smith?"

"Smithy? All I can tell you is, he in my opinion is a murdering wife beating bastard who I hope is rotting in the pits of hell" Nancy spoke bitterly as the hatred she had for that man came to the surface and made her skin prickle.

"Tell me have you ever heard of a man called Pilot"

Nancy remembered Malachi mentioning his name to her the day she arrived home. But pleaded total ignorance.

"No never, why who is he?"

Jonesy rubbed his hands together before mirror imagining Nancy's position.

"You mean I know more than you, wonders will never cease" Jonesy grunted

"Okay stop with the smarmy act, and just tell me" Nancy answered her voice showing her impatience

"Pilot, is how can we put this, hmmmmm….a man who takes no prisoners. He actually makes your family look like pussy cats. We have had him under surveillance for a number of years and Smithy worked for him. But what I think would really interest you is the fact that Sophie has been having an affair with him ever since Danny was about thirteen years old"

Nancy's mouth dropped open

"What, do you mean? "

"I mean Nance, Sophie was fucking her husbands want for a better word boss" Jonesy paused "Look Nance I'm going to put the cards on the table. I know you don't like me and will find it really hard to trust me. But, I'm not the same copper I was all them years ago. In them days at least there was a mutual respect of sorts but nowadays it's so different. I'm different "

Nancy laughed

"What, you mean you're honest at last"

"In actual fact yeah, I'm honest, I'm by the book now Buckland. Well sort of. Look it's pretty obvious you haven't got a fucking clue about what the angst between Joe and Pilot was but the fact remains that you are now caught up in something that had nothing what so ever to do with you. I'm going to ask you this off the record, did you kill Smith?"

Nancy shook her head

"No, no I didn't"

Which wasn't a lie really was it, he fell.

"Do you know anything apart from what I have just told you?"

Nancy once again shook her head

"No, nothing"

"Okay Buckland, for the time being there will be a car parked at the bottom of your drive. But again, off the record, I think you should think about getting everyone away from here. Especially the grandchildren. Like I said Buckland, this bloke is the worst of the worst, he is mindless evil piece of shit, and he will do absolutely anything to get what he wants, and I mean anything."

Nancy frowned and bit on her bottom lip.

"But how can I give him what he wants if I haven't got a clue what the fuck that is?"

Jonesy rested his elbows on the edge of the table.

"Nancy…..Nancy just do as I have said, but please remember he is the sort of bloke to bite first irrelevant of consequences. He has more people in his back pocket than the Queen's guard has blisters. Please Nancy. Please be careful. And if I may say so Nancy it may be time to go back to your roots"

Nancy's eyes widened

"What did you just say?"

"I said be careful he has more people i…."

Nancy angled her body towards him

"No, no the last sentence" she demanded

Jonesy scratched the white bristles on his chin

"Erm, it may be time for you to go back to your roots"

Nancy rose from her seat making sure her decency was being covered and stepped across the kitchen floor to the aga. Her body began to feel cold and shaky and she was hoping the heat from this old antiqued cooking machine would warm her instantly. She turned and faced the old unkempt balding copper.

"You're not the first person to say that."

Chapter 42

Nancy had spent longer than usual in her bath that morning. Her mind in total and utter confusion. She finally concluded that may be Jonesy had changed but could she really trust him like he said?

Both Joe (in her induced coma) and Jonesy had said the exact same thing. 'Go back to your roots. Where were her roots? Back at Ralph's house? But she didn't want to be with Ralph, plus it would have meant sharing her old home with Lucy, and there wasn't a hope in hell of her ever doing that! Her mother's house? But this house now had another family living in it and she was damn sure that they wouldn't appreciate a complete stranger sleeping with them in their beds! Her roots can't be at Joe's as that's where she was. Which left only one other place. 'Grammies'.

Her kitchen was full of life and activity when she finally made the transition from her boudoir. Daisy was feeding Wyatt and scoffing her own breakfast at an extortionate pace. Danny was frying up his breakfast steak. Mal. Oh Mal he, was dancing around the kitchen half naked in nothing but a pair of boxers. Unfortunately it still done nothing to get Nancy's juices flowing (poor Nancy) and Walnut was mixing up some smoothie that looked like someone had just blown their nose into the blender. There were two added bodies for breakfast that morning. Michele and Simon. Michelle was nibbling at the edges of a piece of toast and Simon was trying his hardest not to look at Daisy's ample breast being sucked dry. He wasn't doing it in a perverted way, he was just totally transfixed by how all this motherly stuff worked.

Nancy reached for her favourite pink tea cup

"Morning everyone"

"Oh Nance brilliant I'm glad you're up I need to go over a few things for next year's shows and also both the boys and girls have been booked for a New Year bash but I need to know how long we are going to let everyone have off for Christmas?" Michele spoke with no pauses

"Erm", said Nancy "In all honesty I haven't given the dance troop a second thought and I totally forgot about Christmas….Look Chele I have to go out for the day today can I just leave all the business side of things to you for the moment"

Daisy looked up at her mother

"Where you going Mum? Shall I come with you?"

"Do you want me to drive" enquired Mal

Nancy sipped her tea. She was so unsure of how this day was going to go, in actual fact she was unsure of everything right now

"Just out Daisy and no Mal I think this is best handled alone….But can you all please do me a favour can you all stay together today. And Daisy please phone your sisters and tell them to go to their dads for the day. I will explain I promise but right now I just want you all to do as I tell you…..I think may be, if you could Danny tell all the builders to take a couple of weeks off. I will pay them in full. I just think for everyone's sake they should not be here at the moment"

Nancy gave Danny a hard glare. She hoped he understood what she was saying and the implications that could follow if he didn't.

Daisy tutted

"But Mum you can't stop them working, Poppy and Willows houses are nearly finished and we can then all live close to each other again. Mum what the hell is going on?"

Nancy sighed heavily and brushed her fringe away from her eyes

"I will tell you all very soon, but first I just have to get today out of the way. Just promise to all stay together" Nancy rubbed Michele's arm "And that includes you two"

Nancy walked towards the door of the kitchen and turned to face her extended family

"Please everyone just do as I have told you, I love you all, I will be back as soon as possible and then I will explain everything"

Nancy felt a little anxious getting back behind the wheel of her car, but she felt more nervous about seeing her family again after such a long time. It had been a considerable amount of years since she last visited them, and she wasn't even sure if they would accept her back into their bosom. All she knew was one way or another she had to find out if this was the 'roots' both Joe and Jonesy spoke about. In all honesty she couldn't even be sure if they were still in the same place, but where else could they be? No one would have accepted their sort in the modern world, especially with their history so with fingers toes, legs and eyeballs crossed she carried on driving to the fringe of East Grinstead.

The gates were padlocked as she reached the entrance to their land. Nancy pulled at them trying to see if they would come lose. They didn't.

"Oh bugger it!" she said as she looked around for someone, anyone that may be able to let her in.

"Dat's locked love, you's don't wanna go on dat land" said a tall thin spindly young boy that appeared from behind one of the holly bushes to the side of the gate

"Yeah I gathered that" Nancy answered "Tell me do the Bucklands still own this land?"

"Whose dat, did you's say"

Nancy repeated herself

"The Bucklands"

The spindly boy scratched his ear and tilted his head

"Wos, you wanna know dat for den"

Nancy walked over towards him. He was a handsome lad. Couldn't have been no older than fifteen. His hair was long, very long and was being tied back with an old head scarf. His clothes were grubby with mud smeared down the front of his jeans and you could tell just by looking at his hands that he was used to doing manual labour.

Nancy smiled at him as she reached in her trouser pocket for a crisp twenty pound note. She waved it in front of him.

"Can you please just tell me if the Bucklands still own and live on this land?"

He grabbed the money from her quicker than the Inland Revenue can send out your tax demand.

"Er, yeah, they still live ere's, why do you's wanna know?"

"My name is Nancy, Nancy Buckland, my Grammie is the head of this family, and …..and I've come home"

The young boy stood mouth wide open, rummaging around his dirty jeans pocket for the keys to the padlock. He fumbled ever so slightly as he glanced at Nancy from the corner of his eye. Nancy couldn't help but feel amused by this whole situation and she tried her hardest not to smirk, smile or even laugh out loud. Not once in the last twenty plus years has she had such an effect on a young boy. The poor thing was shaking in his boots.

The scruffy unwashed young-un nodded to her and pointed up the dirt track road. She gave him a courteous smile and climbed into her car. As she watched the scenery pass the memories of so many years ago flashed through her mind. Nothing had really changed. The land was still as she remembered. Even the sycamore tree she climbed as a child that Henry had fallen from and broken his wrist still stood in the centre of the top paddock. Its bark white and branches entwined and free from leaves. She remembered Grammie telling her that 'It was winter when we see nature in its full beauty, as everything is laid bare and not hidden behind camouflage' Oh how Nancy's body yearned to be held in those loving arms again. Apprehension, anxiety and a bad dose of the collywobbles migrated through her body and down her spine, as she parked up in-between a rusty old tin bath and a pile of freshly plucked chicken feathers.

Nancy opened her car door and breathed in deeply to calm her beating heart. Absolutely everything was exactly the same as she had remembered. The hand built weathered log cabin that was big enough to house at least ten families at once stood proudly in front of her. It was such a sizeable building, made from raw natural materials but it did have the addition of solar panels on its roof.

 "Well would you Adam and Eve it, even the Hicks have kept up with technology" grunted her alter ego

But Nancy took no notice and rubbed her hand down the established and familiar wood, she leant forward and sniffed the cortex. It still retained the indistinguishable essence. Tears started forming in her eyes. She had lived in many places, in many homes but her roots lay at where she stood.

"I knew 'twas you" came a quietly spoken voice from behind her

There was no mistaking who it belonged to. Nancy swiveled on her heels and stared right into those wrinkly eyes of Grammie. She fell into her arms and dissolved into tears.

"Oh my ickle poppet, don't you let dose eyes of yours weep. Grammies got ya'" Grammie held Nancy's face in both hands "Bud look at you, all growd up and turned into a beaut-ful woman. We ave so much to gargle bout, come come"

Grammie took hold of Nancy's hand and led her inside. To her left stood the same grandfather clock that chimed the day away.

Neatly stacked to the right were shelves up on shelves of shoes, boots and slippers.

"Outside feet off me dear" Grammie winked

Nancy bend down and untied her timberlands

"Yes Grammie, I remember, everything looks exactly the same Grammie, and it even smells the same"

"Why would'nt it me dear, you's don't go changing wot aint broken. You's will be staying for supper won't you's. Ave had a pig spit roasting since dawn an a lubberly chicken broth on the stove"

The same twinkle shone from Grammies eyes as it always had, as the lines on her face all joined and moulded into one.

The large open planned kitchen and living room only had two extra additions in it. Two very young, sleeping French Mastiffs curled up together in front of the open fire. Nancy being Nancy just couldn't resist and headed straight for them.

"Oi oi oi" shouted Grammie "You know the rules poppet, let the sleeping dogs lie"

But Nancy didn't listen and heaved up one of the sleepy bundles into her arms

"But Grammie they are adorable, and they have puppy breath and everything"

Grammie shook her head as she stirred the simmering broth on the top of the stove

"You's never could do as you's were told. Put's dose pups down and come ave a brew we ave lots to be gargling bout"

Nancy pulled her bottom lip over her top as she laid the puppy back down on the tartan blanket in front of the fire

"But Gram's"

"No buts me dear's you's is not a goat"
Grammie answered sternly

Grammie lifted up her ornately carved walking stick which was hanging on the edge of white painted dresser. Nobody knew how old Grammie was as this families day of birth was never celebrated. But their day of death was a day where the deceased was revered in every manner. At the crack of dawn the body would be carried out into the countryside. Come rain, shine, hail or snow, it would be left there for all to pay their respects too. In the days of old, the body was wrapped tightly in a muslin sheet and encased in woven wicker before being set alight. The funeral party would then dance and be merry until the moon set on the third day, then the ashes were buried deep under the ground. Obviously now all bodies have to be cremated. But the three day celebration of life still occurs……unless, unless you go against the families beliefs as in the case of Nancy's father then your body is buried. There conviction states that a buried body cannot join the after - life instantly and will stay in a limbo state until they can see that the woman has and always will be the sacred feminine.

Grammies movements were as Nancy expected slower than she remembered. Her body looked frail and she had deep furrows on her face and hands. Grammie had never dressed in anything but black. In fact she never dressed in anything but a below knee length black dress that had a v neckline. It always accentuated her ample bust, which still looked as good as Nancy remembered.

Nancy looked around the living space. It too had not changed. There were two butler sinks. One for washing dirty dishes and clothes. Grammie washed everything by hand, she didn't trust washing machines to clean the clothes to her standards and dish washers were for the lazy! The other sink was used to wash and prepare food in. Grammie always used to laugh at the 'rutters' (townsfolk) who constantly said that there sort were dirty. Nancy recalled the day when Grammie had invited a few rutters to theirs for afternoon tea. After they were told to remove their 'outside feet', Grammie made them all wash their hands and faces before tea was served. And when one of them enquired about having two sinks Grammie turned to them and said

"Whys wouldn't you's? You's cant wash your pants in the same place you's wash your food, dats just disgusting! You's will end up with all sorts of germ's in ya mouth!"

Some of the rutters did leave that day with a change of heart but sadly the small minds of some still saw this family as beneath them.

Numerous oil and water colour paintings hung in an orderly fashion around the room. Every one of these was painted by Grammie herself. The watercolours were all of the changing faces of nature but the oils were Grammies memories of a child. When they travelled from town to town, harvesting the crops and tending livestock.

Grammie interrupted Nancy's thoughts as she placed two tea pots on the butterfly table that was situated under a small window on the back wall of the cabin.

"So's my poppet are you going to choose left or right? Are's you's going to choose your's past or your's future?"

Nancy stared at the two pots, as the steam escaped the spouts.

"I don't need to know the reason my past happened the way it did, but do I really want to know my future? "

Grammie moved slowly over to Nancy and rubbed her arm.

"My sweet, sweet, Nancy, you's may not wanna know but I's bloody do! Were choose the right" Grammie cackled and began to pour the tea into a gold rimmed cup. "Drink Drink" she ordered "Don't forget hold's the leafs inside your mouth's, then spit them into the cup, turn the cup upside downsie on the saucer, then Grammie will do's the rest"

Grammie seated herself in a high backed chair to the side of the fire, and Nancy sat once again on the blanket with the puppies. She handed her the cup and saucer. Grammie turned the cup three times in a clockwise direction before observing the shapes and styles of the fallen wet tea leafs.

"My dear's Nancy, there will be blood lost and death will follow. You's has to remember the Buckland blood is strong, but our's bond is stronger. You's ave come back to your roots, my poppet and in life or death Grammie will always take care of you"

Nancy frowned, and stroked each puppy in turn shocked at how neither had moved from the rug even though they were wide awake and fully alert.

"Gram's please don't talk like that, I've only just come home, please don't talk about your death, I just......." Nancy was interrupted by the door to the living area being pushed open.

A burly built man entered first. He was tall with broad shoulders, short dark hair and dark brown eyes. He couldn't have been older than twenty seven. The spindly young man who unlocked the pad lock followed next and as soon as he entered the room the two French mastiffs leapt to their feet and ran straight towards him. Jumping up his legs and whining in a high pitch squeal. He picked both up simultaneously and carried them right back out of the room to the open landscaped outside. There was no mistaking the next two males who entered. Both shared her father's build and distinct features. And finally a man whom Nancy would never forget. His shoulders were of generous size and his arms were sheathed in tattoos. His short salt and pepper hair and stubble accentuated his chiseled face. Yes he was older but there was no mistaking who this was. It was Henry.

Nancy stood from her kneeled position, not knowing if she should speak first or just run and kiss them all. She felt awkward and uncomfortable. But she really didn't need to as both Percival and Pethius each took hold of

Nancy's hands and kissed them concurrently. Percival smiled as he turned to face Henry.

"Would ya look who's come home?"

Henry grunted and walked towards the sink to wash his hands. Nancy just stood staring at the back of his head, then looked at Grammie

"Say ello, to our Nance Henry!" Grammie spoke with authority in her voice. "Ain't she just beaut-ful"

Henry wiped his wet hands down the front of his washed out jeans

"She'd look even better without all that slap on er face, why can't women be as fucking nature intended!"

Grammie gave him an icy glare

"Well she would" he said as he held out his hand for Nancy to shake.

"It's nice to see you too Henry!"

But Henry just raised his eyebrows, looked her up and down and retreated from the room.

Chapter 43

Nancy couldn't help but feel ever so slightly deflated at Henrys cold greeting, but then who could blame him. From a very young age Nancy was his world and he assumed that they would be together for an eternity. Nancy broke his heart and Henry still felt the grief of losing her burn through his soul. Of course Nancy had missed him and on more than one occasion when her children were young she would often imagine herself back at this cabin, with Henry by her side and her daughters calling him Daddy rather than Ralph. But things just didn't turn out that way and now Nancy knew she had so many bridges to build with her childhood sweetheart. Right at this moment she felt like she had committed some extreme act of cruelty and betrayal. The happiness she felt at returning home was slowly being eaten alive by guilt. Once again her over thinking mind was taking hold and she couldn't help but feel ashamed of how she had treated the one man who shared her history and the one man who she knew would have done absolutely anything for her.

"I've been a right bitch haven't I Gram's?" Nancy asked not even worrying about all the other people in the room

Grammie leant forward in her chair, reached over and rubbed Nancy's shoulder

"Oh my poppet, you's not been a bitch, you's just done what your heart told ya too....Dont you's be worrying bout Henry, he's just had he's ego bruised, dats all. Now Nancy, you's tell us all why's you are ere"

Just as Nancy was about to tell everyone the events of the past few months Henry re-entered the room. He walked over to the window seat and sat down. Henry glanced at Nancy out of the corner of his eye and then turned his head to stare out of the window. With a huge sigh Nancy began telling her story.

Percival looked as Percival always looked. Constipated and confused. His face would always screw up and then relax, then screw up and relax again. Pethius eyebrows would rise high on his forehead like two slugs searching for freedom, before realising they couldn't actually crawl higher than they did. Grammie just continued to look at Nancy and occasionally give a nod of the head or make a 'hmmm' sound. The young boy with the French mastiffs just chewed on the sides of his cheeks and stroked the dogs, who obediently sat at his side. The burly man with broad shoulders, dark hair and eyes sipped on a can of beer and just appeared to ogle at nothing but Nancy's breasts. And dear Henry just sat and carried on looking out of that window.

Nancy concluded her story

"So it would appear that Joe has really pissed of some bloke called Pilot wh…."

The young dog whisperer with dirty jeans interrupted her sentence. His voice sharp and high pitched

"Who's did you's say?"

"Pilot" she repeated

With excited exaggeration in his voice the skinny young man jumped up from his seat

"Dats him, dats the one who fights the dogs, dats the one who I nicked these two from" he looked at the two slobbering mutts who were now laying at his feet "He's a nasty, nasty, bit of work, dat one is, he don't care wot he do's he don't, does he Henry, does he!.... He's the one who hurt dat girl isn't he Henry isn't he! If he's after you's then he's aint gona stop till he's got what he wants!"

It was now Nancy's turn to have slugs on her forehead and a confused constipated expression.

"I'm sorry, I don't even know your name, what is your name?"

"My's name is Thomas, but day all call me Critter they do's"

"Well Critter, I haven't got a clue what he wants, all I know is Jonesy is watching our place and to be honest it was his idea I came back here. I just don't know what to do next"

Grammie sighed, pushed up her breast and rested those loving arms across her chest.

"Well seeing I's got two great, great, grand babies and three great, granddaughters I's never met I finks until this is sorted out, you's all need to come stay here for a while. We's got more than enough room and more's than enough eye's and hand's near's by to make sure everyone is taken care of."

The two Buckland brothers both nodded in agreement, mirroring each other's movements in a scary fashion. Once both had stopped looking like a nodding dog you see on the dashboards of peoples cars they both stared at Critter, and nodded to each other.

Grammie spoke directly to him

"Critter, we want's you's to go back with our Nancy, help her sort all she's has too and stay there, at her's place. You's can take you's dogs wiv you's and take's Challenge too, he will's be able to sniff out any rutter quicker than the pup's. Stay out of sight mind you"

Nancy knitted her eyebrows and grimaced

"But Critter is just a boy, and, and, what girl, what did he do?"

Henry stood up from his seated position, his face was steely and cold.

"He's may be a boy Nancy, but he's faster than any person I know and he can stay well-hidden without anyone knowing he's there. After all you didn't see him did ya?"

"No I didn't…..but what girl Henry?" Nancy replied

But neither Henry nor any other person in that room would answer her question. Instead, Grammie rose from her seat picked up her stick and poked Nancy on the knee with it

"Dat's it then, dat's the plan. Now's go get you's stuff Critter and Nancy goes start your's car. We will's be already for all of you's when you's get back"

Chapter 44

Nancy had some explaining to do, when she arrived back at Joe's. There were many sighs and grunts but all understood why it was safer for the time being to move in with Grammie. Michele, Simon, Mal, Walnut, Ralph and the dreaded Lucy were also part of this big move too. Both dance troops were told not to come back to Nancy's until they all had been given the nod to do so by Michele.

Nancy explained everything to Jonesy and his sidekick Ambrose, who were still sitting at the end of her driveway. Both coppers appeared to give a huge sigh of relief when Nancy told them of where everyone would be residing for the foreseeable future. But Jonesy was adamant that they would both still keep up with their surveillance on Nancy's home.

She felt awful leaving Critter there alone with no one but the two pups and Challenge a 58kg male Rottweiler. This dog was a power house and there was nothing Critter could not get him to do. Play dead, he done it, snarl growl and drool, he done it. Even when Nancy's three own dogs were introduced to Critter, they obeyed without so much as a second's hesitation. He was truly a natural when it came to dogs any dogs.

Nancy smiled at him as she climbed into her car for the journey back to Grammie's, but Critter didn't even bat an eyelid as Nancy drove down the drive way. She may have had a menopausal typical female guilt trip travelling through her but Critter seemed not to have a care in the world. The one thing Nancy did ask of him was he was to sleep in the house. He argued with her and had a classic teenage strop at her demands. But Nancy was having none of it and as 2nd in line to the Buckland throne he had to obey her, didn't he?

Christmas was not something the Buckland's celebrated, instead they went for a more ancestral tradition of celebrating Yule. On December 21st Fires were lit in the open fields to celebrate the rebirth of the sun, gifts were exchanged, food drunk and alcohol consumed.

Nancy's own children who had never celebrated this time honoured tradition all agreed that Yule will now be their new Christmas. Even Lucy with her pouting lips and her disgusting kitten heeled slippers seemed to actually appear to enjoy the Yule celebrations. She had even taken to plucking chickens in an artful manner. Wonders will never cease.

Grammies home was once again a bustling settlement. And for hours on end she told stories of her own childhood, their way of life and their beliefs. Grammie had everyone intrigued by her tales of bygone days. And to Nancy it was just like old times, this place never seemed to age. The whole house with its hand carved furniture looked the same. The house with its constant smell of homemade cooking and wax polish smelt the same. The only thing that was different was that everyone had grown a little older, with a few more wrinkles and as much as she hated to admit it, she couldn't help but regret never coming here after leaving her home with her estranged mother and alcoholic dad. This was without a shadow of a doubt her one true home.

Everything was very still and silent when Nancy made her way down to breakfast. It couldn't have been later than five in the morning and the only other person to be awake was Grammie. You see, Grammie never actually slept in a bed but had naps throughout the day in her old high backed chair. Ten minutes here and there was all Grammie needed to re-fresh her aged body and tired bones. But deep in Nancy's heart she knew the main reason Grammie slept in the main living quarters. It was because she was there ready, at any given point of a day to help, nurture, and feed and protect her family.

Nancy poured herself and Grammie a cup of tea and seated herself in front of the open fire at Grammie's feet

"Gram's I'm gona quickly nip back to the house. I need to pick up a few bits and get some paper work as Michele wants to get the dance troops bookings in order. I don't really want to wake anyone to come with me, after all Critter is there and so are Jonesy and Ambrose"

"Okay my dear's, would you's mind if I came wiv you's? I could do's wiv a bit of a change of scenery and would luvs to see's where you's been living"

"Of course I don't mind Grammie. If we leave in a minute we should be back before anyone else has even risen from their beds"?

"Well den" said Grammie "Let's get dis show on da roads shall we. Let Grams just pack her bag. Do I do sandwiches for the journey?"

Nancy smiled and hugged her maternal grandmother's leg.

"No, Grams we don't need any sandwiches"

Nancy left the kitchen and went to do the preferable and necessary bladder emptying. As she returned she saw Grammie place a retractable flick knife in the side pocket of her hand bag.

"Grammie why do you need a blade?" Nancy enquired with a frown

"Oh dis old thing, I takes it everywhere wiv me, you know dat. After all you's never know when you might need to kill some vermin, dose rat's gets everywhere" Grammie chortled

Nancy spoke in a reticent manner

"Or a human?"

For a split second both woman just glared at each other before heading for the door (changing from indoor shoes to outdoor ones)

It was only six fifteen when they arrived at Nancy's. Jonesy's car was nowhere to be seen. But Nancy really didn't expect him to continue a twenty four hour surveillance on her property where there was no body there to protect. Well nobody except Critter.

As she entered her kitchen Nancy's heart began to palpitate. Something just didn't feel quite right. There was no sign of Critter nor the pups or Challenge come to that. Just one single plate with a stale bit of cheese on it and the crust of one of Grammie's homemade loafs lay on the oak table. The house was freezing cold and quieter than a graveyard at midnight. Grammie could see the distress beginning to appear on Nancy's face.

"Don't worry poppet, he's either probably sleeping in the old barn or he's in the wood's. That boy don't like to be locked in. Come rain or shine he's always in the outside world. Running wiv dose dogs of his and just sitting watching as the world goes by"

Nancy gave a tentative nod, and left Grammie to nose about the house whilst she went to pick up some paper work from Joe's old bedroom. She couldn't be bothered to sort out exactly what she wanted so just filled Joe's old black brief case that was resting against the wardrobe.

Nancy placed the briefcase down next to Grammie's rather large old carpet style handbag and called out her name. Grammie did not answer. Nancy searched each of the rooms both down stairs and up and Grammie was nowhere to be seen. An icy shiver cruised through Nancy's bloodstream as she re-entered the kitchen. She stood still trying not to allow her over thinking brain take control. But it already had. Nancy reached inside Grammie's bag, unzipped the inside pocket and grabbed the switch blade. She tucked it down the back of her jeans and made her way outside.

The lights to the converted barn style dance studio were glimmering out from the half opened door. Nancy crept slowly towards it and peered through. She placed her hand over her mouth to stop herself from screaming out loud. Lying in a pool of their own blood was Challenge and one of the pups both with their throats cut. The other pup was hanging from an old beam a steal chain pulled tight around his neck. Sitting tied to two chairs in the centre of the dance studio was Critter and Grammie. Critter's face dripped in fresh blood, his head was lowered. Nancy could not see if he was dead or alive. She swallowed hard as a man, dressed in a plain black single breasted suit, walked over to Grammie. He stroked the sides of her face. He began to mock her, as he whispered into her ear. Grammie did nothing, but sat and smiled at him.

"You's can do's what you's like boy's but let old Grammie give you a warning shall I's. You will not win this." Grammie laughed openly as the man standing by her side, struck her hard across the face with the back of his hand.

Nancy winced, she felt powerless as she watched him hit Grammie over and over again. Nancy pulled out her mobile phone and with shaky hands called the one man she knew she could always rely on. Henry.

"Yup" Came Henry's voice from the telecommunications device

"Henry" she said her voice but a whisper "I'm at Joes, they've got Grammie, and I think Critt……"

A deep husky voice came from behind her.

"Talking to someone love"

Nancy jumped out of her skin and turned
away from the scene she was watching. A man
over six foot six with a bald head and beard
stood before her. He reached out and grabbed
her forcefully by the arm and hoisted her
inside the barn.

"Got her boss" he said as he walked towards
the vile suited man who struck her
grandmother.

"I will give you whatever you want! Just leave
my Grammie alone" Nancy cried as she pulled
herself out of the bearded man's grasp

"Ooooo boys looks like this Buckland wants to
give in before we've even had a fight. Don't
make pykies like they used to, do they boys?"
he convulsed into sarcastic laughter. He
stopped abruptly, "I want my papers! The
ones your arse fucking do gooder stole from
me"

Nancy shook her head in consecutive movements, and pleaded with this bastard of a man.

"I really don't know what you are talking about"

"Really, and I'm expected to believe that am I" he sucked in his teeth and glared at Nancy and nodded to the bald henchman by her side. Who once again took hold of her arm and squeezed it hard. But this time Nancy was ready for him. With her free arm she reached round and pulled out the switch-blade from the back of her jeans, swung her arm around and embedded it into the side of his neck. He instantly let go of her and yanked at the blade that was ingrained inside his body. Nancy stood still for only a moment and glanced at Grammie. Her blood was trickling out the corners of her mouth and her delicate old skin was already showing signs of bruising. Grammie licked her lips, simpered and with the last fragment of energy she had screamed

"RUN"

But Nancy didn't want to run, Nancy didn't want to leave this woman who nurtured her like her own child. She didn't want to leave her alone with these diseased piles of rotten horse shit. But if she stayed she would be dead. She had no choice, she had to flee this place and she had to do it now!

Nancy began running down the long drive way, being closely followed by another man who must have been out of her eye line in the dance studio. He was large and cumbersome but he kept his pace well. Her eyes were blurred with tears and her heart was crying in pain, but somehow she managed to get to the gates just as Jonesy's car with siren blaring joined her.

Ambrose was first out of the unmarked police vehicle and grappled with the man chasing her. Ambrose was fitter and a lot stronger than he looked. In minutes he had her assailant, face down in the dirt. Jonesy tried to take Nancy in his arms, but she pushed herself away from him and gesticulated to Jonesy he had to follow her. Nancy began running back in the same direction as she had just come only to come to a sudden halt when she saw the cold hearted evil monster that battered her Grammie, exit the dance studio. He looked over to Nancy and Jonesy. With one detached stony hearted smile he flicked his petrol lighter and threw it inside. Nancy wailed like a banshee as Jonesy grabbed hold of her and held her tight. In no time at all the barn was in flames and Nancy was left sitting on the dusty road rocking herself like a terrified child.

Nancy's body began to feel numb, even the cold icy winds became invisible to her. She was now trapped in the non-classification moment, where your body goes deep into shock. She couldn't cry, she couldn't feel. She could just sit and stare at the barn being engulfed in the hot amber and red flames. The air was black not just with the smell of a burning building but with the smell of hate.

Henry's 4x4 pulled up alongside Jonesy's car. The sky around him was full of ebony vapour, but his eyes only needed to see one thing. Nancy. And there she was sitting in her transfixed state of nothingness. Henry climbed out of his vehicle without thought he walked over to Nancy. He bent down and in one swift movement lifted her up into his arms. Nancy buried her head in his shoulders as he carried her to his rusty old Land Rover . He laid Nancy down on the back seat and covered her body in an old blanket and stroked the side of her face. Nancy stared at him with bloodshot eyes and tear stained cheeks. Henry gritted his teeth and flared his nostrils and called out to Jonesy. Jonesy came to heel like a well-trained dog.

"I,I,I'm sorry Henry, we didn't see the point in continuing our surveillance during the night as no one was here, I really am sorry"

Henry bit down hard on his bottom lip, and spat by Jonesy's feet

"Are they both dead?" he asked

Jonesy just nodded his head, as Henry once again flared his nostrils

"The bloke in the back of your car, is that one of them?"

Jonesy reached into his jacket pocket, his fingers white with the cold and pulled out a box of matches to light the cigarette he was holding. "Yes" he replied "Henry…..it was Pilot"

Henry rubbed his mouth and looked at the overweight henchman sitting handcuffed in the back of Jonesy's car.

"Here's what you going do Jonesy, you going to take that fucking piece of shit back to our's, then you going to lie through your teeth and tell everyone this was some sort of accident "

Jonesy inhaled deeply on his cigarette.

"But Henry, what am I supposed to say, they know I've been watching this place for weeks now, I, I just can't cover this up, it's, it's a murder!"

"Yeah, ya fucking can mate! You owe us, remember what we did for your daughter!"

Jonesy really didn't want to be reminded of the night his fourteen year old daughter was raped by one of Pilots narcotised abettors. If the truth be known, Jonesy still blamed himself for the violation that happened that night. After all, it was him that was supposed to collect his daughter from the swimming gala, but instead he was in the pub celebrating the nights before drug bust. Who owned the drugs, Pilot, who sold the drugs, Pilot, who will take revenge on any person who gets in his way, Pilot. Who did Jonesy turn to, to seek his own retaliation, the Bucklands. And they did. They followed Pilots cohort back to one of the properties he owned on Stone Quarry Estate. Dragged him out of his bed, took him downstairs and nail gunned his bollocks to a chair, before injecting him with more than enough heroin to kill an elephant. His daughter never really recovered from her ordeal. Being raped, buggered, beaten and thrown out of a moving car, was just too much for her innocent mind to bear. And for the last five years of her life she has been living in a psychiatric unit, doped up to the eyeballs on tranquillizers.

In Jonesy's heart he knew he owed Henry gratitude for something he just couldn't do. And that was to seek revenge for the savage attack on his daughter. To be honest he didn't want to be on the receiving end of any form of vengeance that Henry would bestow on him if he did not accept his instructions.

With a heavy heart Jonesy nodded his head in acceptance, and preceded to make the necessary calls. He left Ambrose to deal with the fire engines and other police officers that turned up at the scene whilst he made a sharp exit with the rotund flunky that was sitting handcuffed in the back of his car.

Everybody's heart began to beat in the same rhythmic fashion as the ancient grandfather's clock in the hall way of the cabin. The muted silence drifted through every rafter and beam. The only thing to be heard was the cackle of the logs burning on the open fire. Sorrow surrounded every person as each deplored the loss of life that had happened just moments ago.

Nancy was sheathed in the same old blanket Henry had wrapped lovingly around her and she was sitting once again on the floor in front of the fire. She was filled with so much remorse that it started to shatter her already broken heart. Nancy picked at the edges of the blanket, and conveyed just how she was feeling.

"It's my fault" she expressed in a soft voice "If I hadn't had come back here none of this would have happened."

Each person looked directly at Nancy. Their eyes filled with the same sorrow and their hearts burning with rage. Percival coughed and cleared his throat.

"Our Nancy, none of this is you's fault. We had upset Pilot years ago so it was going to be sooner rather than later dat, dat scum-bag wanted revenge.....You's my darling was just in the wrong place at the wrong time.....Dont you's go blaming you'self " Percival wavered "But Nance, you's gotta decide whats going to 'appen next, you is the head of this family now, and we, we will do whatever you choose for us to do"

Henry walked over and stood in front of Nancy and held out his hand to her. Nancy took hold of it and searched the entire room for at least one person who would make that decision for her. But no one would. This had to be her decision, this had to be her choice and this was her moment to show if her heart lay in tradition or her heart lay in the trust of the police and modern society.

Nancy allowed the blanket to fall to the ground. With a large exhale Nancy addressed her family

"Now it's our turn"

Chapter 45

The old barn stood approximately two miles from the cabin. Its old greyed wooden rafters merged into the vast landscape of sycamore and birch trees that surrounded it. It had been there for centuries and housed much of the family's livestock during the winter months. It was a proud monument of history. If only it could tell you all it has seen and been witnessed to over the years. Maybe for the Buckland's it's better that it couldn't.

Shafts and rays of sunlight seeped through the vertical cracks in the barns high ceiling, highlighting fragments of straw and dust that were floating abundantly throughout the building. In the far corner were half a dozen pigs, snorting around inside their pen. A very heavily pregnant goat was roaming freely inside, eating the barley straw that smelt as sweet as a summer meadow.

The barn was full of Nancy and her family, the only one not to be there was Simon, who stayed back at the cabin to look after Nancy's grandchildren. He point blankly refused to be part of what was to come. Not because he was scared but because he would faint at one single drop of blood. Michele obviously called him a "fucking pussy" but his fear of blood was stronger than her verbal abuse. To everyone's shock Lucy was well up for being there. She was desperate to see the man who helped to murder Grammie. But she did take things just a little too far. She turned up at the barn wearing a bright yellow sou'wester hat, fisherman style rain coat with matching trousers and a pair of bright red wellington boots. Instead of all eyes being on the accused everyone looked at her in total astonishment.

"Well" she said smoothing down her waterproof jacket "I don't want to get any blood on my Lois Vuitton's do I?"

Lucy then preceded to walk right up to the bald headed henchman, who was standing handcuffed in the centre of the barn. She slapped him across the face. It must be said it wasn't a hard vicious slap more of a feeble minded attempt at trying to be brutal. She then called him "A mother fucking murdering cunt". Which, really did not sound quite as fierce and intense as it should, as her voice squeaked and wavered. But she tried.....Bless her.

Needless to say, her actions and her rhetorical abuse, however feeble, took everyone by surprise. Especially Nancy, who didn't think this plucked, pruned and rather orange spray tanned female had it in her.

Nancy stepped forward and with her head held high walked over to Pilots appointee. The hate and anger she was feeling seared through her heart and pulsed heavily through her veins.

"Strip him" she ordered

Jonesy obeyed.

Nancy eyed him up and down

"You actually look better with your clothes on"

"Fuck you!" he answered as he spat at her feet

Nancy rubbed her tongue over her front teeth

"I'd rather not, you're really not my type" she hissed

He growled at her with spittle frothing at the sides of his mouth

"I'm going to fuck you into next week, you pykey whore, then I'm going to fuck your kids, and fuck anyone else that knows you!"

Nancy turned and faced her on-looking family and shrugged her shoulders. Mal stepped forward his fists clenched into a tight ball. Nancy shook her head at him.

She turned once again to face her opponent. Pethius joined her and stood by her side.

"I take's it from what you's just said you's aint going to be very helpful?" Pethius asked

"Fuck off you pathetic senile little prick!"

Nancy sneered as her eyes travelled to his groin, she mocked him.

"No, my dear sir it's you that has the little prick"

Nancy nodded to Henry as the pair sauntered to the naked man's side. Henry stood eye-balling him and without any hesitation placed the sweetest Glasgow kiss at the centre of his forehead. The henchman fell instantly to his knees as his nose erupted with blood. He looked up at Henry as the blood dripped down his face.

"Is that all you've got, you fucking cream puff!"

Henry took hold of the man's head to stabilise it and thrust his knee into the side of his face. Blood sprayed onto Nancy's jeans as he fell handcuffed to the ground. Nancy looked up at Henry and nodded again. With one swift movement Henry kicked him once to the stomach and once to his groin. There was a pause in the barn as everyone watched this

contemptible man groan and cough. He spat
mouthfuls of claret and lifted himself back to
his bended knees

"Go fuck yourself! You ain't getting fuck all
out of me….fucking pykie scum!"

 Nancy reached inside the pocket of her wax
jacket and pulled out a plastic container full of
sharp cocktail sticks. Apprehension was
building inside her as she walked around the
back of this now blooded and rather bruised
man. Henry pushed down hard on his
shoulders as Nancy grabbed hold of one of his
hands and spontaneously pushed the cocktail
sticks under his nails. He cried out in pain, but
Nancy was relentless in her actions. She
continued driving the sticks further and
further into his nail bed.

Walnut buried her head into Malachi's
shoulders gripping tightly to his chunky knit
sweater

"I,I,Im sorry I can't do this, I just have to get
out of here"

Malachi kissed her forehead and walked her to the open barn door.

"Go back to the cabin Sasha,"

"Are you not coming with me?"

Malachi stoked her cheeks, and kissed her tenderly on the lips

"I can't, I have to see this to the end, I'm sorry"

  Walnut nodded and took her leave whilst Malachi walked over to the pig pen and grabbed hold of an axe that was lying against the barn wall. Its tip glistened as he advanced towards Nancy and Henry. He grasped hold of Nancy's arm pleading her with his eyes to stop. This callous, ignoble woman that stood before him was not the Nancy he loved so deeply.

Nancy felt confused so much hate pulsed through her, so much grief. Throughout the entirety of Nancy's life she never expected to find herself on the receiving end of so much enmity and betrayal. After all for the past twenty five years she was nothing more than a mother and a typical suburban housewife. Doing all the mundane and boring housewife things. No one can argue that the Buckland genes travelled through her soul as easy as a duck swims on water, she just never expected in her lifetime that she would ever need to use them. How quickly another person's actions turn you from what is classed 'as a normal life' into a world where nothing has limitations and nothing is deemed vile and inappropriate. Every person has wanted revenge once in a while but nobody needed it more now than the post-menopausal woman known by Nancy.

Nancy looked up at Henry, Henry looked at Percival. Percival twitched his shoulders.

I think's it's time the room was cleared" he demanded

"I'm not going anywhere" Cried Poppy "I want to see this mother fucker writhe in pain"

Her sisters all nodded in agreement and so did the rest of her extended family.

"It's your call Nance?" said Henry

With eyes as cold as the driving snow Nancy answered

"They stay"

In typical Lucy style she stood clapping like a demented seal waiting for her fish. Overcome with happiness at Nancy's decision.

"Let's do this" Lucy snarled a joyous smile spread across her face

The light in the barn was starting to dim as the weather outside became dank and moist. The gun metal coloured clouds rested above the old barn as if they were sitting waiting patiently for the afternoon's entertainment to begin. The rain began descending at a faster pace the sound of it hitting the old tin roof echoed around them. All eyes were on Malachi as he stood over his victim. His stomach burned with fire, a fire that was lit from the pits of hell. With one fell swoop he bought the axe down. It sliced through the ruthless subordinate's ankle like a knife through butter. The stooge wailed in pain as his leg convulsed and spewed with blood.

Daisy covered her eyes and wretched, but Poppy and Willow just stood and stared as his warm fresh blood soaked into the dry straw that covered the barn floor. Lucy had frozen to the spot her mouth wide open, she was like a corpse that still had a pulse. Ralph placed his arm around her waist and tried to encourage her to walk to the open barn door. For the first time, in like forever, Lucy was silent.

In desperation and agony the battle scared sidekick of Pilots yelled out to his torturers

"STOP, I'll tell you want ever you want, please, please no more, please don't kill me!"

Nancy walked over to him and lifted up his face. Her eyes boring through his soul.

"Where is Pilot?"

"Please get me a Doctor first and I will tell you?" he groaned

"I don't think he quite understands" Nancy said looking at Malachi "Maybe he doesn't want to keep his other foot?" she shrugged

"NO, NO, Please I do, I do……He is staying at his house in Forest Row, but you will never get in, it's guarded 24-7"

 Nancy's voice was full of acid and bitterness "How many men has he got working for him?"

"Please, I feel faint, get me a Doctor, I beg you"

"You haven't answered my question yet, tell me how many men are working for him and I may call you a Doctor"

"Six, there are six of us and then just the ones who guard his house, that's it I promise you, I

promise, now please, please, help me" he
implored

Nancy walked to the open barn door, rotated
on her heels and eyeballed Percival.

"Finish him" she demanded as she stepped
outside into the driving January rain.

Chapter 46

Nobody could under estimate the apathy that a harrowing act of punishment inflicted on another human being would make you feel. For Henry, Percival and Pethius this was their life. This is what they would normally get paid to do, but it was made personal with the deaths of Grammie and Critter. For Nancy's daughters it was just something they had to get used to. Because like it or lump it they were now part of this family's life and their history. One day either one of them could take Nancy's place as head of this family. They had to have the stomach for all that may happen. Or they could just walk away and build their lives free of the brutality and destructiveness that could follow them. Strangely the carefree savagery was not the one thing Nancy could think about, what was, was how easy Malachi butchered Pilot's servant.

Nancy's curiosity got the better of her and she headed for the bathroom where Malachi was showering. She could see Malachi's silhouette behind the glass screen of the shower. The frothing soap suds trickling down his body.

His physique was magnificent, even more so than when she first laid eyes on him in that dingy Rugby club. If anyone had ever told her that one day she would taste his scent she would have laughed in their face. But she did, she tasted him, she caressed him and she made love to him like a woman half her age. Nancy stared as he washed the shampoo out of his long dark hair. Her body began to yearn, it was crying out to be fulfilled.

Her alter ego sarcastically spoke

"He doesn't belong to you, you had your chance!"

Nancy breathed in heavily and tried to calm her desperate need. She didn't want to be made love too, Nancy needed to be fucked, and fucked hard. She needed a man to take away the days torment not treat her like a lady of a certain age. She swallowed and dismissed the burning ache she was feeling.

"Mal"

Malachi wiped the water from his eyes and pulled back the shower screen. His body shimmered as he stepped out and reached for a towel. He pulled it around his waist covering his dignity.

"Nance.....you okay?"

She bit her top lip and folded her arms

"Mal, I need to ask you something, please be honest with me. What you did today where the hell did that come from?"

 Malachi picked up another towel and began rubbing it through his hair

"Nance, I have history too, people are not always what they seem to be, may be that's the attraction between you and I we both have shaded pasts. Can we just leave it there for the time being with no more questions?" Malachi walked over to Nancy and placed his hand on the side of her face "I know this is your life now, but please don't lose your humanity, I love you Nancy Buckland" He kissed her cheek and Nancy felt she was dissolving in his touch "Our love can never go any further than what we have now because I'm going be a dad Nance. Walnut is pregnant."

Nancy stepped away from Malachi's touch, no matter how much she longed for him she would never step in the way of his future happiness.

"As long as you are happy Mal?" Nancy headed for the bathroom door "May be in time you can trust me with your secrets" She gave Malachi a weak smile "Look after her and thank you for what you did today"

Malachi just smiled that sweet 'any time' smile, and closed the bathroom door. He stared at his reflection in the bathroom mirror, whilst a nauseous feeling rose inside his gut. He heaved and rushed to the white porcelain sink. His stomach convulsed and he vomited over and over again. Unlike Nancy he never ever wanted to go back to his roots. But just like the roots of a tree, somehow, they will always find a way to take you back to the source of your creation, and the source of where your life began.

Jonesy had left a few hours earlier and was dubious about how he was going to cover this total mess up. Lucy was still in a shocked state and Ralph was spoon feeding her some homemade chicken soup in the kitchen. Nancy's three daughters, Danny and the babies were all sleeping in the same room. Danny was in an old winged chair, whilst the females and their off spring shared a king sized bed. Nancy peered around the door and mouthed to Danny.

 "Everything okay?" he nodded and pulled out a twelve inch long slicing knife from Grammie's utensils drawer. Nancy nodded back at him and pulled the door closed. She was relieved that this time Danny did not keep going on about Silent Witness and leaving clues. But when Percival arrived back at the house with Pethius, Danny and his inquisitive personality had to ask what they were going to do with the body. Pethius just smacked Danny on the back and told him "Da pigs would feed well tonight, they's are chewing through his bones quicker than you could eat a rib eye steak with chips" Danny did not ask any more questions after that!

Percival and Pethius were sitting outside on two rickety chairs planning Grammie's and Critter's celebration of life ceremony, and Henry was standing by the old sycamore tree chatting to the broad shouldered man with dark hair and dark eyes Nancy saw the day she arrived. Her three German Shepherds were running around the large paddock living in the moment. She whistled loudly and they all came to heel. She bent down and stroked them and the vision of seeing Challenge and the French Mastiff pup with their throats cut haunted her conscious mind. How she would die if anything happened to her fur babies. She loved them like her own children. Fear began permeating throughout her body and the rancour for Pilot was growing to a disproportionate degree.

Henry's voice came as a welcome break to her thoughts.

"Shall we walk?"

Nancy bowed her head in response

"I need to put the dogs inside first"

Nancy kissed both Percival and Pethius on the head before taking the dogs into the living area with Ralph and a chicken soup slurping Lucy.

"Keep the dogs inside please Ralph"

Ralph could do nothing but give her a cold harsh stare. Throughout the years he had been with Nancy, he knew some of her history but what he did not know was to what extent her family would go too. Well now he did. He was stunned to think that this mild mannered woman who gave birth to his children, cleaned his house, washed his underpants and took care of him for all these years could perform and engage in such acts of barbarism.

Henry was speaking quietly to Percival and Pethius as Nancy exited the cabin. He stopped talking abruptly and held out his hand to Nancy. She took it willingly. His hands engulfed Nancy's and were the total opposite of her smooth skin. They were strong hands, they were hands that had partaken in many acts of violence but they were also hands that still gripped hold of Nancy's heart. Nancy felt her body shift and her blood pump faster than ever before. Ralph ignited some of her desire, Malachi even more. But Henry, well he was different. He was the missing piece that made her connect once again to who she once was.

The rain of the afternoon had given way to a crisp January evening. The full moon above their heads shone brightly down on the forest below, lighting their path as they walked deeper into its mysterious landscape. Henry let go of Nancy's hand and lent against a robust oak tree.

"So tell me, what is it with you and pretty boy?"

"It's nothing Henry, he just gave me a helping hand that's all?" Nancy really didn't want to tell him he had given her a hand, a finger and what he had between his legs! "He's a friend Henry nothing more"

Henry just stared at the empty branches of the oak above his head and reached inside his pocket for his cigarettes. He flicked his petrol lighter as his eyes fell onto the middle aged woman who stood not four feet away from him. Nancy stared back with a profound intenseness building in her senses. His expansive shoulders stretched the fabric of his jacket and she could see the thickness of his thighs through the taut denim. Nancy unbuckled her belt and slid it through the loops of her jeans. Without leaving Henry's eye-line she walked towards him. Henry threw down his cigarette and stood motionless watching her. Nancy took hold of his hands and wrapped the strap around them, she pulled tight as the clasp secured both ends together. She lifted his arms above his head and hooked the belt over a branch. Nancy rubbed her hands down his chest and delicately her fingers brushed the top of his jeans. Henry's erection throbbed as Nancy stroked the length of his shaft through the denim. With nimble fingers she undone the buttons on his 501's and slid her hand inside, he moaned with pleasure. Nancy dropped to her knees. The light touch of her tongue made his hips thrust forward. She was the mantis devouring her prey. There was no mistaking it Henry was her ambrosia, he was the nectar she needed and desired. She rose and stood before him. Her breathing quickened as she undid her blood spattered jeans and yanked them to the ground. With ease and precision Henry was now inside her. Their bodies were conjoined and Nancy fucked Henry hard and fast. Her heart raced, her breathing quickened and her body was out of control. Her mind was closed from the day's events as pure pleasure took her to the point of no return. Nancy fell against Henry's firm chest as the sacred feminine pulsed through her veins and her body spasms sent her to the utopia she craved so desperately. Nancy had now come home…..literally!!!

Malachi was shouting loudly at Percival when Nancy and Henry arrived back at the cabin. His fists slamming down hard on the oak table in the kitchen.

"WHAT THE FUCK AM I SUPPOSED TO THINK? I CANT JUST STAND AROUND HERE TWIDDLING MY FUCKING THUMBS!"

Nancy rushed into the kitchen and took hold of Malachi's wrists.

"Mal, for fuck sake what's the matter?"

Malachi grabbed hold of his hair and held it tight in his fingers. His eyes glistening with tears.

"Walnuts missing. Nobody has seen her since she left the barn earlier, I thought she was in our room sleeping so I didn't disturb her, but she's not there. I've looked everywhere"

Nancy took Malachi in her arms and squeezed him tight. She had fear in her eyes as she turned her head to look at Percival. Henry clenched his fists and walked to the far end of the kitchen.

"Is your car still parked at the back of the cabin?"

"Of course it fucking is Henry, don't you think that's the first thing I checked!"

Percival itched the whiskers on his chin, and stroked Nancy's arm

"If dis is Pilot's work he won't stop till you's have giving him whats he wants"

Nancy let her grasp go of Malachi and joined Henry at the other side of the room

"But I don't fucking know what that is! All I know is it's a letter or something like that" Nancy paused and took hold of Henrys hand. She squeezed it hard "Everyone has to leave tonight! Percival go wake everyone up, and tell them to pack. And that includes you and Pethius too"

"I's not going anywhere Nance! this is me home!

Nancy let go of Henry's hand and pulled back her shoulders. She spoke in an autocratic manner.

"I am the head of this family! Not you! You will do as I ask! Now go wake everyone up and pack your bags!"

Nancy began rubbing the centre of her palm with her thumb and walked back to Malachis side

"Mal, we will find her I promise." Nancy turned and faced Henry "We are going to need some more muscle Henry. The three of us can't do this alone"

Malachi wiped his eyes with his tea shirt gulped down the thick taste of disgust and rage he had in his mouth. He picked up his mobile phone and held it to his ear. He moistened his lips with tongue

"Ciao Alberto, its Malachi, I need your help"

Chapter 47

Dawn was breaking when every person in the cabin was packed and ready to leave. The rain had returned and a soaking wet Nancy was kissing her daughters goodbye. Each one had tears falling fast down their cheeks. Nancy did not know when or even if she would see them again. All she knew was she had to get them all as far away from the cabin as possible and that included her dogs too. She sweet talked Percival and Pethius around and told them that they had to go with her family to protect them and keep them safe from danger. The real reason was both these men were old and fragile and she didn't want their deaths on her already over bearing conscience too. Nancy's daughters were not stupid they knew this may be the last time they held their mother in their arms and the pain of knowing this sent each ones heart to the edge of despair.

Ralph prized Daisy's arms from Nancy's neck and dragged her to the waiting car.

"Mummy, please, please don't let him hurt you!"

Nancy felt as if she was being choked from the inside as her raw unblemished tears stained her cheeks. She licked her lips and could taste the salty flavour of each one as it fell. She wiped her nose on her sleeve and held herself tight as the procession of cars drove off down the muddy drive. Nancy had never felt so empty in all her life. But right now she couldn't think of her own sorrow she had to find her bollocks and be Nancy Buckland. A woman that nobody messed with and a woman who had to learn fear was not an acceptable trait.

The absence of sound in the cabin made it eerie and ominous. The only noise that could be heard was their breathing and the grandfather clock ticking away in the hall. Neither Nancy, Henry nor Malachi had slept in over twenty four hours but neither one had the urge and desire to sleep. Nancy broke the silence

"Mal, are you going to tell us now who it was you called?"

Malachi picked up Henry's cigarettes and shook the packet in front of Henry

"May I?"

Henry nodded. Mal lit it and took a huge draw on it.

"I phoned my uncle, Alberto Travaglini. He should be here with one of my cousins in a couple hours…..Nance, don't ask any more, and just accept the help they offer. Like I said we both have history"

After the tribulations of the day Nancy was not going to ask any more. No doubt Malachi would tell her all when the time was right. She was willing to accept any help to over throw the vile and contemptible Pilot. Even if it meant her actions were no better than his. Nancy just smiled and left Henry and Malachi alone whilst she headed to the bathroom.

Nancy pulled back the shower screen and turned on the taps. She removed her top, her blood splattered jeans and left them in a pile on the floor. Goosebumps instantly appeared on her skin as Nancy stepped under the flow of cascading water. She shuddered and as the water fell so did her tears. It had finally hit her. Grammie was dead, Critter was dead and if it wasn't for Grammie taking her old knife with her Nancy's body also could have been nothing but a pile of dust. Her children, grandchildren, Ralph her dogs and her best friend, were being whisked away to a travelers site in Wales, in a bid to keep them safe. She was frightened but somehow she had to control the fear and trepidation that was oiling her bones and penetrating her body. Nancy placed her hands on the tiles in front of her and lowered her head, allowing the water to run down the back of her neck. She was lost in the space between sadness and anger. There was only one way this whole situation was going to go. Death.

As Nancy tried to control the utter confusion and grief inside her a finger traced the contours of her spine. Nancy began to dissolve under the touch as a hand stoked her thigh and glided to the parts that she didn't ever think Heineken could enlighten again. But she didn't need a lager to make things come alive, she only needed the man who stood in the shower with her. Henry.

Nancy melted as he kissed the back of her neck. Henry gently raised his leg and eased Nancy's legs apart. Without wasting one second he was inside her. His hips moving in precision and rhythm to Nancy's heartbeat. Nancy rasped as her head fell onto her hands. He rode her like the experienced carefree man he was. Migrating deeper and deeper inside until simultaneously they reached their meridians.

Out of breath and panting Nancy turned to face him and run her hand down the side of his face. Henry lowered his head and their lips touched and their tongues danced in each other's mouth like a well-choreographed musical. It was at that point Nancy realised Henry was all she needed to find the strength and tenacity to deal with what was to come.

Nancy stood and stared out of the cabin window as a silver BMW X5 drew to a stop just feet from the cabin. Two men exited. One, was in his late fifties, silver hair. He was dressed in a tatty old pair of jeans and a tight fitting grey marl t-shirt. Nancy had never seen biceps that big before and her mouth dropped open as she ogled this specimen of a man. The other man was the spitting image of Malachi, a little shorter may be but nether less, he could have passed as his twin. He too was dressed in a pair of jeans that were ripped and stained and even though the weather was damp and cold he was wearing a scoop neckline line, racer cut back vest with a bold typed 'Infinity' across the front.   His well-toned stomach was visible through the soft touch jersey material. Nancy was not only catching flies with her open mouth she was now giving herself a face lift with her highly raised eyebrows.

"Oh I say" she said smiling in Henry's direction

Henry shook his head

"Your mine now Nancy, look but do not touch!"

Nancy grinned. Yes she was his……..but window shopping isn't illegal is it?

Henry joined Nancy at the window as she continued to gaze at these highly muscular and rather dashing men. They opened the boot of the X5 and took out two ruck sacks and two very expensive looking crossbows.

Nancy looked up at Henry frowning and questioning the weapons

"Crossbows?"

Henry just shrugged and gripped Nancy around her waist. Quite possibly in a bid to make the visitors realise she was off limits and HIS!

Alberto was first to introduce himself to Nancy. He took hold of her hand and kissed it. Henry's presence didn't make a blind bit of difference to him. Even though Henry gave

him that 'glare'. You know the one that most
Neanderthal men do from time to time. Nancy
had expected Henry to 'ugg' and grunt a
disapproving comment, but he just gave 'the
look'.

Malachi's double ganger was next to take hold
of Nancy's hand, he stared into Nancy's eyes
lifted her hand and kissed it in the same
manner as Alberto

"Bellissimo"

Nancy blushed. Not a hot flush blush more of
a 'holy shit balls, I think I've died and gone to
heaven' blush. She now knew where Malachi
got his good manners and his Adonis body
from! She was without a shadow of a doubt,
having to control just what was happening in
her down stairs region. She felt hotter than
Mount St Helens on July 22nd 1980! Malachi
turned the key but Henry had finally unlocked
the barren space between her legs. She was a
forty plus woman who felt hornier than a
rutting deer.

Her lustful ardour was soon halted when Jonesy barged into the cabins kitchen. His scruffy unwashed and unkempt appearance turned her rather over heated lady bits colder than an Eskimos kiss in minus 36 degrees. The pale subdued face of Ambrose followed him in.

Jonesy handed Henry a slip of paper, and gave Nancy Joes old stuffed Briefcase and Grammies carpet bag.

"That's Pilots address in Forest Row. But I'm not sure if he is there or at his rented house in Hollands Way on Stone Quarry" Jonesy looked at Henry with a questioning face "Look, I don't want to know what you are going to do, but I do need to know that no innocents are going be hurt along the way?"

Henry lit a cigarette, his face held no expression as he stared at the address on the piece of paper in front of him

"No innocents? Like Grammie and Critter you mean?"

"I'm sorry Henry, I didn't mean..."

"I know what you meant Jonesy."

Nancy walked over to Ambrose. He looked so young and intimidated by the burly men in the room. She felt her motherly aspect rise in her chest and began rubbing his back

"Are you okay?"

He answered her in a matter of fact manner

"I'm fine. I just can't wait for that cunt to be dead!"

Nancy puckered her eyebrows and stared curiously at Ambrose

"Why would you want him dead, he hasn't done anything to you....has he?"

Jonesy walked over and stood by the side of Ambrose and placed a hand on the tense boys shoulder.

"Nancy" Jonesy said his voice dull and un-moving "Ambrose is my son. It's his sister that got raped. They are twins Nance and he wants revenge just as much as the rest of us. If not more so."

Ambrose lifted his head to face his fathers and nodded to him before scanning the other faces in the room.

Alberto was sat in Grammies chair. He didn't seem moved or affected by the rise in emotions. In fact he had a look of total boredom on his face. Gone was his Italian accent as he spoke to the room.

"So when are we going to kick some arse then?"

Malachi smirked, and so did his double ganger Dante who was fingering his crossbow.

"That's a neat crossbow" Ambrose said as if to try and break free from the distressing mental state he was feeling.

Dante nodded his head and held his crossbow out for Ambrose to glance over

"Yep sure is, it's a Ten point carbon deluxe extra with an ACU Draw. One of the best on the market, and it fires like a complete bitch!"

All the men in the room now had their eyes on Dante's armament. And the conversation had turned into how quick it fired, its revolutionary carbon barrel and its draw crank cocking aid. Nancy's enthusiasm for his weapon of choice was hard for her to understand or even get excited about. She was more used to weapons being of the 'what's in the tool box variety'. Not expensive shiny toys like the one that was before her eyes. She tried her hardest to be involved in the conversation, and before she realised what she was saying she turned to the red hot bloodied males and exclaimed.

"I do like a man with a sizeable weapon"

This statement to say the least ended the manly banter that was taking place.

Whoops!

Chapter 48

Nancy searched everywhere for her extremely old but highly comfortable, favourite pair of Doctor Marten boots. She knew she had bought them with her, but where she left them was anyone's idea! She sat on her bed trying her hardest to remember where she last saw them. Her eyes scanned her room and they fell on a wonky legged walnut lamp table. On top of it was the suitcase full of paper work that she hurriedly packed at Joe's. Nancy walked over to it and clicked the two latches. She trawled through one invoice after another. Some of which were years old that Joe had kept. At least rummaging around this old case full of documents had taken her mind of what was possibly going to happen that night. She felt uncomfortable, as her heart palpitated with the prospect of coming eye to eye with the man she loathed so much.

The case fell on the floor as Nancy pulled out the final document that was resting inside it. May be it was because of its age or just the force that it had hit the ground but the bottom of it fell out. And along with it an envelope stuffed full of photos and letters

Nancy riffled through each photo in turn.

"FUCKING HELL"

She ran from her room the photos and letters held tight in her hands. She found Malachi, Henry and the two Travaglini's packing up the BMW with the crossbows and a knife or three.

Nancy waved the snapshots in front of their eyes. Her voice was highly excited and almost childlike.

"I think I have found what Pilot wants"

Each one ogled the prints as Nancy began reading out one of the letters.

I just wanted to say thank you so much for last night. It was most enjoyable. May be next time we could

possibly find a younger male to join us.

Please find enclosed some photographs of our night. But for both our sakes PLEASE keep these safe and away from the media and prying eyes.

Rt Hon Sir Hubert Finkle

Henry grabbed hold of the photographs, stared and it has to be said winced at each one in turn.

"Well fuck me into next Tuesday! But how the hell did Joe get hold of these?"

Nancy shrugged her shoulders

"Your guess is as good as mine, Joe had his fingers in lots of pies

Henry tilted his head

"Obviously not muff pie"

Nancy giggled

"But who would have guessed Pilot likes a bit of arse......... and banana's and oranges and cucumbers and please don't tell me that is corn on the cob?"

Malachi rubbed his nose and lifted his eyebrows

"Well at least he is into healthy eating and gets his five a day!"

Alberto gave Mal an old fashioned glare. He had nothing against people's sexual preferences but he did draw the line at using elongated vegetables for gratification purposes!

"Well we best keep these safe" Nancy declared as she put each one back into the envelope "You never know we might need a bit of leverage with the Rt Hon Sir Hubert? He is still the MP for these parts isn't he?"

Henry nodded as Nancy watched him put a pair of coveralls into the X5. He gazed at Nancy watching the expression on her face drop from childish giggles to unease.

"You don't have to come Nance"

Nancy ground her teeth and bit her top lip. Her face was now glowing a deep red and the tension through her body triggered yet another palpitation.

"Yes….Yes I do"

Dante was not showing one ounce of dread or concern as he patted Nancy on the backside

"Let's get this show on the road then shall we"

Alberto parked the BMW at a layby approximately fifty yards from the private lane that Pilots house was situated in. The four of them walked up the wooded area which was adjacent to his property. Nancy had found her good old faithful Doctor Martens and was so pleased she did. They held their grip well to the fast freezing mud and fallen leaves she was walking on. All she could think about was not the fact that someone was quite possibly going to get hurt tonight or even killed. It was that, she was glad Danny was not here, waffling on about Silent Witness and leaving clues. Countless other thoughts escaped her mind, and guilt rose inside her as she hadn't even given Grammie and Critter a proper Buckland family send-off yet.

Alter ego stepped in

"Let's get this sorted first shall we. And Nancy Buckland for both our sakes please hold it together!"

Pilot's house was set on a nice and quiet private road not far from Colemans Hatch. It was built in the early part of the 20th century and retained many of its original features. The garden and grounds were about 1.75 acres and were exceptionally maintained. Even in the middle of winter they were tidy and looked stunning especially with the frost glistening like diamonds on the well-manicured grass.

Matured shrubs and trees lined the driveway and would have easily led your mind to believe you were not in the heart of Sussex but some mystical forest filled with fairies and wood nymphs.

The raw wintry wind howled through Nancy's clothes and sent shivers through her body as they finally came to a halt. The four of them stood behind a well-established eight foot tall Daphne shrub. Nancy couldn't help herself as she bent forward touched the leaves and inhaled its remarkable scent. The three men all gazed at her with amusement.

"When you've finished sniffing bushes would it be possible to actually carry on with the job in hand?" Henry pronounced

Nancy let go of the leaves and continued to follow the regime of the men by her side.

The house was quiet. Too quiet. They had been told by Jonesy that there were approximately four Rottweiler guard dogs that roamed the grounds. Yet they hadn't seen or heard one. He had also told them that there was always two men that stood at the front entrance, but there was no one guarding or standing at the main door.

The thick oak front door was slightly ajar as the quartet tacitly entered the house. A range of six dimly lit wall lights enlightened the space. Dante changed his stance and allowed his crossbow to hang in his hands by his side. He raised and contracted his shoulders as the floor boards squeaked beneath his feet. He pointed to the others that he was going back out the same entrance they had just come in. Alberto responded with a gesture of the head.

Henry moved closer to a glow of light that was coming from beneath a closed door to their left. Slowly and gingerly they headed towards it. Henry turned the handle and pushed the door wide open. Sitting on a rather overly floral couch in this exquisite but pretentious abode were two of Pilot's henchman. Both men had sewn off AYA 12 bore shotguns held tightly in their hands.

Nancy recognised one of them immediately. It was the same one she stabbed in the neck in the dance studio. He smirked at her as he lifted his shot gun in her direction.

"Well, well, well, if it isn't the old slag from the poof's house. Bet you thought you'd done me good and proper didn't ya?"

Nancy flared her nostrils and exhaled deeply, the immense detest for this bastard was building inside her, as her anger and hatred began to flow to the surface.

"No I just hoped I had"

Pilot's accessory sucked in his teeth as his eyes looked Nancy up and down.

"Did you lot really think you could just waltz in here and expect it to be as easy as pissing in the wind? You are a fucking joke the lot of ya! see you don't ever trust a copper especially when we have his wife and his mental daughter locked up!" he laughed out loud and winked at the man who was sitting next to him "I do like a bit of mother and daughter action don't you?"

Nancy stepped forward as he cocked his gun at her

"You vile piece of shit!" she screamed "You disgust me, you are the lowest form of pond scum that has ever been born!"

He ginned a sarcastic arrogant grin

"And you my little pykie princess are about to die"

Nancy watched her life flash through her mind. There was no way she was going to die at the hands of this man. She wasn't ready, she had her life in front of her. She stood tall and pulled back her shoulders.

"But my dear sweet little fuck wit, if you kill me, Pilot will never know where I've hidden the letters and pictures. I'm sure the tabloids will love to see Sir Hubert Finkle with corn on

the cob being shoved in his arse by Pilot."
Nancy smiled in a very pleased of herself way.

Pilot's flunky lowered his weapon and bit
down on his bottom lip. He looked at his
assailant by his side who was texting someone
on his mobile phone and waiting for the
answer to his question to arrive.

Nancy observed the room she was standing in.
The French navy blue walls clashed terribly
with the accessories in the room. The whole
room was not to her taste and reminded her of
some back street knocking shop. All it needed
was a few nipple clamps, a choker collar and
matching cuffs to set the distasteful room
alight. Her observational transit was
interrupted by a woman entering the room.
She was tall, blonde and heavily made up.
Four inches of matt foundation covered her
face and her lips were painted in the brightest
of red lipsticks, which bled into the creases
around her mouth. Henry looked at her, then
at Mal and Alberto. All eyes then travelled to
the open leaded light French doors. Where a
smiling Dante was standing. His crossbow

aimed precisely at the back of the head of the man who Nancy stabbed. Nancy took two paces to her left so Dante could not be seen with their peripheral vision. Henry put his hand inside his jacket pocket, as Mal edged a couple of steps closer to the seated men.

"So what's occurring then?" the female asked as the man placed down his phone

He cleared his throat and once again lifted the gun in the air.

"It would appear that I'm to kill the groupies and then take the pykey whore to where our boss is"

Alberto nodded to Dante who fired his crossbow. The arrow was silent as it flew through the air and landed in its target. The subordinates head slumped forward and before his accomplice had time to react Alberto fired his crossbow. The arrow grounded itself into the man's shoulder, pinning him to the back of the couch. Malachi rushed forward, snatched the gun and aimed it at the man's head.

Nancy gloated as she stepped closer to him.

"So tell me, what was it you were going to do with us" she laughed openly as she pulled her bottom lip over her top and twisted the arrow in his shoulder. He eyeballed her and spat in her face. "Now, now that's not a very gentlemanly way to behave is it" She wiped away the spit with the back of her hand "Now, tell me where I can find Pilot?"

He said nothing. Nancy twerked his nose.

"Over to you Henry"

Henry stood towering above this man as Alberto and Malachi held his shoulders tight. Henry bent down and undone the man's trousers and pulled down his boxers.

In Henry's hand he held a curved stainless steel blade. With finger grooved black rubber over-mold handle. He kissed the tip of it.

"This is my favourite weapon of choice. I used to use it for castrating cattle, but I have found it works just as good on humans. I'm feeling generous today which one of your bollocks would you like to keep?"

"Fuck you!"

"No, fucking is the one thing you won't be doing for a while. I think the left first don't you?"

Mal and Alberto gripped tighter to the man's shoulders as Henry very accurately inserted the tip of the knife into his left nut sack. He sliced through it like butter. Alberto winced. Nancy just stared as he screamed in pain.

"Now" she said "Where is Walnut and where is Pilot hiding?"

The tall transvestite looking female spoke as she opened a silver cigarette box she held in her hands. She lifted a cigarette to her red stained lips. She spoke in a monochrome way.

"They don't know where they are. I'm the only one who does. But as you are more than aware Miss Buckland, if you hurt me, you know I will never tell you anything. We are cut from the same cloth you and I, we both do what we have too to survive"

Nancy eyed up this woman with curiosity

"And who the fuck are you?"

The woman inhaled deeply on her Marlbrough lite and toyed with her lighter in her fingers.

"Maybe Henry would like to tell you" she questioned as she walked closer to him

"Henry?" Nancy asked "What the fuck is going on?"

Henry breathed out and looked at all the faces in the room, each one now staring at him looking for the answers to Nancy's question.

"She, shes, my wife" Henry announced

"WHAT!" Nancy screeched "But your wife died in child birth along with your son......you never married again did you?"

Henry stood staring at Nancy, he shook his head

"No Nance I never married again" he paused and walked over to Nancy taking her hand in his "My wife never died in the physical sense. You see the baby she lost at birth wasn't actually mine. This fucking immoral and noxious tramp was fucking Pilot at the same time she was bedding me."

"I'm sorry I'm confused, how do you know the baby wasn't yours? What, why" Nancy stuttered.

"Look Nance" Henry continued "I may be a bit thick but it's not fucking rocket science to work out that I couldn't have been the father, you see I was working away in Wales at the time. Unless my cock can travel alone, or I can impregnate someone from a wank. I could not have been the father. Adriana was fucking around even before I married her. But dear old sweet Addy, isn't and wasn't just into cock, she liked licking some other woman's cunt dry too especially your son in laws mother, Sophie"

Nancy just stood in total shock of what she was hearing. But her thoughts were soon interrupted by the bollock less accomplice that had more claret running down his leg than one of Draculas victims.

"Excuse me, I'm actually dying hear, can your family history lesson wait for another day" he pleaded

In unison all the occupants of that room shouted together.

"NO!"

Adriana extinguished her cigarette in a crystal glass ashtray and trotted like a horny mare to where Nancy was standing. She ran her fingers down Nancy's face and allowed them to keep travelling to tip of Nancy's cleavage.

"Aww what's the matter Nance, are you feeling guilty for leaving your poor little Henry all those years ago in my careless hands?"

Nancy took hold of Adriana's hand, gripped it tight and started to walk out of the overly decorated room.

"Nance" henry shouted, but Nancy did not answer him. Instead she carried on walking, slamming the door behind her.

Nancy walked to the end of the hallway and into a modern style designer kitchen with glossy black doors, and shiny stainless steel finishes. She let go of Adriana's hand as she closed the door behind them.

Adriana once again opened her silver cigarette holder and lit another Marlborough. She sat down on a black vinyl and chrome high backed stool at the breakfast bar, like a budgerigar on a perch.

"So" she said "In all honesty my dear sweet Nancy, that golden Buckland throne actually belongs to me, because Grammie never annulled my marriage to Henry."

Nancy went to the sink and filled a cut crystal glass of water. She gulped it down, turned and walked towards Henry's, for all intense and purposes, wife. Nancy prized Adriana's legs apart and stood in between them. She ran her hands down Adriana's long heavily dyed hair. Bent forward and kissed her lips.

"I don't understand, what are you doing?" An inquisitive Adriana asked

Nancy provocatively licked her lips, and began unbuttoning Adriana's blouse

"You like women, I'm a woman and you said yourself if I hurt you then you won't tell me where my friends are. So.....If I'm nice to you, maybe you could be just an insy winsy bit helpful to me....maybe?"

Adriana pouted her lips and moved Nancy's hand down between her legs. Nancy slowly and methodically caressed the crotch of Adriana's lace French knickers.

Adriana groaned with pleasure.

"Well, Miss Buckland it seems you have many hidden talents, no wonder Henry has never ever forgotten about you"

Nancy smirked and bent down on her knees. And with the lightest of touches stroked Adriana's already swollen clitoris with her tongue. Nancy paused and looked up into her lubricious face.

"Where is Pilot and my friends?" she asked

Adriana stood and pulled off her French knickers.

"Oh no, no, no, no my dear Nancy you will have to do better than that"

Nancy stood from bended knees lifted her right hand and spat on her fingers before inserting two of them deep inside Adriana. Adriana squirmed with delight as her head tilted backwards Nancy placed a single kiss on the taut skin of Adriana's throat. Nancy removed her fingers from the wet dark pudenda, moved her hand to the front pocket of her jeans and pulled out Grammies knife. Nancy whispered into Adriana's ear

"You want me to continue, my darling Adriana, tell me where are Pilot and my friends?"

Adrianna tilted her head back to face Nancy and whispered

"They are at the Quarry house, please, please finish me off" she begged

Nancy stroked Addy's cheek and smiled a devilish sweat sickly smile.

"Oh my darling I intend to"

Nancy lifted her blade and sliced at an angle right through Adrianna's femoral artery. Adrianna screamed and tried to stop the flow of blood with her hands. Nancy just stood and watched as the pulsating crimson stream flowed effortlessly out of the gaping wound.

Nancy wiped the blood from the knife down her jeans, and watched as Adriana fell to the kitchen floor. Right at the point before Adriana fell into an unconscious state, Nancy bent down and spoke in the quietest of voices.

"This is my family and you will never get your pathetic, slutish hands on them. When you get to the other side, mind your back as Grammie will be waiting for you, you skanky fucking vile piece of shit"

Nancy arose and headed for the door. The men in the living room hadn't even moved from their places since Nancy departed the space.

"They are at the Quarry house" Nancy said as she walked over to the man whose scrotum lay shriveled up in a nice bloody mess at the foot of the couch. She kissed Henry's cheek, and gave Henry one single nod of the head. Henry didn't need to be told twice.

"You've been a loyal dog, but time to go sleepy bye's"

With one swift movement Henry dragged his knife across the henchman's throat. He gargled and spluttered a sea of red crimson as Henry patted him on the head like a sheep dog after a hard day in the fields.

Chapter 49

Stone Quarry was still and silent and the remaining street lamps that worked flickered brightly into the winter night sky. The quartet drove up Quarry Rise and past the cherry blossom trees that lined the entrance to the estate.

Alberto slowed down so Nancy could dictate just where he had to go.

"Turn right at the row of shops, then turn left when you see the kid's park in front of you. According to Jonesy there should be a post office and a small layby adjacent to it."

Nancy smiled widely at Henry and stuck out her tongue to him as Alberto pulled in behind a car they all knew.

"See women can give directions" She said as she reached for the handle of the door

Jonesy was sitting at the steering wheel of his car and as he wound down the window a waft of whisky and cigarettes escaped the confinement. He was even more unkempt than usual. His hands shaking worse than Nancy had ever seen before and by the state of what he looked like and smelt like he hadn't slept, showered or shaved for days.

He spoke directly to Nancy, stuttering his words whilst a trail of spit formed in the creases of his mouth.

"I'm, I'm so sorry Nance I didn't mean to say anything I, I"

Nancy could see and feel the distress he was in and her eyes began to fill with tears. She rubbed his shoulder. She didn't like him but understood why he had done what he had done.

"It's okay Jonesy, so far we are all still alive and kicking. To be honest we all most probably would have done the same thing in your shoes. Now, which house is it and who is in there?"

Jonesy sighed deeply and pointed to a house straight opposite the Post Office. It had a brick paved drive and an old VW Golf parked on it.

"Pilot's in there and as far as I'm aware the last of his lackeys are to." Jonesy paused and struggled to hold a lighter still enough to ignite his cigarette. Henry held onto Jonesy's arm to stop the shaking.

"Thank you" Jonesy said "I managed to get the dogs impounded, as people were complaining about their extensive barking…..but…but my wife and daughter are in there Nance!"

An impatient Malachi stepped closer to the window and leaned inside

"Walnut, is Walnut in there?

"I'm sorry, I really don't know, please, please get my wife and daughter out of there"

Malachi thumped the roof of Jonesy's car, as Nancy tried her hardest not to show her fear that Walnut may already be dead.

"We are going to try, but where is Ambrose?"

"He's at the nick trying to cover up some lose ends and get everybody off my back. At least I know he is safe there"

Alberto started to walk to the house closely followed by Dante and Malachi.

"Stop" Nancy yelled "It's me and these letters he wants, he doesn't know the others are dead or you lot are even alive or even here. Let me go to the house alone. Give me ten minutes and then make your presence felt."

Henry was not happy and tried to grab hold of Nancy's arm as she pulled out his curved knife from his pocket.

"Nance I don't want you going in there, let us sort this"

"Henry stop! I will be fine I promise"

"But Nancy.."

"But nothing……Ten minutes that's all"

Nancy stood at the front door and banged
hard on it. No answer. So she banged again.
The door was opened by a young man no
older than eighteen. His head had been shaved
and he was chewing gum like a deranged
camel who had smoked too much Mary Jane.

"You alone" he questioned"

"Yes, the others couldn't find anywhere to
park so have had to drive down the road"

"Why didn't they just park on the drive?"

"Look" Nancy said sternly "I don't fucking
know, now it's been a long night and I've got
what Pilot wants, so just hurry the fuck up and
let me in!"

The boy moved away from the opening of the door and Nancy entered. The house stunk of skunk and cigarettes and it didn't look like it had been cleaned for a month.

As Nancy stood in the hallway another man walked down the stairs zipping up his trousers.

"That young un, is a good fuck" he laughed "But her mother is as tight as a choir boys arse!"

Nancy vomited in her mouth and swallowed it back. The revulsion was spreading faster round her veins than her blood could flow. He walked to Nancy's side and grabbed hold of her crotch.

"Bet your cunt could do with a fucking good shag"

"There won't be a day I'm alive that you or your cock goes anywhere near my cunt. Now where is Pilot?"

He laughed, bent forward and licked the side of her face. Nancy just stood there. Her eyes not leaving his glare.

"One day bitch!"

Nancy did not respond she just waked towards an open door to her right. And there he was. Standing with his back to the door by an old two bar electric fire. Was the man she hated more than anything else in the world. He turned to face her. His cold icy stare bore through her clothes and made her stomach churn spasmodically.

Nancy reached behind into the back of her jeans and pulled out the stuffed envelope full of photos and letters

"I will give you these, if and only if you release Walnut and Jonesy's wife and daughter"

Pilot licked his lips and smiled an arrogant smile

"You are in no position to bargain with me love"

"Oh but I am. You see before I left for your place tonight I made copies of every letter and as I had all the negatives too I thought I should use them for an extra piece of security. They are right now sitting with a friend of mine and if they do not hear from me by 6am I have told them to go to the trashiest tabloid out there"

Alter ego spoke loud and clear in her head

"Good call girl, just don't have a hot flush or he will know your lying through your teeth!"

 Nancy tried to compose her breathing and keep that dreaded hot flush at bay. The menopause had been kind to her since the accident and she did not want a bad dose of nerves bringing a damn flush back right now.

The young eighteen year old ripped out the envelope from her hand and gave it to Pilot. He browsed through the pictures and letters before placing them in a tin waste paper basket by his feet.

"Okay" he looked at the sex pest by the door and ushered him to get Jonesy's family from the upstairs room. "I will let them go. But you are going to take me to where the copies are, or" He walked to a dark corner of the room reached out his hand and pulled a young girl up from a chair. Her hair was matted and her face bruised. She held her arms across her stomach and her tears fell. The disheveled child was Walnut.

"If you've laid one finger on her by god I will kill you!"

"I normally like them a bit riper" He stroked her tiny compact baby bump "But as she was one of your bitches I just couldn't stop myself from having a little taste"

Nancy watched as Pilot took hold of Walnut's arm and pulled her into the centre of the room.

"Shall we go?" he mocked.

As they got to the bottom of the stairs the messed up sights of Jonesy's wife and daughter joined them. Nancy was in disbelief of what she saw. Fresh blood trickled from their mouths, their clothes where torn and they smelt like sex and faeces.

"You lot are worse than animals" she hissed as the eighteen year old boy pulled down the latch of the front door.

Nancy quickly and nimble footedly stepped in-between Pilot and Walnut. As Pilot lunged forward Nancy took hold of Henry's knife and slashed it down the side of his face.

"You fucking whore" he denounced

The sex fiend who had zipped up his trousers just moments before went to grab hold of Nancy's arm. She sliced the blade straight across his throat. His blood sprayed all in its range. Jonesy's daughter screamed as his wife forcibly pushed the young lad out of the way. Mother and daughter ran out of the house into the waiting arms of Alberto.

Pilot threw his full body weight onto Nancy's petite frame. Both fell to the ground as Walnut froze in terror. Malachi lurched into sight, followed closely by Henry. They bounded over to Pilot and Henry lifted him up by his shirt, whilst Malachi's fists pummeled him until Nancy shouted.

"STOP!"

Malachi gasped in oxygen his breathing fast and rapid and stood staring at Nancy.

"Take care of Walnut, Pilot is mine!" She looked up into the angry incensed eyes of Henry "Take this piece of filth to the car"

Henry instantly done as he was told whilst Alberto pointed to the cock-sure teen.

"And what about this arse sniffing peasant?"

"Grease his arse with WD40 shove your crossbow up it and kill the little fucker, then torch the whole fucking house!" Nancy affirmed as she walked to the waiting car with its sadistic cargo.

Malachi had taken Walnut straight to the local hospital with Jonesy, his wife and daughter. Dante had been told to tag along to keep a close eye on Jonesy, and what cock and bull story he was going to tell the authorities. Nobody wanted to assume that he would grass up the Buckland's but that was not something anyone wanted to take the chance with. The Hollands Way house was now full of murdered occupants and fully ablaze, so whatever Jonesy was thinking it had better be good.

The others drove the short distance to the Buckland's. But they did not stop at the cabin but drove to the familiar barn. Alberto hauled a battered Pilot out from the car and inched him forward to the open barn door. Nancy and Henry trailed behind. No words or glances were exchanged as they entered the building.

Henry pulled out a plastic chair from behind a bale of straw and Alberto forced Pilot to sit. Nancy just stood staring at him. Her mind thinking about nothing but the need and desire to hurt this man, this murderer, this rapist this untamed mammalian that she abhorred.

"Henry, can you and Alberto please leave us alone for a while?"

Alberto placed a can of petrol on the barn floor by Nancy's feet.

"I don't think that's a good idea Miss Nancy"

"Please, just leave I will be fine, I will do a typical high pitched girly scream if I'm not!"

Henry handed Nancy his jacket "Put this on then you look freezing. And Nancy, We will be just outside okay?"

Nancy just smiled as both men retreated. She stood staring at Pilot. He really didn't look anything special. She noticed a few straggling grey hairs he had missed when shaving his head. His teeth were yellowing and chipped and what would have once been a muscular body, had sagging flesh hanging from its biceps and a stomach that dropped over the top of his trousers. Pilot licked his lips and spat at Nancy's feet.

"You know Critter cried like a girl when I sliced the throats of those dogs, your Grammie was a little different she didn't moan once. I admire her for that" he growled and sucked in his teeth "But when I took that pregnant bitches pussy in my hands she screamed like a whore being fucked in the arse by twenty men" Pilot lifted his finger to his nose "I can still smell her juice on my hands"

Nancy just stared right into his eyes as she held Henry's nut cracking blade between her fingers.

Pilot grinned at Nancy

"You haven't got the bollocks love"

Nancy walked closer to him bent down and whispered into his ear as she stuck the knife into his groin. She twisted and sliced it through his flesh.

"Neither have you" she said as his scarlet plasma dripped from his crutch

Pilot grimaced and gritted his teeth. Nancy was not fazed by the personal pantomime Pilot was building around him.

"You can mock and laugh all you like Pilot, but I am a Buckland, and my blood is stronger and thicker than yours. Unlike that whore you call your Mrs."

Pilot snarled like the savage animal he was.

"If you've laid one fucking finger on Adriana I will rip out your insides with my bare hands and have great enjoyment squeezing the very last bit of blood out of your fucking heart"

Nancy sniggered and sneered and lent over Pilot's dismembered body. She lifted her fingers to his nose

"Take a good sniff Pilot, you may still be able to smell the pungent odour of her cunt on my fingers, because I made her squirm like the bitch she was. Right before I twisted my knife into her thigh and watched her bleed to death"

Pilot tried to grab hold of Nancy, but Nancy was the one with the bollocks not him and she sidestepped more nimbly than Ann Pavlova danced the dying swan.

Nancy bent down as Pilot salivated and cursed her every movement. She unscrewed the lid from the petrol can and began pouring it over Pilot's body. He coughed as it dripped down his face and into his open mouth. Nancy began heading for the door as Pilot shouted in her direction.

"TYPICAL FUCKING BUCKLAND, ALWAYS GETTING SOMEONE ELSE TO FINISH THE JOB. YOU FUCKING SKANK!"

Nancy stopped swiveled on her heels and turned back to face Pilot.

"I will see you in hell" she said as she pulled out Henry's petrol lighter, flicked open the lid, sparked it and threw it onto Pilots petrol soaked body.

Epilogue

One month later.

The fires in the top paddock were all but embers now as the celebration of life ceremonies were complete. They may not have had the bodies of Grammie and Critter to mourn over. But in typical Buckland style they gave them the richest of send-off's to the next life.

The last three days had been spent with music and dancing, happy memories and more importantly a family who admired and adored each other more than life itself.

There was nothing Nancy would not do to protect each member of her family even if it meant she had to become the cold hearted murderer she had. But now as she stared around the happy smiling faces of her loved ones she realised that life does not get better than this.

They held each other tight, they remembered the good times, the hard times, the murderous times and they also remembered that 'Good old Nancy' may be a fickle, hot flushed female whose hormones took control of her soul and her vagina more often than they all cared to remember. But she had proven she was as strong as any male, as cunning as any fox and as malicious and forceful as she needed to be.

Malachi had not let Walnut out of his sight since she got the all clear from the hospital. Her physical wounds were beginning to heal but the emotional ones would take a lot longer. If they would ever heal at all. But right now she was protected by the father of her unborn child and his unmistakable tenacious family.

Jonesy didn't ask nor neither did he question the fact that nobody had seen Pilot since that dreadful night in Holland's way. He was just grateful his family were safe and once again reunited. He lied through his teeth obviously to his superiors and for some miracle of the modern world they never even pushed for the real truth. To be brutally honest I think they were glad to finally see the back of Pilot, his diseased henchman and all he stood for. After all now that he was out of the picture it made their life's a hell of a lot easier. Nancy as she always does, when someone needs a helping hand, had booked Jonesy's daughter into one of the country's leading psychiatric hospitals. Where she was now receiving the best quality care she could get. And even after this short period of time she was showing remarkable progress.

Nancy's daughters were just pleased that their mother was safe. They too did not ask too many probing questions but knew in time the truth will come out. It always does. And as for Ralph and Lucy, well they seemed a perfect match. Lucy had exchanged her short fitted skirts and dresses for a very tight fitting pair of dungarees. Obviously designer. She even mucked out the pigs daily, but couldn't quite bring herself to lose her Louis Vuitton's and nobody could hide their smirks when she was seen every morning scraping the pig shit off her shoes.

As for Henry well he was just happy that Nancy was finally back in his life and back each night in his bed. After all these years he knew that nothing would ever take his Nancy from his embrace again.

The two elderly Buckland brothers stood at the door of the family cabin and ushered Nancy to follow them. She did, with Henry and the rest of the family following closely behind. They led the Buckland descendants and the extra adopted family members down the cabins corridor to a locked room. Henry was the one who reached inside his pocket and unlocked the sealed door.

The room was vast with nothing more than a highly polished solid oak table and matching chairs. A glass water decanter and upturned glasses were positioned in the centre of it.

Henry and the Buckland brothers walked to the end of the table and Henry pulled out the chair.

"Nancy, this chair belongs to you, Please take your seat as head of this household and this family"

Nancy walked forward, her head held high. She stood still and looked at the smiling faces that were all staring straight at her, before taking her seat on the family throne dedicated to the sacred feminine known as Nancy Buckland.

15059090R00353

Printed in Great Britain
by Amazon.co.uk, Ltd.,
Marston Gate.